Dear Reader,

February is Black History Month, a time when we pay special tribute to the triumphs and achievements of African Americans in this country and in the world at large. Writing is but one of the many contributions black Americans have made— from Zora Neale Hurston to Terry McMillan. African American writers bring to you stories that are steeped in the rich and wonderful tapestry of African American tradition and culture.

To coincide with Black History Month, Harlequin has included my romantic suspense novel, *Crime of Passion*, in this month's selection.

As an African American writer, I feel a special sense of pride in being able to bring to you stories of romance and adventure featuring today's contemporary black men and women. I hope my stories also show you that love comes in all colors.

I love to hear from readers. You may write to me at: P.O. Box 5397, Springfield, IL 62705.

Warmest regards,

Maggie Ferguson

Maggie Ferguson

ABOUT THE AUTHOR

Maggie Ferguson has always been an avid reader with a strong desire to write. Her writing experience was limited, however, until a close friend started penning a romantic suspense novel and encouraged Maggie to do the same. *Looks Are Deceiving*, her first Harlequin Intrigue title, was the result. Maggie says she loves to write stories with a special twist, and that's exactly what you'll find in her latest romantic intrigue, *Fever Rising*.

When she isn't writing or reading, Maggie enjoys watching Alfred Hitchcock movies, horror movies, attending the theater, drawing and spending weekends in St. Louis.

Maggie loves to hear from readers. You may write to her at: P.O. Box 5397, Springfield, IL 62705.

Books by Maggie Ferguson

HARLEQUIN INTRIGUE
284—LOOKS ARE DECEIVING
347—CRIME OF PASSION

Fever Rising
Maggie Ferguson

Harlequin Books

TORONTO • NEW YORK • LONDON
AMSTERDAM • PARIS • SYDNEY • HAMBURG
STOCKHOLM • ATHENS • TOKYO • MILAN
MADRID • WARSAW • BUDAPEST • AUCKLAND

To Margie, Layle, Brenda and Carla
for their friendship and support.

ISBN 0-373-22408-7

FEVER RISING

Copyright © 1997 by Anita Williams

Highland Park •

Evanston •

• Oak Park

Lake Michigan

• Chicago Memorial
Hospital

Lake Shore Drive

N

Rev. Walters'
Shop
•

CHICAGO

Nature's Cure
(Raven's shop)
•

Sears Tower
•

Police Station
•

• Flynn Imports-Exports

CAST OF CHARACTERS

Raven Delaney—The lovely young herbalist has devised an herbal treatment for a deadly disease, but will she really want Jeff to use it?

Dr. Jeffrey Knight—Will his adherence to conventional medicine jeopardize his relationship with Raven, not to mention the very lives of his patients?

Detective Nick Valentine—The ambitious homicide detective. Was he overlooking valuable evidence in his rush to make an arrest?

Rev. Charles Walters—He was the only alternative health care practitioner who treated both Lauren Connor and Eleanor Parker. Had his herbal concoction proved to be a deadly brew?

Harry Flynn—The importer-exporter. He claimed he wanted to help Raven and Jeff identify the deadly microbe, but his actions made it clear he had the opposite in mind.

Calvin Parker—His wife was critically ill. Yet he didn't seem at all concerned. Was it because he knew more about her "condition" than he was telling?

Mark Daniels—How far would this Romeo go to stay out of jail?

Chapter One

It was too soon to panic.

Dr. Jeffrey Knight had no clear-cut evidence that the infection afflicting Lauren Connor was the same one that had struck his other two patients or, indeed, that it was a life-threatening microbe. Until he did, he shouldn't even think along those lines. But after working the last two years for the World Health Organization as an infectious disease specialist, it was inevitable that thoughts of deadly viruses would instantly spring to mind. But this was Chicago, not the African rain forest; hence, it was unlikely he was dealing with some exotic disease. He'd left that world behind him when he'd accepted the teaching position four months ago at Chicago Memorial Hospital. The best thing he could do now was to make his patient as comfortable as possible while he tried to unravel this medical mystery.

But Jeff was hard-pressed to feel any semblance of confidence as he looked down at Lauren Connor. Her color was ashen, her blue eyes feverish, and her thick, auburn hair was plastered to her head. Severe dehydration had given her skin a coarse, dry look, belying her youth—she was only twenty-nine. Several feet of tubing hung from the IV bag and fed into a needle positioned in her right arm.

He looked at her medical chart, as the facts of the case ran through his mind. Lauren Connor's illness had begun two days ago with a headache and fever, followed by abdominal pain, vomiting and diarrhea. The vomiting had gotten so bad, she'd not been able to keep anything down, not even water; but it was only when her fever had gotten dangerously high and she had become delirious that her husband had rushed her to the hospital.

Glenn Myers had been the resident on duty the night before in the emergency room. At first, he had thought it was a simple case of food poisoning, but that test had come back negative. Then he'd tested for several other intestinal ailments, but those tests had also come back negative. Mystified, he'd asked Jeff, the attending physician, if he would take a look at her.

Jeff had noticed immediately that her symptoms were uncannily like those of two other patients—Eleanor Parker and Julie Hartman. Both women had been admitted the week before with the exact same symptoms exhibited by Lauren Connor. But that was where the similarities ended. Eleanor Parker and Julie Hartman were both black; Lauren Connor was white. Eleanor Parker was a married, sixty-two-year-old elementary schoolteacher. Julie Hartman was thirty-five, single, and a freelance writer. Lauren Connor was twenty-nine, married with two children, and worked as a teller in a bank in the Loop. They lived in different parts of the city and, from all accounts, didn't know each other. Yet all three women had been admitted in the last two weeks, all apparent victims of the same mysterious illness.

Jeff handed the chart to Dr. Myers and smiled down at the patient. "I know you're not feeling well, but I need to examine you again," he said. He pulled the stethoscope from around his shoulders. "I'll try to be as gentle as possible, but let me know if there's any discomfort. Okay?"

Lauren Connor nodded weakly, whispering through parched lips. "All right, doctor."

The nurse steadied her as Jeff listened to her heart, then

checked her lungs. Straightening, he pulled the stethoscope from his ears, tucked it into the pocket of his lab coat, then gently palpated Mrs. Connor's abdomen. Her skin was hot and had that peculiar doughy feel characteristic of severe dehydration and protein-wasting. It was like kneading flour without enough water. The liver and spleen areas were also tender because even a gentle pressure made her flinch. Jeff lifted his hand from her abdomen and noticed the tiny bumps for the first time. They were brilliant red and spread across her lower abdomen. Just like they'd been on Julie Hartman and Eleanor Parker. There was no doubt about it now, he thought, Lauren Connor had been exposed to the same infectious agent as the other women. But what in God's name could it be?

A WEEK LATER Jeff still didn't have an answer. He tossed down two aspirins, followed by a swallow of water. His headache had long progressed from the nagging stage to the four-star splitting category. He took a moment to flex his shoulders and look around his office. At the moment, he hated the place. In the last ten days, he'd spent more time here than at his apartment. It would probably be that way until he had a handle on this thing.

Jeff leaned back in his chair and studied Eleanor Parker's vital signs sheet. According to the report, her blood pressure was falling and her temperature was rising. In addition, she had a low white count, a low ESR and low thrombocytes. Even her EKG showed mild abnormalities. Further complicating the matter, she was a diabetic. Unless he came up with some kind of treatment—and soon—she wasn't going to make it.

He propped his elbows on his desk and rubbed his temples. He had hoped this latest antibiotic would buy her some time, but unlike Lauren Connor and Julie Hartman, she hadn't responded. Maybe if he knew more about her medical background and her movements in the days leading up to the illness, he'd have a better chance of devising a course of treatment. But, unlike the other women, Mrs. Parker was too ill to question, and they hadn't been able to locate her husband. An abrasion under her right eye, along with other bruises, had made him wonder if there might be violence in the marriage. Maybe that was the reason Calvin Parker had yet to visit his wife in the hospital.

He sighed and set the report aside. Nothing about this infection made any sense. According to the information he had collected from the patients and their families, he was sure that the period from exposure to onset of the illness was extremely short, less than five days. The problem with that theory was that it would suggest a huge overwhelming infectious dose, which seemed unlikely.

Another point of curiosity was the method of transmission of the infection. It didn't appear to be contagious. Nor was it spread through the air or by bites from mosquitoes, insects, rodents or animals, or person-to-person contact. Yet, three unrelated women had been exposed to the same infectious agent. But if that was the case, then it was very selective in who it struck. None of the patients' family members, friends or co-workers had exhibited signs of illness. It didn't make sense.

At this point, he leaned toward the theory that it was some kind of bacterial contaminant transmitted by ingestion, and that there was some connection between his patients. Maybe if he knew what that connection was, he could get to the source of the problem. But he'd had no luck in that area, either.

He leaned back in his chair and closed his eyes. They felt gritty from lack of sleep. Could it be some new virus? he wondered. Just last year there had been an outbreak in the Southwest of hantavirus, an airborne viral infection carried by rats and field mice. Thirty-two people had died before the virus and its source had been isolated. And then there was Legionnaires' disease, so named because the first outbreak occurred at an American Legion convention in

Philadelphia in 1976. After being dormant for decades, the bacteria had suddenly burst onto the scene and killed fifty-one before it was finally identified. What if this was something like that? Or worse?

He couldn't discount the possibility. With the vast network of airline routes connecting all the major cities of the world, a virus from the African rain forest could shoot anywhere in a day—Paris, Tokyo, New York, Los Angeles, Chicago, wherever planes flew. A shiver went down Jeff's spine as he thought of the possibilities.

He gave himself a mental shake. He was just being an alarmist. If there was any new virus, he'd have heard about it. News like that generally traveled rapidly in the medical community. Instead of being a pessimist, he ought to look on the bright side of things. Two of his patients were showing signs of improvement. There was a chance things could turn around for Mrs. Parker, as well. Yet even as he tried to view the situation in the best possible light, he couldn't rid himself of the feeling that there was something about this infection, about the way the women had all fallen sick within days of each other, that felt—it wasn't easy to find a word for it—*unnatural.*

He leaned forward, kneading the stiff muscles in his neck. He guessed he would call it a day. He'd run by the hospital, check on Eleanor Parker, then grab something to eat. After that he'd head over to the medical school library for a few hours and check the latest journals to see if there was anything in the literature. After all, it wasn't as if there was anyone at home waiting for him.

Not that he wouldn't have wished it was otherwise. He was thirty-four years old, and ready to start a family. He sighed. However, that required a wife. And his list of candidates was nil. Working these last few years in remote locations left little opportunity for a social life. And since he'd been back, he'd been too busy with his classes and patients to think about dating. Hell, he wasn't even sure there was a woman out there who could deal with the long hours and pressures of his work.

Well, that wasn't exactly true, he thought, as the image of a smiling, petite woman with midnight-black hair and caramel-colored skin flashed before his hazel eyes. For a moment, he let the memories wash over him before quickly pushing them back into the recesses of his mind. Once, a long time ago, he thought he'd found that special someone...but he'd been dead wrong.

His troubled thoughts were interrupted by the jingling of the phone, and he reached for it with reluctance.

"Yeah," he said wearily.

"Grace Wells is in the waiting room," his nurse said. He could hear the irritation in her voice. "I told her the office was closed, that you weren't seeing patients, but she says it's imperative that she see you."

Jeff sighed. He was tired, hungry and in no mood to deal with a cantankerous hypochondriac like Grace Wells. Every ache, every pain was blown out of proportion. A sniffle was pneumonia. A cough was tuberculosis. In the three months since she'd been his patient, he had seen her at least nine times. He'd run every test imaginable but he never found anything. And he didn't think he'd find anything this time, either. The woman was as healthy as a horse.

"Do you want me to tell her you're not here?"

"No." He sighed again. "She'll just start bugging the answering service or take herself to the emergency room. Put her in examination room two. I'll be with her in a few minutes."

"Will do. I'll pull her file and bring it in so you can review it."

Jeff didn't need the file, but he took it when the nurse brought it in. He took a few moments to skim the nurse's notes before heading out the door.

A moment later, he knocked, then entered the examination room. A tall, wire-thin woman looked up as he entered. Grace Wells wasn't old, no more than fifty or so, but streaks of gray dulled her dark hair and deep lines in her tobacco-brown-skinned face made her appear much older. There was also a certain hardness around Grace Wells's brown eyes and thin lips that made Jeff think she got little pleasure out of life. She was wearing her usual garb—a dark blue jacket and skirt and a utilitarian white shirt. All in all, the image she projected was that of a spinster with no family and few close friends. Perhaps that was the problem. Maybe if she had someone or something to care about, she wouldn't spend so much time obsessing about her health.

"I understand you're not feeling well, Grace," he said as he took a seat on a stool across from her. "What seems to be the problem?"

"I've got this terrible pain," she whined. "It started yesterday afternoon and has gotten progressively worse."

"Can you describe the pain for me?" Even before the words were out of his mouth, he wondered why he even bothered asking. Her complaints were always of a general nature. What he should be asking was what book she'd just finished reading or what television program she'd watched the day before. Whatever it had been, it was no doubt the source of her imaginary illness.

"Well, the pain is sharp and very intense," she said, pointing to an area just below her breastbone. "It feels like a knife cutting into my insides, especially when I take a deep breath."

"I see," Jeff said. "Does the pain go anywhere? Does it move around?"

Grace shook her head.

"Do you have pain in your back or in your teeth or in either of your arms?"

"Not recently," she said.

He questioned her for several more minutes, in which he determined that there were no symptoms of cardiac arrest or problems with the lungs. He leaned over and took

a thermometer from its container on the table next to him
and stuck it into Grace's mouth. While he waited for the
thermometer to equilibrate, he wrapped a blood pressure
cuff around her arm.

"Your blood pressure is normal and you don't have a
temperature," he said a few moments later. "I don't think
there's a problem. But why don't I examine you, just to
be sure." He asked the nurse to step in the room while he
examined Grace. As he suspected, he didn't find anything
wrong.

"But that can't be," Grace insisted. "Something is definitely wrong. If you'd just run some tests—"

He shook his head. "I think we can dispense with any
testing at this time. It was probably just heartburn." He
walked to a small desk on the other side of the room and
opened the top drawer. He took out a small bottle containing a half-dozen white pills. It was a placebo, a dummy
drug, but Grace didn't need to know that. As long as she
thought it would work, it would. "I think these pills should
do the trick. I want you to take one before each meal, three
times a day for the next two days."

"Well, if you think this is all I need," she sniffed, taking the bottle and slipping it into her purse. "I just hope
you're right about this being heartburn and I haven't got
what poor Eleanor has."

He looked up from her medical chart and frowned.
"Eleanor?"

"Eleanor Parker," Grace said by way of explanation.
"She's one of your patients. I hear she's real sick."

So that's where the symptoms were coming from. He
gave her a wry smile. "I don't think you have to worry
about that."

"Dr. Knight, I wish I shared your confidence, but I
don't." She paused, giving him a pointed look before adding, "And you wouldn't, either, if you knew what I
knew."

He looked at her sharply. He could see she was dying

for him to ask what she meant by her cryptic comment. Okay, he'd bite. "And what's that?"

"Well, it's about Eleanor's illness," she began. "It's been preying on my mind. I want to do the right thing, but…" Her voice trailed off.

"Go on," he prompted.

"Dr. Knight, I promised Eleanor that I wouldn't say anything, but under the circumstances surely she has to understand that I can't keep a secret like that." Grace clutched her purse to her bosom. "She should have told you herself."

Jeff's eyes narrowed. Knowing Grace, she was probably blowing things out of proportion, but if she could provide any information on Mrs. Parker's health or movements prior to the onset of her illness, he'd like to hear it. "Mrs. Parker is very ill and is not up to talking about much of anything," he said. "If you can shed any light on her condition then I suggest you do so."

"You're right." She nodded. "It's my civic duty to do what I can to help. I just hope it's not too late for her…and me." She looked up at him, her eyes wide, frightened. "I've got it, too! I just know it!"

Jeff released an exasperated breath. "Grace, you're getting yourself all worked up for nothing. You don't have what Eleanor has."

"Are you sure?" Her eyes searched his face.

"Yes, Grace, I'm sure. You're fine and you're going to stay that way, but tell me about Mrs. Parker."

She drew a deep breath. "Well," she said in a calmer tone. "You don't know Eleanor the way I do. She's very superstitious. She's always going to see psychics and faith healers, trying to get someone to give her a love potion to keep that poor excuse of a husband of hers at home. The latest one is this woman in the Windwood Mall."

Jeff's head snapped up. Windwood Mall? Lauren Connor had been there right before she'd taken ill. Could that be the connection? He leaned forward, listening closely now to her narrative.

"Well, anyway," Grace continued, "Eleanor asked me if I'd go with her to this place called Nature's Cure. I wanted to say no, but I couldn't. Not with our being friends and all but…" Her voice broke and tears filled her eyes. She drew out a tissue and blew her nose. "I'll never forgive myself," she sniffed after a moment. "If I'd just said no, none of this would have happened."

A chill of foreboding went up his spine at her words. "Grace," he said, trying to still his pounding heart, "what wouldn't have happened?"

Once again her eyes filled with tears. "Eleanor wouldn't have gotten herself poisoned."

He'd been right! It was something all three had ingested. "Do you remember what she ate?" he asked, trying to keep his excitement under wraps.

Grace snorted. "It wasn't what she ate that made her sick. It was what she drank."

"Which was?" he asked impatiently.

"Well, I don't rightly know. It was a light brown liquid. It had a foul, bitter taste." She scrunched up her nose in distaste. "I just took a sip and didn't drink any more, but Eleanor drank all of hers. *She claimed* it was just some kind of herbal tea to help calm the nerves. Frankly, I think that kind of stuff is just so much bunk. I told Eleanor she was wasting her money, but she wouldn't listen. She has a lot of faith in that woman—"

Jeff frowned. "What woman? Who are you talking about?"

"The one that runs the herbal shop in the Windwood Mall. Raven Delaney."

Jeff felt as if he'd just taken a punch in the solar plexus.

Raven was here in Chicago? He took a deep breath and tried to ignore the pain that had settled in his gut. Old memories die hard. And some never quite made it to oblivion.

Raven Delaney was that kind of memory. It had been nearly four years since he'd seen her, but her image was still as clear in his mind as if it had been yesterday: large, almond-shaped brown eyes, an oval face, and honey-colored skin.

She'd been a hospital nurse, working on combined degrees in pharmacology and nutrition, when they'd met. She had been everything Jeff wanted in a woman—bright, pretty, charming. He had fallen for her like a ton of bricks. It had made no difference that their views on medicine were diametrically opposed—she a staunch believer in herbal medicine and he a student of conventional medicine.

Naively, he'd told himself those differences didn't matter, that their love was strong enough to weather any storm. And for a time, it had been. Then she'd spoiled everything. She began to question the prescribed treatments for several patients at the hospital. Things had come to a head when she had expressed a desire to use an herbal concoction to treat Nelson Redmond. He had let her know in no uncertain terms his position on the matter and had thought that was the end of it. He'd never thought she would actually go against his directives and hospital policy. But another nurse had observed her giving Mr. Redmond an herbal concoction, and the nurse had reported it to Jeff.

At the time, he'd thought it was bad enough that the man had nearly died, but, to make matters worse, when he confronted her, she'd lied, denying having given anything to Mr. Redmond. He had covered for her. The patient had survived, but their relationship was over.

Seeing her every day at the hospital but not being able to be with her had been too painful, so shortly after their breakup he'd taken a position with a hospital in New York, then later with the World Health Organization. But even now, four years later, the pain was still there. God, how he'd loved her....

Grace Wells's raspy voice slowly penetrated Jeff's thoughts.

"I'm sorry, Grace," he said, pulling himself together. "What did you say?"

"I said it's strange. Eleanor drank that stuff the Delaney woman gave her, then less than twenty-four hours later, *boom*, she's deathly ill." She gave him a knowing look. "That's just too much of a coincidence for me, if you know what I mean."

He knew exactly what she meant. The same thought had occurred to him, but he wasn't going to let her know that.

"Now, Grace, let's not jump to conclusions," he said reasonably.

"Conclusions my foot." She wagged a thin, bony finger in his face. "It's as plain as the nose on your face. There was something in that drink that made Eleanor sick. I'm sure of it."

He shook his head. "Well, I'm not. You drank the same thing and you're fine. How do you explain that?"

She folded her arms across her chest and gave him a stormy look. "I can't, but I know what I know."

He raked a hand over his hair in frustration. "How can you be so sure? You said yourself that Mrs. Parker runs from one practitioner to the next. If that's the case, then how do you know that it was Ms. Delaney that made her ill?"

"Because another friend of mine, Lauren Connor, also went to see her and now she's deathly ill, too."

"DOES THAT HURT?" Raven Delaney asked the elderly man as she slowly extended his right leg forward about three inches.

Wayne Simmons leaned forward in the wing chair and smiled down at her. "Doesn't hurt at all," he said.

"Good." She lowered his leg back to the carpeted floor. She rose from her crouched position on the floor and returned to her seat behind the large cherry desk. "There doesn't appear to be as much inflammation or stiffness in the knee. I think we'll continue with the echinacea tea and the eucalyptus ointment. Don't forget, rub the ointment over the entire leg, not just the kneecap. Any questions?''

Wayne Simmons shook his head again. ''No. That sounds simple enough.''

''Okay, but call me if you have any questions. How's the visualization coming?''

''It's getting easier,'' he said. ''I thought it was going to be hard setting aside thirty minutes every day to meditate, but it's not too bad.'' He looked at her with something close to amazement. ''I don't understand it, but it's the darnest thing. Since I started your herbal treatments and the visualization, my arthritis is a whole lot better. It's like magic.''

She chuckled. ''There's nothing magical at all about it. Our mind and body are inextricably linked together. Therefore, every physiological change in our body is accompanied by a corresponding change in our mental state. Likewise, every change in our perceptions, attitudes and emotions is translated by the body into an altered state. By visualizing your leg healthy and strong, your subconscious mind seeks to create that reality.''

''Well, you've made a believer out of me,'' he said. ''I've had arthritis in my left leg for years, so bad that I couldn't bend it without a lot of pain. Now, in four short months, I'm able to walk a block without any pain. That's something I haven't been able to do for a very long time.''

Raven smiled. ''I'm glad you're feeling better, but we need to take things slowly. So don't overdo it, and use your cane when you go out walking. I'll see you in six weeks.''

Raven drew a sigh of relief as Wayne Simmons walked through the doorway. He was her last client for the day.

In the now quiet shop, Raven allowed the tranquility to wash over her. She set about restoring order to the small room just off the main part of the shop that served as a private consultation area and storage room. Even though she'd been on her feet since nine that morning, testimonials like Wayne Simmons's made the hard work and long hours worth it.

She thought back over the last four years. They'd been rough. She had known it wasn't going to be easy, but she hadn't been prepared for the level of hostility she'd initially encountered—from both the local medical community and people in the area who feared she was just a quack. But finally things were beginning to turn around. Nature's Cure was showing a bigger profit every month, to the extent that she'd been able to move from her tiny cramped quarters to this spacious, two-room shop six months ago. She'd even been able to hire a part-time employee.

One of the things that had helped was that she didn't try to compete with the medical community. As far as she was concerned there was room for both views—their traditional view of medicine and her own more unorthodox view.

She walked over to the long rectangular counter that served as her worktable. At the moment, it was covered with herbs, packaged for potpourri, for tea and for culinary uses, as well as several tubes of ointments and a number of ceramic canisters. A floor-to-ceiling cabinet directly behind the counter housed her herbs and other products. She picked up a canister and placed it back on the cabinet shelf.

"Here, let me help you with that," a female voice said from behind her.

She glanced over her right shoulder to see Phyllis Weston, her employee, standing in the doorway. Phyllis was a small, pretty, dark-haired woman in her mid-fifties. "I thought I told you to go home."

"And desert you?" Phyllis said. "Not on your life. Besides, staying here to help you is the only way I know you'll get out of here at a decent hour." She picked up a canister and passed it to Raven.

Raven slid the canister onto the shelf then looked back at Phyllis. "I appreciate the help, but I can't take advantage of you like this. Until I can afford to bring you on full-time, I don't think you should put in so many extra hours."

"Let me worry about that," Phyllis said good-naturedly. "But you do work too hard. You're twenty-seven. Too young and beautiful to be cooped up in this shop until all hours of the night. You should be out enjoying yourself. Why don't you let me fix you up with my nephew?"

Raven smiled. Phyllis, who'd been married more than three decades, was an incurable romantic who saw it as her life's goal to pair up every unmarried person she knew. Instead of answering Phyllis's question, she asked, "How are you feeling?"

"In other words, you aren't interested." Phyllis chuckled. "But in answer to your question, I feel great. That licorice root tea you prepared for me knocked that cold right out of me." She grinned. "Not a sniffle all day."

"Good, I thought it would do the trick," Raven said as she tightened the cap on a tube of ointment. "That particular herb kills germs and clears up cold symptoms quicker than a lot of prescription drugs and over-the-counter medicines."

"Not to mention being a lot more cost-effective." Phyllis paused and looked at her. "Is that why herbs play such a large part in your treatments, because they're so affordable?"

"Well, that's one of the reasons," Raven replied. "But, more importantly, my treatments emphasize prevention and go after the cause of the illness rather than merely treating the symptoms. Additionally, herbs assist your own body in healing itself, instead of introducing strong drugs to do it for you."

Phyllis shook her head. "You'd think more doctors—"

The tinkling of the old-fashioned bell above the front door of the shop interrupted what she was about to say.

"Oops," Phyllis said. "Looks like I forgot to put up the Closed sign. Be right back."

Raven smiled as she watched the other woman scurry through the open doorway into the front room. A moment later, she heard Phyllis say, "I'm sorry, but we were just about to close."

Then came a man's voice, strong, husky...and familiar, like an old love song. The tube of ointment slid from her fingers to the floor as every cell in her body screamed in recognition. Jeff Knight? It couldn't be. He was in Africa. She was losing it, imagining things. Maybe Phyllis was right. She was working too hard and her mind was playing tricks on her. But even as the thought crossed her mind, she was moving across the room. At the doorway she paused and stared at the back of the man talking to Phyllis. As if he could feel her eyes boring into his back, he slowly began to turn toward her.

She waited, her body tense, not daring to breathe. Waited until he faced her, and Raven found herself rooted to the spot as Jeff's hazel eyes fastened on her own startled brown ones—fastened and held her mesmerized.

Time seemed to stand still. She didn't move. She didn't blink. She didn't dare breathe as images splattered before her mind's eye—the two of them laughing, sprawled on the floor in Jeff's apartment making love, planning their future. Things had been perfect. Then her whole world had come tumbling down. Jeff had accused her of giving an herbal mixture to one of his patients. She hadn't, and she'd told him so. But he hadn't believed her. It had been terrible. He couldn't have loved her, not like she'd loved him or he wouldn't have believed Teresa's lies....

She drew a deep, steadying breath, trying to regain her composure. But it was hard. It was terribly hard. A thousand sleepless nights she'd wondered if her memories of him were accurate. If his smile was really so captivating, if his hair actually fell in lush, dark waves about his high forehead, framing his classical features. Now she knew just how deceptive memories could be. They hadn't done him justice.

He was even more handsome than she remembered. She turned the word over in her mind—handsome—the word didn't begin to describe the man who stood before her. Jeff Knight was gorgeous. His features were flawlessly chiseled, his hair curly and jet black, his skin a smooth dark bronze, reflecting his African-American heritage. His eyes were deep-set and totally riveting. They were green, with golden brown flecks, and could mesmerize with sparkling brilliance or melt into hot embers with dark swirling passion. His nose was strong, not hawkish, but decisively masculine, as was his squarish jawline. Sharply defined, prominent cheekbones made his glorious mouth all the more fascinating because it was so sensuously molded, provocative in the fullness of his lower lip and exciting in the elongated curve of the upper one.

He was tall, over six feet, with a lean, muscular build that was essentially athletic. His hips were narrow, his shoulders broad, and his chest wide.

But it wasn't just good looks that brought the sensitive hairs all over her body to attention. He exuded a virility that was all male animal.

Even from several feet away, she could feel the impact of her former lover's powerful presence. It was as if a magnetic current were running back and forth between them. She wondered fleetingly if he felt it, too. She certainly hoped not.

"I thought you were in Africa," she said, moving slowly into the room.

"I left the World Health Organization about four months ago," Jeff said. His deep voice was still husky. "I'm teaching a class over at Chicago Memorial, seeing a few patients."

Phyllis cleared her throat, obviously wondering what the hell was going on between her boss and the handsome stranger. "I'm Phyllis Weston, salesperson and chief bottle washer around here," she said, "Looks like you already know the boss."

"Yes," he said, giving the older woman a warm smile. "Raven and I are…old friends. In fact, that's why I'm here. There's a private matter I'd like to discuss with her."

Phyllis threw Raven a sly wink and grinned. "Oh, sure. I was just leaving."

Raven groaned inwardly. She could see the wheels turning in Phyllis's matchmaking mind. Before she could say anything to clarify the situation, Phyllis had moved behind the cash register counter, grabbed her purse and was headed for the door. "See you in the morning, Raven," she called as she sailed through the door.

The shop door closed, leaving behind a cloud of silence. Raven struggled for composure. She didn't know why Jeff was here, but she dared not let him know how his presence was affecting her.

"I see you got your wish," he said, looking about the attractively decorated shop. "It's very nice."

A compliment? She looked at him, surprised. A compliment was the last thing she'd expected from him, but she'd also never expected to see him again. Or to feel this same pull of attraction. She shook off her feelings and reminded herself that whatever they had once shared had died a long time ago. At least it had for him.

"I'm sure you didn't come here to comment on my shop," she said coolly. "We both know your feelings on that score."

For a moment a flash of pain appeared in his hazel eyes, and then it was gone so quickly she was sure she'd imagined it.

"Look, why don't we just get to the reason you're here," she said curtly.

One dark brow rose sardonically. "Aren't you going to offer me a seat?"

Her mouth tightened. "This way, please," she said,

amazed at how calm she sounded as she turned and walked across the room. He fell into step beside her, matching her stride. The smell of him assaulted her senses. A clean smell, soap and aftershave, and something more. That unmistakable musk that had always clung to him like a personal aura, a permanent badge of his masculinity. She quickened her steps, forcing him to fall back a step. Then she realized that having him walk slightly behind her was just as bad. She could feel his eyes on her, watching every quiver of her body through the navy slacks. She moved still more rapidly. God, the sooner they got this meeting over with, the better she'd like it.

She led him into the small sitting room and was about to offer him the wing chair next to the desk, when she noticed the tube of ointment lying on the floor. She knelt to pick it up.

"Here, I'll get it." He crouched down next to her and they reached for the tube at the same time, his fingers lightly brushing against her own.

A jolt of electricity shot through her, curling her toes. She jerked her hand away, frightened by the feelings that accompanied something so meaningless as an incidental touch.

"No, that's okay," she said, trying to lessen the sexual tension that swirled around them. "I've got it."

"Of course," he said, straightening.

She also stood, but that was just as bad. He was close, too close. She could feel the warmth of his body radiating toward her, almost reaching out to her.

"Ah...why don't you have a seat?" she said, pointing to the wing chair. Then she seated herself behind the desk.

For a moment, neither spoke. They sat staring at each other for painfully long minutes. Raven's stomach muscles tightened. She would not be the first to speak. If this was going to be a game of who blinks first, she was prepared to sit there until hell froze over. Looking into his hazel eyes, she knew he could, too.

"Do you have something to say?" she finally blurted out.

Jeff shifted uncomfortably in his chair. "It's my understanding that Eleanor Parker and Lauren Connor are clients of yours." His voice was soft, but there was an edge to it, like a well-tempered blade.

Her first thought was not to answer, but the look on Jeff's face told her his question was not posed out of idle curiosity. "That's correct," she replied guardedly.

"What about Julie Hartman? Is she also one of your clients?"

The question came quickly, demanding an answer. "The name doesn't sound familiar, but it's possible," she said. "What is this about?"

Instead of answering her question, he fired off another of his own, "What are you treating Mrs. Parker for?"

The edge in his voice had grown sharper, and Raven didn't like it. "I'm not treating her for anything. She was only here once. I suggested an herb called motherwort to calm her nerves and to help her sleep."

"And Lauren Connor? What are you treating her for?"

"Pretty much the same thing." She folded her arms across her chest and looked at him coolly. "I'm not answering any more questions until you tell me what this is all about."

He must have known she meant it, because he said, "It's about three women who all wound up in Chicago Memorial. All seriously ill, all suffering from the same infectious agent, characterized by a fever, headache, abdominal pains, vomiting and diarrhea. Thus far, we've had no luck in identifying the infection. However, in trying to determine the method of transmission of this thing, we discovered a link between at least two of the patients." He paused for a fraction of a second, then added, "That link is you."

Raven's mouth dropped open. Stunned, she had to struggle to find her voice. "I don't like your implication," she said. "I certainly had nothing to do with their health problems."

"I'm not saying you did," Jeff said quickly. "I'm just trying to get to the bottom of their illness."

"Oh, sure you are," she said sarcastically. "That's why you immediately ran over here after hearing Lauren and Eleanor had been to see me."

"I just want to ask you a few questions."

Raven's blood pressure shot skyward. Jeff Knight hadn't changed one iota. He was still willing to believe the worst about her. "Don't give me that. This is about what happened four years ago. I didn't do anything then or now. I admit seeing Lauren Connor and Eleanor Parker and giving them the same herbal tea, but I certainly didn't do anything to cause their illness. My herbs are natural products, free of any chemicals or preservatives."

"I'm sure they are," he said in a placating voice. "But there are a number of herbs that can be quite harmful if prepared incorrectly. Maybe that's what happened in this case. Maybe you made a mistake."

"I did no such thing!" she snapped. "I'm not incompetent. Those herbs were properly prepared."

"That may be, but that still doesn't mean they couldn't have been laced with some kind of bacterial contaminant."

She rolled her eyes. "Give me a break. There was nothing wrong with my herbs."

"How do you know?" he barked. "Did you grow them?"

She could tell he was having difficulty hanging on to his temper. Well, so was she. Her chin rose a fraction. "No, but I'm quite familiar with my supplier and there's no way he would sell contaminated products. I know you don't think much of me or other alternative practitioners, but we're not irresponsible or a bunch of incompetent boobs."

"That's a pretty little speech, but it doesn't square with the facts. The truth is, most of you so-called alternative practitioners, with your claim of miracle cures, are just a bunch of snake oil salesmen preying on the sick and the elderly strictly for financial gain.''

She stared at him coldly. ''You know this is not about money.''

Her frigid stare didn't faze him. ''No, you're a true believer, which probably makes you a hell of a lot more dangerous than your counterparts.''

She curled her fingers into her palm, struggling to hang on to her temper when what she wanted to do was slap his arrogant face. ''The only one of us that is dangerous is you. With your close-minded, outdated ideas about patient care.'' Her voice was so low, so filled with suppressed anger, that he blinked. ''You talk a good story but that's all it is. Talk.''

''And what's that suppose to mean?'' he said hotly.

''You spend almost no time talking to patients, let alone listening to them. Then, on the basis of virtually no information, you're ready to prescribe a course of treatment. A treatment, I might add, that focuses solely on symptoms and consists of toxic drugs. In my book that's irresponsible. I'm not surprised you don't know what's wrong with these women.''

Her remark must have hit home. ''Don't preach to me about responsibility,'' he snarled. ''I've got three seriously ill patients, one of whom is probably not going to make it. I've been working my butt off for the last two weeks, trying to figure out what's wrong with them. Everything we've tested them for has come back negative. We don't know what this thing is or how they contracted it. So when I found a link between you and two of my patients, I had to check it out. If my questions offended you, then that's too damn bad!''

For a moment neither spoke.

''Look.'' She sighed. ''I'm sorry about Mrs. Parker and the other women, but I assure you there is nothing wrong with my herbs.''

"Can you prove it?" His eyes were hard, challenging.

She stood and walked over to the storage area. She could feel his eyes on her as she located the canister containing the herbs she'd used to brew the tea she'd given Eleanor Parker and Lauren Connor. She turned and walked back across the room until she was standing directly in front of him. "Take it," she said, thrusting the canister into his hands. "Run all the tests you want, but you won't find anything. Now—" she stepped back and pointed toward the door "—get out!"

He stood and walked across the room, but in the doorway, he paused. "For your sake, I hope you're right," he said. Then he turned and walked through the doorway. A moment later, she heard the front door open and then close.

A tiny shiver went through Raven. God, her herbs couldn't have caused this illness, could they?

Chapter Two

"Damn!" Raven swore at the overturned canisters and the herbs strewn about on the counter in front of her. Her eyes flew to the clock on the wall. It was almost ten, and she was only half-done with completing Kevin Miller's order. Miller was a nervous, impatient man but he was also one of her best customers. He could be counted on for a minimum purchase of two hundred dollars a month. It wouldn't do to keep him waiting. But she was so darned angry, she couldn't see straight, let alone concentrate.

She'd had all night to stew over Jeff's words, and the more she thought about his outrageous allegation, the angrier she became. Jeff Knight was a narrow-minded, cynical, self-righteous bastard. She'd love to—

"You okay?"

Raven looked up from the mess in front of her to find Harry Flynn, her landlord and business colleague, scrutinizing her.

"Uh...yeah," Raven stammered. With an effort, she banished Jeff from her mind and gave her friend a faint smile. "I was just thinking."

"Obviously not very pleasant thoughts," he said, moving into the room.

Harry was shrewdly observant, a quality that was an asset in his profession as an importer-exporter. But as a friend, he could be disconcerting. "Just give me a minute to finish up here," she said.

"Sure, take your time."

Raven scooped up the remaining herbs and dumped them back into the ceramic canister. Out of the corner of her eye, she saw Harry prowling the room. It was unlike him to drop by this time of day. Then she smiled. He was the most structured person she knew. An attractive man of forty-five, tall and slender, with dark eyes and thick, wavy hair that was more silver than gray, he looked like an investment banker, but he wasn't stuffy or pompous. He had a relaxed, easygoing manner.

She had liked him on sight when they met a year ago when he'd become her herb supplier. Then, six months ago, he had become her landlord. His obvious interest in alternative medicine had solidified the bond between them. She considered him a good friend.

She knew he'd like the relationship to be otherwise, but she'd made it plain she wasn't interested in anything other than friendship. For one thing, she was too busy trying to get her business off the ground and didn't have time for socializing. For another, she simply couldn't imagine herself becoming romantically involved with him. Handsome and charming he was, but for her the chemistry was missing. For that matter, she hadn't met anyone in a very long time who made her heart beat double time. Her girlfriends laughed and called her an incurable romantic. Maybe she was, but she'd decided long ago that the man she married had to make her heart flutter. She didn't think it was ridiculous to want the passion, the heights. She'd had that kind of relationship...once. A flood of memories washed over her.

She shook them off. Jeff was the last man she should be thinking about. But she couldn't get him out of her mind. Seeing him again had stirred deep-seated feelings that she'd thought long since buried. God, she needed her head examined. How could she still have feelings for a man who not only didn't respect her profession, but who also thought she personally was irresponsible—that she could endanger someone's life?

All this flashed through her mind in an instant while Harry Flynn perched on the stool in front of the counter.

He regarded her thoughtfully for a moment, then said, "Look, Raven, I don't mean to pry. I considered not even telling you this, but if it were the other way around, I'd want to know." He sounded serious.

"What is it?" she asked cautiously.

"I had a visitor this morning," he said. "A cop by the name of Valentine. He wanted to know what I knew about you. If you were a responsible and stable individual."

"He...*what?*"

Harry nodded. "There's more. He also asked what kind of tenant you were—if you paid your rent on time, if I'd ever had any problems with you. When I said I had no complaints, he hemmed and hawed and finally asked if I'd ever heard of anyone getting sick after taking one of your herbal treatments."

Raven's mouth fell open as sudden fury swept through her. "I can't believe he has the police checking me out!"

"I know it's none of my business, but I'm curious as hell. Want to talk about it?"

Raven released a long sigh, then recounted her meeting with Jeff.

"*What?*" Harry's voice was a shocked squeal. "He believes you're responsible for the illness of these women?"

Raven nodded, her face grim.

"That's ridiculous," he said. "I know a couple of alternative practitioners that tangled with some folks in the medical profession. But it was over some pretty innocuous stuff. I've never heard of anything like this."

"I know." She sighed. "But Dr. Knight has a particularly low opinion of herbs and herbalists. He thinks we're a bunch of dangerous quacks."

"Well, I guess you can't expect anything else. He's a

doctor," Harry said, as if that explained it. "They understand things like cancer, heart disease and broken bones. But they aren't quick to grasp things outside the normal range of standard medicine. The concept of herbal healing isn't in Dr. Knight's world."

Raven shook her head. "I know, but it doesn't make sense. He deals with prescription drugs every day. Doesn't he understand that a large percentage of those drugs are derived from the very herbs he disdains?"

Harry shrugged. "It's the nature of the beast. The sad fact is, the typical American physician's only real exposure to herbal healing involves the small but steady stream of medical journal articles reporting harm from the irresponsible use of herbs."

"Yeah, but the number of people harmed by herbs is only a tiny fraction of the number harmed by prescription drugs."

"But the average doctor doesn't know that," Harry countered. "When you start talking about herbs to treat serious illnesses, even the most open-minded doctors find that hard to swallow. And the others immediately assume you're nuts or, worse yet, a quack out to take some poor schmo to the cleaners. It's not what they're taught in medical school so it's outside their frame of reference. I'm sure you haven't always been a true believer, either. At some point in your life you probably held some of these same views."

"I was skeptical at first," she admitted, "but at least I was willing to consider the possibility."

Harry smiled. "It's that objectivity and open-mindedness that probably makes you such a good herbalist."

"Thanks for the vote of confidence," she said, returning his smile.

"I'm just calling it the way I see it." He cleared his throat. "Er...Raven, you know I think you're a very levelheaded person and would never intentionally do anything that would endanger anyone's life. Oh, hell, there's no easy way to say this," he said quickly, "but is it possible you could have made a mistake in the preparation of the herbal tea you gave those women?"

She shook her head. "No. I've gone over it a thousand times in my mind, and I'm sure on each occasion I prepared it the way I always do. Just to be on the safe side, I called the three other clients whom I gave tea from that batch, and they're fine."

"Ah...well," Harry began, then he looked down at his hands. "You know, there is one other possibility."

Raven knew immediately what he was getting at. She took both of his hands in hers and squeezed. "No, there isn't," she said. "I know you didn't sell me contaminated herbs."

"So, why do I hear a *but* in there?"

"I also know Jeff," she said bleakly. "He's very thorough. He must believe the method of transmission of this thing is from herbs. What if he's right? What if there is some kind of contaminant in the herbs out there?"

Harry's eyebrows shot up. "That's a pretty scary thought, and one that I don't buy. But in the meantime, you've got a very serious problem. If that cop questioned me, it's a sure bet he's questioning other people associated with you. There's bound to be talk—talk that will hurt your business because people are going to assume the same thing that guy Knight did, that your herbs are making people sick."

"I won't let that happen!" she cried, jumping to her feet.

He shook his head. "I don't know how you're going to stop it. It would be different if you had a longer track record, but you don't. You've only been in the business a few years."

"I've worked too hard to sit back and do nothing." As she talked she rubbed her hands on her arms and paced, her arms folded tightly. "I'm going to have to do something to clear my name."

"Yeah, but that's easier said than done," he replied. "How can you prove a negative—that you *didn't* do something? It seems to me the only way that could happen is if this Dr. Knight gave you a clean bill of health."

"Or," she said, pausing in her pacing and looking across the counter at him, "if I figure out what's wrong with these women myself."

Harry smiled. "That's true," he said, "but to do that you're going to need help from someone in the medical community, and I don't see that happening. No one is going to want to get involved in this mess. Since they're Knight's patients, getting him to help you would probably be your best bet, but from what you've said, I can't see him rushing to help you or including you in any investigation. Without someone within the medical community helping you, you're dead in the water."

"I don't think so," she said, shaking her head. "I've got an idea."

"Good," he said. "Let's hear it."

She leaned forward, her eyes sparkling with excitement. "It's a sure bet that if Eleanor Parker and Lauren Connor came to see me, then they've probably seen other alternative practitioners in the past. What if they continued seeing them? It's possible that's where the exposure to this herbal contaminant—if indeed that's what it boils down to—occurred."

"Yeah, it's possible," Harry said slowly, "but how are you going to find these people?"

"From my client records. I always take a medical history on anyone coming for a consultation. As soon as I finish up here, I'm going to review my write-ups on Parker and Connor to see if I can find anything."

"Good luck," he said. "But don't be surprised if you find that your clients haven't been entirely candid with either you or Dr. Knight. It's been my experience that the truth is more likely somewhere in the middle." He looked at his watch. "Well…I'd better get back to the office." He leaned across the counter and laid his hand over Raven's. "If there's anything I can do, let me know."

She smiled. He really was a kind man. "Thanks, Harry."

"I mean it. Call me if you need anything." He slid his slender frame from the stool and sauntered out of the room.

After he left, Raven tried to get back to work, but it was no use. She was too keyed up. Once again, the more she thought about Jeff's allegation, the angrier she became. She stood and paced the brightly lit room, seething with anger at the thought that Jeff had actually had a cop checking up on her. He had some nerve! He probably hadn't even considered the possibility that she had nothing to do with Lauren's and Eleanor's health problems. It was just like four years ago all over again, she thought bitterly. On the basis of questionable information, he'd tried and convicted her. How did he expect to get to the root of his patients' sickness if he was couldn't separate fact from fiction?

Well, he'd get no help from her.

Then she thought about Lauren and Eleanor and their mysterious illness, and her anger subsided. If the women had been exposed to some kind of bacterial contaminant, as Jeff surmised, there would be other victims. Maybe even some deaths. *They* would be the ones who would suffer from Jeff's attitude. Could she live with herself if she did nothing?

"SO YOU DIDN'T TELL Grace Wells that Raven Delaney had poisoned Eleanor Parker?"

"Of course not," Jeff said as he regarded the man who sat across the desk from him. Detective Nick Valentine could have passed for a college student with his boyish good looks. He was an athletic-looking man with blond hair, cut military short. Despite his youthful appearance, Jeff sensed he was no pushover.

"Then how do you suppose she came to that conclusion?"

Jeff shifted his weight uneasily, rubbing at the tension building in his gut. "Grace is a highly emotional woman," he said, choosing his words carefully. "She's very upset about her friend's illness. In a case like this, where someone is critically ill, it's not unusual for the patient's family and friends to seek to blame someone else for their loved one's condition. It's their way of coping with the situation."

"Hmm," Detective Valentine mused. He leaned back and tapped his finger on the arm of the chair as he considered Jeff's words. "So you think that's what happened here, that Ms. Wells is focusing on the Delaney woman because she needs someone to blame?"

"I'm saying it's one explanation," Jeff said cautiously. "Just before Mrs. Parker was hospitalized, she and Grace went to see Raven Delaney. After Mrs. Parker was hospitalized, another of Grace's friends, a woman who'd also seen Ms. Delaney, was hospitalized. Now she's convinced herself that Ms. Delaney is behind Eleanor's illness."

"I see," Detective Valentine said slowly. "By the way, what's Mrs. Parker's prognosis?"

Jeff issued a weary sigh. "I can't go into any details because of doctor-patient confidentiality. I can tell you that she's gravely ill and hasn't responded to treatment."

"So there's nothing suspicious about her illness? No sign of criminal activity or foul play?"

Jeff shook his head. "There's no evidence to support that claim." That was true. He was still waiting for the lab results on Raven's herbs so he had no evidence that they were behind the mysterious illness. And even if they were, in his book that certainly didn't amount to criminal activity. "I'm afraid Grace misunderstood what I said."

Detective Valentine gave him a quizzical look. "Is she prone to jumping to conclusions?"

Jeff's mouth curved into a smile. "You met her. What do you think?"

"That I'd hate to have to deal with that woman on a regular basis," Detective Valentine said, closing his notebook. "We didn't think there was anything to her claim, but you understand we had to check it out."

Jeff felt an incredible sense of relief. "Frankly, I'm surprised," he said, relaxing for the first time since the interview had begun. "Isn't it a little unusual for a homicide detective to be checking out this kind of claim? Seems to me it didn't merit more than a few discreet phone calls by a rookie cop."

"You're right. Generally, that's the way we would have played it." His face breaking into a grin, Detective Valentine added, "I was in the squad room when Ms. Wells stormed in making all kinds of noises to the effect that if we didn't check out her claim she'd go to the newspapers and then the governor."

Jeff grinned. He could imagine the ruckus she'd caused.

"Unfortunately, the mayor and a slew of reporters were due any moment. Naturally, the captain wanted her out of there ASAP. Being relatively new to the force, I needed to get acclimated to the city and saw an opportunity to get some brownie points, so I told the captain I'd make a few inquiries."

"And?" Jeff was careful to keep his voice and facial expression neutral.

"You confirmed what others said about Ms. Delaney. I think we can close this matter. There's no evidence to suggest this is anything other than the ranting of a hysterical woman." Detective Valentine tucked his notebook inside the breast pocket of his jacket, then stood. He reached across the desk and offered his hand. "Well, thank you for your time, doctor. You've been a lot of help."

Jeff stood and took his hand. "Anytime."

When the door closed behind the young detective, Jeff walked over to the window and stared bleakly out at the street below, his thoughts in turmoil. If things weren't complicated enough, now this. He raked his hand over his hair in frustration. He should have seen it coming, spent more time allaying Grace's fears. But after she'd dropped her bombshell, all he could think about was Raven. What it was like to hold her, her scent, her lovely smile....

He closed his eyes, seeing again the expression on her face, a mixture of apprehension and innate pride. He'd thought he had prepared himself for the meeting, that he could handle it. But at the sight of her, the gut-wrenching desire had returned, the relentless yearning that he'd always felt. So he'd taken refuge in icy politeness, then anger, discussing a medical problem with the one woman he had never been able to forget. Lord, why couldn't he forget her?

When they'd first broken up, he'd tried. First by dating a slew of women, later by enmeshing himself in his work. And when that hadn't worked, he had moved halfway around the world, but still she'd remained in his subconscious mind—haunting his thoughts, his dreams.

How many nights had he lain awake, wondering what it would be like to see her again? Wondering if the relentless heartache would still wring the life from him, the way it had in the first painful weeks and months after their breakup. Well, now he knew. It wasn't a damn bit easier today than it had been then. If anything, it was worse.

He rubbed his temple. He had to stop thinking about her. No matter how much he might still be attracted to her, he still couldn't reconcile her belief in herbal medicine. It went against everything he believed in. Hell, this wasn't getting him anywhere. He turned and looked at the pile of work on his desk. He had a million things to do, including preparing for a meeting with Shay Alexander, the head of the hospital's medical research lab, to discuss the three cases. Shay had promised to have the results of the latest tests ready within the hour.

He turned away from the window, sat down, and propped his feet on the corner of his desk. He opened the first report and forced himself to concentrate. It was difficult at first, but gradually his thoughts turned to the matter at hand. Twenty minutes later, he looked up as Shay Alexander entered the room. Jeff set his feet on the floor and sat up. "Did you find anything?"

"Nothing that helps us much," Shay said as he dropped into the chair flanking Jeff's desk. The two men had first met in medical school and had kept in touch over the years. It had been Shay who had convinced him to take the teaching position at Chicago Memorial. Shay was thirty-seven, six foot one, with a lean, strong build. His mouth was wide, his blue eyes merry, and his strawberry-blond hair thick and wavy. He was witty and intelligent, and Jeff got the impression that Shay could find the silver lining in almost any situation. From his grim expression, however, this was not one of them.

"Frankly, I'm stumped," Shay muttered. "I've been an epidemiologist for seven years and I've never seen anything like this before."

Jeff groaned in frustration. "I was hoping for a different answer."

"You and me both." Shay consulted the notes he'd pulled out of a slim manila folder. "Everything we've tested has been negative—blood cultures, urine cultures, sputum cultures, stool cultures, even cerebrospinal fluid cultures. We thought about malaria and actually tested for it. Not surprising, the blood smears were negative for the parasite. We even tested for typhoid. But, just like with all the other tests, the results came back negative."

Jeff frowned. "Can you tell me anything?"

"Well, I can tell you what it's not. It's not yellow fever, dengue hemorrhagic fever, or dysentery. Just to cover the bases, we tested for a number of enteroviral, arboviral, and adenoviral infections, and came up with zilch.''

Jeff sighed. ''So you're saying we don't know much more than we did two weeks ago?''

''Afraid not.''

''I take it then that you haven't made much progress in the therapeutic realm either, or for that matter, determined why Hartman and Connor seem better equipped to fight this thing off than Mrs. Parker?''

Shay shook his head. ''Not really. My guess is that as the oldest of the three, she simply has the weakest immune system. And her condition is further complicated by her diabetes. The only bright spot,'' he said with a grimace, ''if you wish to call it that, is that I was able to track down Mrs. Parker's errant husband. He was able to help us fill in some of the gaps regarding her movements in the days preceding the onset of the illness.'' He leaned over and handed Jeff the report.

Jeff flipped through the pages, stopping on a section entitled ''History of the Present Illness.'' One item immediately jumped out at him. One week prior to admission, she'd been bitten by a *Cercopithecus aethiops*. He asked Shay about it.

''It's a type of monkey,'' his friend replied.

Jeff gave him a sour look. ''I know that, but how the hell does someone in Chicago get bitten by a monkey?''

Shay shrugged. ''I gather it was some kind of freak accident. Mrs. Parker took her Sunday school class on a field trip to the Brookfield Zoo. While they were there, one of the monkeys got loose and during the ensuing fracas, she was bitten by the primate. The monkey's been quarantined, but there's no indication that it was the source of the infection.''

Jeff nodded and continued reading. Two days before Mrs. Parker was hospitalized, she had been mugged while walking home from church. She'd hit her cheek on the pavement. Well, that explained the bruises, he thought.

He scanned the remaining pages. Finding nothing of interest, he tossed the report on the desk and looked at Shay. "Well, that didn't tell us very much. But we'd better find something that does. We've got to come up with some way of combating this infection."

"Jeff, I understand your frustration but I don't know what to tell you. I can test for every known bacterial and viral infection, but that will take some time."

"And time is what we don't have."

"Then give me something to go on," the other man said. "Otherwise, it's like looking for a needle in a haystack when you don't know what a haystack looks like."

Jeff rubbed his temples. "I know," he said wearily.

For a moment neither man spoke.

"What about bringing the Centers for Disease Control in on this?" Shay asked after a while.

Jeff shook his head. "I suggested it, but Brockman vetoed the idea." His hazel eyes clouded as he recalled the hospital's chief of staff's reaction. He'd seemed to Jeff to be unduly concerned about bad publicity and its effect on the hospital's financial status. "He doesn't want to bring them into this until it is absolutely necessary."

"Well, we're almost there," Shay said dryly.

Jeff nodded. "We'll give it a few more days. If something doesn't break by then, I'll notify the CDC."

"Okay, how do you want to proceed from here?"

"I think we should concentrate on prevention, which, at this point, means determining the origin of the current cases."

"You and I think along the same lines," Shay said.

Jeff cleared his throat. "Ah...what about those herbs that I asked you to analyse? Is it possible they contained some kind of contaminant that could have caused these symptoms?"

"There was nothing in what I tested," Shay said with a slight shake of his head.

Jeff slowly released his breath. "Are you sure?"

Shay cocked his head to the side and gave his friend a speculative look. "Why this sudden interest in herbs? And don't try to give me some cock-and-bull story about being interested in herbal medicine, because I know your views on the subject."

Jeff shifted uncomfortably in his seat, but he knew Shay wouldn't give up until he'd heard at least part of the story. So he gave him a slightly abbreviated version, concluding with his visit from Nick Valentine.

Shay digested his words for a moment. "So you think this is some kind of bacterial contaminant transmitted by a particular herb?"

"I think it's a possibility," Jeff said.

"It's not a bad theory," Shay said slowly. "I think you should pursue it."

Jeff's head snapped up. "I thought you said Raven's herbs were clean."

"Raven?" Shay's eyebrows lifted and a grin began working at the corners of his mouth. "It's like that, is it?"

"I'd drop the subject if I were you," Jeff warned.

Shay put on an injured expression. "Well, if you feel that way about it."

"I do."

Shay sighed. "All right, all right. But on the subject of herbs, I just meant you might be on the right track, that there might be some contaminated herbs out there. Frankly, at this stage I don't think we can rule anything in or out. I can handle the lab aspect, but I think you should pursue the herb angle." He looked at Jeff and grinned. "Maybe if you apologize nicely, you can get *Raven* to help you."

"What? You've got to be kidding."

"Hear me out before you go ballistic," he said, all traces of levity now gone. "You need to check out that angle and you need somebody who knows that world to help—"

"Not on your life," Jeff interrupted.

Shay's eyes remained on Jeff's for a long moment as if he were considering his next words. "I think you should reconsider your answer."

Jeff's brow pulled down. "Why would I want to do that?"

"Look at this," Shay said, handing him a small file from his manila folder. "I didn't want to say anything until I was absolutely sure of the facts, but I did some checking with the other hospitals in the area. Over the last seven weeks there have been at least four other cases admitted, all with the same symptoms as our patients..."

A ripple of apprehension coursed through Jeff. "And?"

Shay's eyes didn't waver from his. "They're all dead. Whatever this is we're dealing with, it's one hundred percent fatal."

Chapter Three

"But, I just want—"

Click! The phone at the other end of the line was slammed down with such force, Raven thought she might suffer a permanent hearing loss. She leaned back in her chair and crossed Fred Baxter's name off the list. He was the third person to hang up on her. The moment she mentioned two of their clients had been hospitalized and that the culprit might be an herbal contaminant, no one wanted to talk. Hence, few of the half dozen or so alternative practitioners whose names she'd found in the notes from her sessions with Eleanor Parker and Lauren Connor would talk to her. And those who did were either suffering from a lapse in memory or flat-out denied ever treating the women. While she couldn't completely blame them for not wanting to get involved, it was still frustrating as hell.

Raven looked at the skimpy notes in front of her and sighed. She'd spent the better part of the day on the phone, running down leads, and all she had to show for her efforts was one name—Reverend Charles Walters. At least it was a pretty good lead. From all accounts, he was the only alternative practitioner that both women had seen, and he also had a questionable reputation. Walters was a practitioner of naturopathic medicine, a form of alternative health care that uses the body's own inherent ability to heal itself. A more apt description, she thought, might be that of separating people from their money. Over the years, Walters had been in and out of trouble with the law. However, she gathered his problems in the past related to fraudulent claims and questionable treatments for cancer and AIDS. That was a far cry from using contaminated herbs. She sighed again. It was going to be darn hard connecting him to Lauren's and Eleanor's illness if this was all she had to go on.

She was frustrated and couldn't help but blame Jeff for that frustration. If he'd come to her for help, together they might have been able to identify this mysterious illness. As it was, she felt as if she were beating her head against a brick wall—

Her thoughts were interrupted by a sharp knock on the outside of the doorjamb. She looked up and was surprised to see the object of her thoughts standing in the doorway.

She was immediately flooded by a tide of mixed feelings, the overriding one being anger—anger at herself for feeling a stirring of attraction, anger at his patronizing attitude, anger at him for having the police check up on her. The man had some nerve!

"What do you want?"

Jeff cleared his throat. "If you've got a couple of minutes, I'd like to talk to you."

"Me?" Raven's eyes widened in mock surprise. "I'm surprised. I didn't think you thought it was safe to breathe the same air as an infamous poisoner."

"Unless you're also a mind reader, how could you possibly know my thoughts?" Jeff pushed himself away from the doorjamb and moved into the room.

Raven's gaze narrowed at the sarcasm in his voice as he moved into her office with a casual, masculine grace. An image of a panther flashed through her mind, causing her to shiver. She knew the image was in no way an illusion—he was certainly as dangerous as a panther. "I would have to be brain-dead not to have known what you were thinking," she snapped, irritated with herself for not being able to take her eyes off him. "You acted like I was some kind of Lucrezia Borgia."

"Well, Raven," he said, coming to stand next to her desk, "you have to admit things did look pretty incriminating."

"You have your reality, I have mine," she said, throwing back at him a comment he'd made all those years ago.

The strong planes of his handsome face shifted as he grinned. Oddly enough it seemed to be a grin of admiration. "Touché," he said. "As for my personal safety, I came prepared..." His voice trailed off as he patted his left side. "I've got a tranquilizer gun handy in case you try anything funny."

She stared at him, not at all impressed by his attempt at humor. "That's real smart of you, Knight, but don't press your luck. I'd like nothing better than to deck you."

His grin widened. "I didn't think you were the violent type."

She bolted from her chair, planting her hands on her hips. "You think a lot of things without much evidence, don't you? Where do you get off having the cops question my friends and colleagues about me?"

He at least had the grace to look uncomfortable. "I didn't," he said. "Look, I know your herbs didn't play any role in Eleanor's and Lauren's illness, and that's exactly what I told Detective Valentine." He then briefly explained Grace Wells's trip to the police station and his visit from the young detective. "I'm sorry if I caused you any embarrassment."

"Embarrassment!" she snapped. "After four years of struggling, my business is finally beginning to show a profit, then this happens. Rumors like this could jeopardize my business."

"I'm really sorry. I'll talk to Detective Valentine again."

"What good would that do?" she muttered. "The damage is already done." Just then she noticed how the lights from the overhead fixture caught his blue-black hair, turning it to glistening ebony. Her pulse quickened. What was wrong with her? How could she be attracted to a man who'd made it plain he thought she was a misguided flake?

"Can I talk to you?" he asked again.

She didn't offer him a seat. Even though he'd apologized, she wasn't quite ready to let him off the hook. "What about?"

"Lauren and Eleanor and their mysterious illness," he said quietly. "This thing has me really stumped. If you have a few minutes, I'd like to talk to you about it."

Raven's fury fizzled out like a firecracker. He'd said exactly the right thing, in exactly the right way. She indicated the vacant chair next to her desk, then watched as he sat. Even though he sat a few feet away, she could feel the sexual magnetism that radiated from him like heat waves, pulling her closer. Suddenly, the room seemed awfully small. She shivered.

He frowned. "Is something wrong?"

She shook her head. As she leaned back in her swivel chair, she felt the barrette at the back of her head loosen, and her hair tumbled free. "Damn!" she muttered under her breath. She grabbed the barrette and quickly put her hair back up.

Jeff was watching her closely. "You have beautiful hair. You ought to wear it down, the way you used to," he said softly, as if speaking to himself.

At his husky words, a shiver worked its way up Raven's spine. She shifted uncomfortably and decided it would be prudent to get the conversation back to the matter at hand. "Thank you," she mumbled, then cleared her throat. "Uh, how are Lauren and Eleanor?"

"Not good."

"What's your guess?" Raven asked.

"I don't even have a guess," he admitted. "It's obviously a severe febrile illness, characterized by headache, fever, abdominal pain, vomiting, diarrhea. From those symptoms we surmised it's some kind of bacterial infection. But that's about all we know." He hesitated, then added, "In addition to my three patients, there have been at least four other cases in the last seven weeks—all terminal."

"My God!" Raven exclaimed. "It sounds as if you're dealing with some kind of epidemic."

"It's a possibility," he said. "We usually see a few infectious disease cases each year in the U.S., but they generally occur in warmer climates such as Florida and California, and they're mostly things like malaria and hepatitis B. We certainly haven't seen anything like this before. But with the destruction of the African rain forest, and the emergence of newly discovered diseases like AIDS and Ebola, I suppose it's only a matter of time before we're faced with some kind of catastrophic epidemic."

Raven shivered at his words. "That's a frightening thought," she said, then added, "Has the media been notified?"

Jeff shook his head. "You've worked in hospitals. You know how public-relations conscious they are. The board has made it plain that they want to keep a lid on things."

"But shouldn't the public be alerted?" Raven pressed.

Jeff shook his head again. "I don't think so. At this stage, we don't know what we're dealing with. By sensationalizing it, the media could make things worse. The mere mention of words like *mysterious illness* and *deadly virus* could evoke panic, and that would be counterproductive."

"Maybe," Raven said. "But I bet people would feel differently if there was a chance they could avoid coming down with this thing if they were forewarned."

"Well, the question is academic," Jeff said. "There's no way the hospital is going public with this. Hell, at this point they're not even willing to bring in the CDC or Public Health."

She frowned. "Is this thing contagious?"

He shook his head. "It doesn't appear to be. Nor is it spread through the air, or by bites from mosquitoes, insects, rodents or animals, or by person-to-person contact. Because of the symptoms the patients have exhibited, we think it may be transmitted by ingestion. Possibly by some contaminated food product. Though I'm not sure where in the process the contamination occurred. It could be with the grower, the supplier or the customer store."

"If there's anything I can do to help, just let me know," she said.

He gave her a dazzling smile, causing her heart to skip a beat. "That's what I was hoping you would say." He pulled out a notepad. "We know all seven patients came into contact with the same contaminant. We don't know if the source is herbs or not, but at this point it's the only thing we have to go on. We also don't know where in the process the contamination occurred so for the sake of brevity I'd like to start with the suppliers. That's where your help comes in, Ray."

She felt a warm glow. It was the first time he'd called her by the old nickname, and it lent an odd intimacy to the meeting.

"My knowledge of herbs is pretty shaky and I don't know anything about the suppliers in this area. Any suggestions on how I should begin?" he asked.

"I have a couple of books I can lend you that should give you a working knowledge of the subject. I can also give you the names of a few suppliers and some mail-order companies." She spent several minutes going through the Rolodex on her desk, writing down names and addresses. When she was done, she handed him the list.

"Thanks," he said. Again, he punctated his reply with a warm smile and her heart began to pound double time.

She shifted uncomfortably. "Ah...I don't think it's suppliers that you have to worry about. You might want to reconsider the possibility of an unscrupulous alternative health care practitioner."

One dark eyebrow rose. "Oh, really?"

Her chin rose a fraction. "We're no different from any other profession. We have our share of bad apples."

"Yeah, but how do we find him and connect him to not three patients, but seven?" He shook his head. "In a city the size of Chicago there would be too many to check out. Then you've also got to consider the ones in Cook County and the surrounding area. Added to that there's got to be an unknown number of storefront practitioners. Tracking them all down and checking them out could take weeks, months even."

"Not necessarily," Raven said. Her eyes sparkled with excitement. "People in this profession have a pretty good idea of who's competent and who isn't. I've been on the phone most of the day, and I got a couple of names. I then matched those names with information I got from Lauren and Eleanor and I came up with one person. It seems both women saw a Reverend Walters before coming to see me."

He looked at her with something close to admiration. "Very good."

"It gets better," she said, barely able to contain her excitement. "Walters has a reputation for using substandard products."

His eyebrow arched. "Now that's interesting."

"It is, isn't it?" She glanced her watch. "It's probably too late to see him today, and tomorrow is Sunday. We'll have to wait until later in the week—"

"We?" Jeff interrupted.

She speared him with a hard look. "Yes, *we*." She took a deep breath, determined to stand her ground. "I want to get to the bottom of this mysterious illness just as badly as you do."

"I appreciate your interest, but I work alone."

"Not this time," she said, shaking her head. "I'm not any more thrilled at the prospect of working with you. But you're the one who got me into this mess. You come barreling into my shop, accusing me of poisoning your patients—''

"I never used the word *poison!*''

"It doesn't matter what your exact words were. Because of you, my reputation has been damaged. I want to be a part of this investigation. I want an opportunity to clear my name. You owe me that much.'' His eyes narrowed, but she sensed she had the advantage, and pressed on. "Besides, I know this world. I can help you check out herb suppliers, interview Reverend Walters, even introduce you to my friend, Harry Flynn. He's my herb supplier. If there is anyone who knows what's going on in this business, it's Harry. You have my word that I won't say anything about the investigation. What do you say?''

He stared at her for a long moment without speaking. "Okay,'' he said finally, "I'll pick you up Monday morning. We'll go see your friend Harry. In the meantime, here's what I'd like you to do....''

AFTER JEFF LEFT Raven's, he drove around for a while, finally parking his car at a spot overlooking Lake Michigan. He leaned his head against the headrest and sighed. He should have said no, he thought. He should have gotten the information he came for, thanked Raven for her help, then gotten the hell out of there.

But no, he was too much of a damn fool for that. Instead of looking out for himself, instead of protecting his heart, he'd agreed to let her be a part of the investigation.

He sighed again. Everything she had said was true about the role she could play in the investigation. She would be invaluable in checking out herb suppliers and interviewing this guy Walters. But it was just that he felt so damn vulnerable. Emotionally, he wasn't sure if he could handle spending a lot of time alone with her.

Then again, maybe spending time with her was exactly what he should do. Maybe it would help him put their relationship behind him once and for all. They were both mature adults. Surely, he could spend time in her company, investigating this case, without going off the deep end. The more he thought about it, the more convinced he became that he could do it.

One thing he damn well wasn't going to do was fall under her spell again. But even as he told himself that, he wasn't sure if he believed it.

AT SEVEN-THIRTY Sunday evening, he was exactly where he was supposed to be, where The Plan said that he must be—standing in front of one of the large picture windows that overlooked the library parking lot below. Except for an occasional patron passing by, he was alone. He liked it that way. It fit in nicely with his Plan.

Now all he had to do was wait for her to show. He took a sip of coffee and grimaced. He hated the stuff, but the thermos, the coffee, it was all part of The Plan. He picked up his camera, crossed to the window, and stared out at the parking lot.

A few minutes later, a late model Mustang pulled into the lot and a tall, slender blonde stepped out. He glanced at his watch and smiled. Right on time. For a moment he was afraid she might have parked in the back lot and entered the building through the rear door. If she'd done that, he probably would have had to hang around until midnight and catch her as she left, since the pictures had to be taken tonight. The Plan was specific. It didn't allow for variations.

He had to get everything nailed down tonight. Tomorrow, he would be working with an even shorter time frame than usual. He'd have to finish up here by 8:45 in order to make it to Smitty's by nine. Two pigeons in one night would be tough, but he was confident he could do it.

He lifted the camera and began to shoot, one picture after another. The Nikon's motor whirred, clicking away as the blonde walked toward the building. Although she wasn't in the first group, she was a necessary part of The

Plan. He continued to shoot, not stopping until she disappeared from view.

He put the camera back into the case and leaned against the windowsill, pleased with what he'd accomplished. The pictures would be nice, he thought, considering the dozen or so black-and-white shots he'd taken. Color was fine for certain situations, but not this one. He glanced at his watch. He'd give her a few minutes to get situated. While he waited, he pulled out of his knapsack the books he'd lifted from a law student outside the University of Chicago Law School two days ago. A few minutes later he pushed away from the window and walked slowly toward the law library's study section.

He entered the alcove. The blonde was already seated at one of the two tables in this area. He walked past her and paused at the other table, where a lone, pimply-faced brunette had settled herself. His eyes took in books, paper and a foam cup filled with steaming, hot coffee. She was hunched over her books, deep in thought.

"Excuse me," he whispered. "I hope you don't mind my sitting here?"

The woman looked up from the Q and A book. He knew she did mind and he wanted to laugh. Like the blonde, she'd most likely picked this back, secluded area of the library for privacy. The bar exam was a week away, and she probably still had a lot of material to go through. No doubt that was why she was here tonight instead of at home. She looked anxious, cracking under the pressure of the exam that loomed ahead. Three years of law school and it all came down to this one exam. Pass it, and a job at some high-powered law firm was hers; fail it, and the last three years would have all been for nothing. That fear was probably what brought her to the law library night after night.

She was on the verge of asking him to sit somewhere else, when she noticed the bar review books in his arms. He could almost read her mind. Another law student, she thought, and felt a twinge of guilt for hogging the entire table. She knew how hard it was to find a nice quiet place to study.

It took all his willpower not to snicker when she said grudgingly, "I guess you can sit there."

He knew she expected him to take one of the seats across from her, but instead he plopped down in the chair next to her. He was crowding her but he didn't care. This seat gave him an unobstructed view of the blonde, and that was all that mattered. The brunette muttered something under her breath as she slid her materials closer to her side, careful not to spill any of the coffee in the foam cup.

He made a show of pulling out a legal pad, fountain pen and a thermos from his knapsack. He poured himself a cup of coffee and took a sip as he surreptitiously studied the blonde. She was totally engrossed in her studies.

A moment later the woman next to him also returned to the Q and A book. Soon she'd totally forgotten he was there. Periodically, he would look up at the blonde, but she wasn't paying any attention to him or anyone else, for that matter. She was totally oblivious to her surroundings. He could have set off a bomb and she wouldn't notice, he thought, twirling his fountain pen between his fingers. And it would be the same tomorrow night. He would sit next to her and she wouldn't notice him. God, it was almost too easy.

He watched the blonde for several more minutes then picked up his things and sauntered out of the library, whistling softly. His practice run had gone well. Tomorrow night would be the real thing. He had no fear, no concern. As his father used to say, it was going to be a piece of cake.

Chapter Four

Harry Flynn was not at all what Jeff had expected. Though exactly what that was he really couldn't say, but it was certainly not the distinguished-looking man who stood in the doorway of the opulently furnished office. He looked as if he'd just stepped out of the pages of a *GQ* magazine. Everything about him reeked of money—from his custom-made suit to his Rolex watch.

"My dear, I'm so glad you decided to take me up on my offer." Flynn walked toward them, confident, self-assured. A muscle ticked in Jeff's jaw as he watched Flynn take both of Raven's hands in his, then he lean over and kissed her on the cheek. "How are you holding up under this?"

"I'm fine," she said, casting an anxious look over her shoulder at Jeff. "I'm just glad you were able to see us this morning." Raven turned toward Jeff. "Harry Flynn, this is Dr. Jeffrey Knight."

"Dr. Knight." He tipped his head toward Jeff before turning his attention back to Raven. "Why don't we step into my office?" he said. Jeff watched as Flynn slid an arm around Raven's shoulder and led her back through the doorway he'd just exited.

He might as well not be in the room for all the notice the other man took, Jeff thought as he trailed after them. He made himself keep a healthy distance away. He was afraid that if he got too close, he would do something stupid, like knock the other man's hand away.

You're jealous, an inner voice whispered. No way, he thought. He just didn't like the way the guy was fawning over her. To take his mind off the scene in front of him, Jeff surveyed the large office. It was huge and lavishly furnished, steeped in an atmosphere of quiet luxury. The entire back wall was glass and offered a magnificent view of Lake Michigan. The other walls were covered with expensive-looking watercolors. The import-export business was apparently a lot more lucrative than he would have imagined.

"Why don't we sit down?" Flynn pointed to two white leather chairs flanking a huge elaborately carved Chinese table that served as a desk and which Flynn took a seat behind. "Raven told me about your allegations," Flynn said coolly. "I'm glad to see that you realize how ridiculous those charges were. Why, everyone who knows Raven knows she's an outstanding herbalist—but then," he paused and gave Jeff a cool stare, "you're not particularly fond of alternative health care practitioners, are you?"

Jeff stared at the other man for a full minute before he spoke. "We're not here to discuss my views on the alternative health care industry. Besides, I really don't think that's any of your business."

Flynn blinked owlishly but maintained a cool air. "It is when you accuse a close friend of being irresponsible. However, as you say, that's not the point of this meeting. I just hope you can curb this tendency to jump to conclusions during this investigation."

Jeff was just about to issue an angry reply when he felt Raven's hand on his arm. Her brown eyes met his, and he saw in them her silent plea for him to hold his temper. Words had never been necessary between them. Suddenly, he was thrust back in time. For a moment he gave in to the memories before pushing them back to the recesses of his mind.

"I want you to know," Flynn was saying, clearly unaware of the private drama being played out between them, "I'll do everything in my power to help get to the bottom of this thing." He then offered Raven what Jeff presumed was his best smile. "If you like, I'll go around with you and introduce you to the other suppliers, pave the way, so to speak."

Raven returned his smile. "That would be—"

"I don't think that's necessary," Jeff said coolly. "All we need is some information." Even if the other man didn't grate on his nerves, he still wouldn't want him tagging along. Until he knew exactly what they were dealing with, the fewer people who knew what was going on, the better.

But Flynn was not so easily dissuaded. "I suppose you think you can just waltz in and the suppliers will tell you everything you want to know?"

"That's exactly what we're going to do," Jeff said smoothly. That and flash Public Health inspectors' badges he'd obtained from a friend. He'd had to call in quite a few favors to obtain them, but it was worth it. Armed with a health inspector badge no one would dare deny them access to their warehouses or refuse to answer questions, but he wasn't going to tell Flynn that. Instead he said, "If they have nothing to hide, they should have no problems answering our questions."

A muscle worked in Flynn's jaw but when he spoke his voice didn't betray his inner thoughts. "What kind of information are you looking for?"

Jeff shrugged. "Anything and everything you can tell me about the other suppliers in the area, particularly those who sell whole herbs."

Harry waved his hand dismissively. "There really isn't very much I can tell you. There are probably about two dozen suppliers, but I would guess only about eight deal in whole herbs. The others sell herbs exclusively in prepackaged and capsule form, and only to health food and grocery stores.''

Raven looked at Jeff. "I think we can eliminate all but those eight." At his nod, she turned back to Flynn. "What can you tell us about them?"

"They're smaller distributors, so in order to compete with the larger suppliers, they deal in more exotic and specialized products, such as whole herbs."

"And these herbs, are they imported?"

Harry frowned. "I doubt it. The red tape involved in something like that would be too big of a headache, and I can't imagine that it would be particularly cost-effective. There can't be that much of a demand for imported whole herbs. Besides, most people who want whole herbs grow their own." He leaned back in his chair and regarded Jeff coolly. "Which makes me wonder if you aren't jumping the gun here. From what I gather from Raven, you have no evidence connecting your patients' illnesses to a particular herb or supplier. This is strictly speculation on your part."

"That's right," Jeff said, giving him an equally cool stare, "but I think it's well founded. From the symptoms which at least two, maybe all three of my patients exhibit, there's a strong probability they came into contact with some kind of bacterial contaminant."

"And just how did this *supposed* contamination occur, huh?" Flynn challenged. "From a pesticide? An herbicide? During the growing process?" He looked over at Raven and grinned. "Don't you think that sounds rather far-fetched?"

Jeff would have liked nothing better than to knock that smug smile off his face, but he held on to his temper. He sensed the other man was stonewalling and wondered why. "Not at all," he said smoothly. "You, of all people, should know that some herbs can be contaminated in any number of ways."

"Perhaps," the other man conceded. "It's just hard for

me to believe any of the suppliers around here would deal in contaminated herbs. They're more responsible than that.''

''I don't know why you find that so hard to believe,'' Jeff said tersely. ''The alternative health care business is an unregulated industry, which makes it ripe for all kinds of unscrupulous individuals to use to make a quick buck.''

Harry gave him a superior little smile. ''That may be in the case of you doctors who practice standard medicine, but people who go into alternative health care do so because they believe in what they're doing.''

''So, you're all a bunch of Boy Scouts?'' Jeff's voice was laced with sarcasm. ''I wonder what the Health Department would find if they made an unannounced visit here?'' It was a throwaway accusation, meant to insult rather than to elicit a response. But from Flynn's reaction, the remark hit home.

''Just what the hell are you suggesting?'' Flynn snarled, his face suddenly transformed into a mask of rage. Suddenly, he looked older, meaner, brimming with hostility. Quite different from the amicable charmer who had invited them into the office minutes before. Which made Jeff wonder just what the hell he was afraid of.

''We're not accusing you or anyone of anything,'' Raven said quickly. She glared at Jeff. ''Are we?''

He rubbed his hand over his hair in irritation. ''No, of course not. Hell, I doubt if the particular supplier—if that proves to be the source of this contaminant—even knows what's happening. But sticking your head in the sand and pretending something like this couldn't happen is also not very productive.''

Harry scowled and cleared his throat. ''I was simply pointing out what I believe to be the fallacy in your logic in order to save you from wasting time checking out herb suppliers.''

Jeff didn't buy his answer for one moment.

"You may be right," Raven said, "but Dr. Knight feels it's a necessary part of our investigation."

Harry snorted. "Or a way of laying blame on an already much maligned industry. I would imagine you find us a handy scapegoat for your medical shortcomings."

Jeff felt his temper rising, but before he could say anything, Raven surprised him by coming to his defense. "Jeff may not be an advocate of alternative health care, but I know he's not vindictive and will be fair in his investigation."

Harry rolled his eyes as if to say he doubted it.

"And Harry," she continued, "I want you to know that we wouldn't be here if we didn't think you could be of assistance. You've been in this business a long time and are in a position to know what's going on. We'd like to hear your thoughts on the other suppliers in the area." She punctuated her words with a warm smile.

Flynn fairly beamed at her words then launched into a discussion of the suppliers. Although he talked for about ten minutes, from what Jeff gathered, the information amounted to nothing more than a series of interesting but worthless anecdotes. But from Raven's rapt expression, he wasn't sure if she realized her friend was just going through the motions. Flynn concluded by again stating that he thought interviewing herb suppliers was a waste of time.

"You were saying there are only eight suppliers that seem to fit our profile," Raven said. "Are you aware of any problems any of them may have been having?"

Flynn waved his hand dismissively. "Oh, there are a couple of suppliers that I'd tell you to stay away from. But that's only because their products are overpriced and the quality isn't what it should be."

Jeff frowned. He'd been hoping for something more substantive than that. "What about allegations of impropriety?" he asked. "Has anyone been accused of doing anything illegal?"

"Hendricks and Sons had some problems with some creditors and the IRS."

Flynn knew good and well that wasn't what Jeff was getting at. It was yet another example of his stonewalling. "What about Food and Drug Administration concerns? Anyone having any problems with them?"

"Well, a couple of people did have some problems a while back with the FDA," Flynn admitted grudgingly. "But it was nothing very serious."

"Why don't you let us be the judge of that?" Jeff said crisply.

Flynn cleared his throat. "Well, I think it had something to do with...ah, importing herbs from the Far East."

Jeff looked at him incredulously. "You don't consider buying herbs from countries that still spray their crops with dangerous pesticides a serious problem?"

Flynn shifted uncomfortably in his seat. "Well...ah, yes, but there was no harm done. No one died."

"That time," Jeff snapped. "We may not have been so lucky this time. You want to give me the names of these suppliers?"

In a strained voice, Flynn named several suppliers. Jeff refrained from mentioning that they were not among the eight he'd previously identified. That made twelve suppliers they needed to take a look at.

He spent several more minutes questioning Flynn about the suppliers who had gotten into trouble, but as hard as he pressed, he didn't get any more information out of him. Again he had the impression that Flynn was hiding something. He would have liked to question him about his own business, but he didn't think Raven would put up with it.

"I guess that's it for me," he said, then turned to Raven. "What about you? Any questions?"

"Just a couple," she said. "Harry, you're familiar with a Reverend Walters, aren't you? He has a shop just off Madison in the Loop."

"Why, yes," Harry answered, clearly relieved they'd

gotten off the subject of suppliers. "I met him about eight, no, maybe nine months ago. He was new in town, needed a supplier and said he was willing to pay top dollar."

"And did you help him out?"

"For a while. But I stopped supplying him after about two months when he fell behind in his account."

"Do you know who supplies him now?"

"International Imports supplied him for a short time, but they also dropped him for nonpayment. As far as I know, no one is supplying him. It's my understanding he grows his own herbs."

Jeff looked at Raven. Now that was an interesting bit of information, he thought.

"You ever hear any talk about him?" Raven asked.

Harry chuckled. "Quite a bit, but probably nothing that could be substantiated...." His voice trailed off and suddenly he looked from Raven to Jeff, realization dawning "You think Walters is the source of this, don't you?"

Raven hesitated, then shrugged. "It's a possibility. He's a man who plays fast and loose with the facts, and that's landed him in trouble with the law on more than one occasion. He's also known for using substandard products."

Flynn nodded slowly. "I wouldn't be the least bit surprised if you found he *was* the source. He always did strike me as something of a sleazy character. I hope you're going to check him out."

Jeff's eyes narrowed. He was a little surprised at how quickly the other man had jumped on the idea of Reverend Walters being the source of the mysterious illness. "You didn't know about his criminal record, then?" Jeff asked.

"Absolutely not," Harry insisted. "I don't do business with convicted felons. I have a good reputation, and I plan to keep it that way."

"One last thing," Jeff said. "Would you mind if a couple of staff members from the hospital come over and took samples of your herbs?"

The only indication that Flynn had been affected by his

words was a slight tremor of his hand. He'd make a hell of a poker player, Jeff thought.

"Not at all," Flynn said.

"Is that really necessary—" Raven began.

"It's all right, my dear," Flynn said smoothly. "Dr. Knight would be remiss if he didn't consider all the possibilities. I have nothing to hide."

"Glad to hear it," Jeff said curtly. "Someone from the hospital will be here in about fifteen minutes to begin collecting samples." Flynn visibly paled at his words. Now he was glad he'd decided to have a team ready to come in as soon as each interview was completed. He didn't want Flynn or any of the suppliers to start running scared and begin removing any herbs from the premises.

Raven got to her feet and Jeff followed suit. "Thanks for your help, Harry," she said. "If we have any further questions, we'll get back to you."

Jeff did not offer his hand and neither did Flynn.

The moment they were outside, Raven turned on him, her eyes blazing. "What was that all about in there?"

Jeff's eyes narrowed, not liking the direction the conversation was going. "What do you mean?"

"That performance in there," she snapped. "You were out of line. Harry is my friend and I don't appreciate you treating him like some common criminal."

"Well, someone had to ask the hard questions, you certainly weren't going to. You were treating the guy with kid gloves."

"How else was I supposed to treat him?" she retorted. "He's a friend who offered to help us. I certainly don't think it was necessary to come down so hard on him."

"As far as I'm concerned, until his herbs are tested and given a clean bill of health, he's no different from the other suppliers." At the stormy look she threw him, Jeff sighed in frustration. "Look, I wouldn't have come down so hard on the guy if he'd been more forthcoming. But he was stonewalling."

"That's because you came on like gangbusters. You put him on the defensive."

He gave her a hard look. "Who are you trying to kid? For all his talk about wanting to help, that's the last thing he was doing."

She looked at him, her expression bleak, and for a moment he wanted to wrap his arms around her. A few seconds later, she drew a deep sigh and nodded. "I don't understand it. Harry is one of the most straightforward individuals I know. Why would he be uncooperative?"

Why indeed? Jeff thought, but aloud he said, "Let's go check out those suppliers."

THEY DREW BLANKS with the first two suppliers, as well as with the third. By the time they left the fourth supplier, Raven's anger had subsided and been replaced with frustration. Posing as Public Health inspectors, they'd gained access to the suppliers, as well as free rein to inspect their warehouses. She'd been surprised when Jeff had produced two official-looking badges. But even under that guise, they always seemed to hit a brick wall.

Basically everyone told the same story—none of them imported herbs, all had certificates from local growers certifying the herbs were chemical, herbicide and irradiation free. Nor had any of them received any customer complaints in the last thirty days relating to herb ingestion. A few grumbled when Jeff requested a list of their growers and customers, as well as samples of their herbs, but they all complied. They were too intimidated by a visit from Public Health officials to do otherwise.

Their only promising lead came from a place called Hunan Imports. The owner claimed not to know anything about contaminated herbs, but said he thought they ought to check out a bootleg supplier known as Jackson Produce. He said he'd heard talk about them in connection with bad herbs. But talk was apparently all it was. Jackson was a small mom-and-pop operation and didn't even sell whole herbs.

By the time they completed interviewing all twelve suppliers, Raven's belief that one of the local suppliers was the source of the bacterial contaminant was more than a little shaken. While she knew you couldn't tell anything from a sight inspection alone, she'd been in the business long enough to draw some conclusions about herb quality. And from what she could see, the herbs seemed to be healthy. And if the documentation the suppliers had produced was to be believed, they were all strictly sanitary and aboveboard. If Jeff had any such misgivings he was keeping them to himself.

She looked at the handsome man seated across the restaurant table from her, and wondered, once again, about the events leading up to their having dinner together. It certainly hadn't been her intention to spend any time alone with Jeff, other than that which was absolutely necessary in the course of the investigation.

Spending the day with him had proved to be more difficult than she'd imagined. Difficult because she'd been forced to spend time with a man who'd not only rejected her as a woman but who had openly scoffed at everything she believed in. Difficult because she'd had to face the fact that she had misjudged him so absolutely, that four years ago she hadn't really known him at all. Difficult because she was now having to face the constant reminder of the pain he had caused her. Difficult because she was being forced to confront her own stupidity every time she looked into Jeff's hazel eyes and felt her heart leap and her pulse kick into double time.

She'd been prepared for that. What she had not been prepared for was the memories. They crept into her subconscious at odd moments, like when he teased her during lunch, it made her think of romantic lunches they'd shared in his office and when he'd brush a stray hair from her face, she recalled how he would stroke her hair after love-making. She shook her head, banishing the thoughts.

She didn't want to remember the good times. She didn't want to remember how much she'd respected him or how much she'd wanted him or loved him. She'd planned to spend the evening going over what they'd learned, as well as putting her jumbled feelings about Jeff into some kind of perspective. But as they stood outside her shop, he'd suggested that they get together later that evening and review the events of the day while conversations and impressions were still fresh in both their minds. It sounded like a good idea, and if it had been anyone but Jeff, she'd have readily agreed. But she'd hesitated. Being with him that day had been both heaven and hell.

She'd wanted to say no. She'd been extremely tempted to do just that, but in the end she knew she couldn't. Aside from the fact that helping with the investigation could save lives and maybe repair her reputation, perhaps daily contact with Jeff would help her put the past behind her, enable her to have a conversation with him without her heart rate going into the danger zone. If she backed out of the investigation now, she'd always wonder how many people died from ingesting this herbal contaminant because she was too chicken to spend a little time with Jeff Knight.

That was the only reason she now found herself sitting in Saavedra, a fashionable restaurant in the Chicago Loop, having dinner with a man who had almost destroyed her.

She glanced up to find Jeff studying her. And just like so many times that day, her heartbeat accelerated and she felt a wave of heat wash over her. Why did he have to be so damn good-looking? And why couldn't she put the past behind her? She had no future with Jeff and she'd do well to remember that.

Praying that her voice wouldn't give away her inner turmoil, she looked at him and sighed. "I've never felt so frustrated in my life."

He gave her a lopsided grin, which once again sent her

pulse racing uncontrollably. "Now you know how I've been feeling for the past week."

"We had the element of surprise on our side," she said, trying to avoid looking directly into his hypnotic hazel eyes. "No one knew we were coming, yet it still doesn't look as if we came up with anything. They were all either telling the truth or else they're all participants in a massive conspiracy of silence."

Jeff shrugged. "Could be a little of both. People are so lawsuit conscious these days, and they often realize that being completely forthcoming isn't always in their best interest—especially in a case like this when they don't know exactly what we're looking for."

She nodded. "Well, whatever the reason, we'll know soon enough. We've got a list of their growers and customers, as well as samples of their herbs."

Jeff took a sip of his drink. "Right, and with that information we should be able to make a conclusive determination about the source of this contaminant, and hopefully find out who else might be at risk." He gave her a quizzical look. "So, why don't you sound happy?"

"Because my gut tells me we've hit a brick wall."

His eyes narrowed. "Is that your gut or your friend Harry Flynn talking?"

She decided to ignore his sarcasm. "Admit it, Jeff, you feel the same way. It doesn't mean we're wrong," she added quickly. "It just means we may not be able to connect this illness to a particular supplier, grower or business. It would certainly make things a lot easier if we could, but you've got to consider the possibility that we won't be able to."

For a moment he didn't say anything, then he nodded and sighed wearily. "I guess I should have known that this wasn't going to be easy. Nothing else has been."

"How long before we know anything?" she asked gently.

"Shay and his people finished collecting samples a couple of hours ago and by now they've begun testing the herbs. They plan to work around the clock. Hopefully, we'll know something in a day or so."

Raven pursed her lips. "In the meantime, we can check out Reverend Walters. I think there's a good chance he could be the source of the contaminant. I made a few phone calls after you dropped me off at the shop. Besides being something of a weirdo, he's totally irresponsible in the claims he makes. Not only is he supposed to be able to effect miraculous cures, but he also claims he can predict the future."

Jeff gave her a faint smile. "Quite a talent. He may be the weirdest person on the planet, but I don't see how he could be the source of contaminated herbs."

She looked at him, frowning. "What is it with you? I don't recall you having these reservations when you were accusing me of using contaminated herbs."

"At that time we had three, not seven patients, two of which I could connect to you." Jeff shrugged. "It seems more speculative now."

"But the man clearly knows next to nothing about alternative medicine, yet he's out there treating patients with God knows what. And remember what Harry said about him growing his own herbs."

"Yeah, good ol' Harry," Jeff said with a twinge of sarcasm. "Maybe he just didn't want us focusing too closely on *him*."

"That's ridiculous."

"Is it?" he challenged.

"Of course." She glowered at him. "I've known Harry for over a year. He's a good man. A little arrogant at times, but basically a nice guy. He has nothing to hide."

"Yeah, but even you have to admit, he seems to be doing his level best to steer us away from checking out local suppliers. If he's clean, then what is he afraid of?"

"I can't imagine he's afraid of anything. You said yourself my herbs were clean. Doesn't that mean Harry's are, too?"

Jeff shook his head. "Not necessarily. Maybe yours came from a different batch."

Raven rolled her eyes. "And pigs fly. Why don't you just admit it, you don't like Harry."

He shifted uncomfortably. "This has nothing to do with my personal feelings about the guy. There's something about his business he's afraid we're going to find out." He gave her a sharp glance. "Just what *does* he import and export?"

Raven chewed thoughtfully on her lower lip. "I know he imports jewelry, art and some furniture, but, other than that, I'm not really sure."

Jeff raised his eyebrows. "That's it?" he asked in obvious disbelief.

Raven shrugged. "Harry and I really haven't talked that much about his business."

"I guess you've been too busy doing other things," he said dryly.

If she hadn't known better, she could almost believe he was jealous, but that was ridiculous.

"It's certainly not for me to say who you can and cannot date," he continued, "but it seems to me that you ought to be a little more circumspect about who you go out with."

That was too much. "Thanks for pointing out what a lousy judge of character I am," she snapped. "It wouldn't be the first time I've misjudged a man. Four years ago, I totally misjudged you, too."

"I'm sorry," he said. His voice was low and filled with some undefined emotion. "I was out of line." He looked down at his hands. "I know you don't consider me a friend, but I still consider you one, and I don't want to see you get hurt." He looked and sounded completely sincere.

"There's nothing between Harry and me," she said softly. "He's just a good friend."

Jeff's face broke into a broad smile. "Good," he said.

She couldn't stop her heart from racing when he smiled at her that way. And for a moment she felt disoriented and thought it best to change the topic. "Ah...how are Lauren and Eleanor doing?"

Her question sobered him. "I wish I could say better, but the opposite seems to be the case." He drew a weary sigh. "Since we have no idea what we're dealing with, we haven't been able to come up with any kind of effective treatment. Both women are critical. So is the third patient, Julie Hartman. I'm afraid if we don't get a break—and soon—we're going to lose them."

His expression was so bleak that before she could stop herself, she reached across the table and squeezed his hand. "I know you're going to beat this thing."

He gave her a faint smile before covering her hand with his own. His hand was warm and firm and, for a moment, she let herself enjoy the feelings coursing through her, before sliding her hand into her lap.

She lowered her gaze. She didn't want to tremble at Jeff's touch, didn't want to feel the old desire inside her rising up like smoke and stealing her breath away. She didn't want to, but she did.

"Thanks for your vote of confidence," he was saying, "but the cards seem to be stacked against us. I've spent two years with the World Health Organization, studying some of the most virulent diseases on the planet, and I've never seen anything like this before. It hasn't responded to any treatment we've tried to date. It's not natural."

A chill went up her spine at his words. "What do you mean, not natural?"

He shook his head. "I can't put my finger on it, but this thing just doesn't feel right. It's not behaving like any infectious disease I've ever encountered."

She looked at him, frowning. "What do you mean?"

"From the symptoms the patients exhibit, it appears to

be a bacterial infection, but it's not responding to the antibiotics."

Her frown deepened. "What about the autopsies on the four who died earlier? Weren't they able to tell you anything?"

He shook his head again. "Unfortunately, only one autopsy was performed, and it was something of a botched job."

Her mouth dropped open. "You're kidding? Why weren't autopsies performed on the other three?"

"In one case the family refused to allow it because of religious convictions. In the other two, none was performed because in each case the attending physicians listed a cause of death and didn't request one. Short of exhuming the bodies, we're stuck with just the tissues from the one autopsy."

She drew a quick intake of breath. "That's awful."

Jeff shrugged. "It's regrettable, but understandable. I spoke to both doctors and what it boils down to is a case of wanting to spare the families any further pain."

Or themselves from a malpractice lawsuit, she thought, but aloud she said, "The reason doesn't matter. No doctor has the right to lie about something like that. The families have a right to know."

He shrugged again. "Maybe, but doctors frequently make those kinds of judgment calls. Remember the period prior to the identification of the AIDS virus? A lot of patients that we now know died of that disease, their death certificates list the cause of death as pneumonia or cancer. No doubt the doctors felt they had to list a cause of death to bring closure to the situation. And I'm sure that during the time you worked in the hospital, you probably encountered the case where a teenager's death was listed as accidental, even though the doctors and the entire nursing staff knew the kid probably committed suicide. I'm not saying that it's right or that I personally subscribe to that philosophy, I'm simply saying that it happens."

It wasn't that it happened that bothered her. It was his attitude. He saw nothing wrong with this Godlike attitude on his part and that of his colleagues, but she held her tongue. It was just another reminder that her own and Jeff's views on health care were diametrically opposed, another reminder why a relationship between the two of them would never work.

"Tell me again what the symptoms of this illness are?" she asked, changing the subject.

He hesitated as if he were considering how much he should tell her. "It begins with a headache and fever," he said finally. "Followed by severe abdominal cramps, vomiting and diarrhea. Then there is a general wasting away of the person's immune system. Once the immune system is impaired, other organs are affected."

"That sounds ominous. So what course of treatment are you following?"

He issued a frustrated sigh. "You should be asking what treatment we haven't tried. They've run the gamut of antibiotics. I don't know what we're going to do if they don't respond to this latest one."

"You know," she said, weighing her words carefully, "there have been some amazing results with certain herbs in repairing the body's immune system. Since you've had no luck with conventional treatment, what about trying an unconventional one?"

His eyes narrowed. "If you're suggesting we use some off-the-wall, alternative health care treatment, forget it."

Her chin rose a fraction. "Why not? You've got nothing to lose."

"That's not the point!" he snapped. "We don't experiment on people."

"Who said anything about experimenting?" she asked, trying to hang on to her temper. "There is an abundance of literature on the subject. These are methods that are generally recognized by alternative health care practitioners, as well as a number of medical doctors."

Jeff groaned in frustration. "Look, we've had this argument more times than I care to remember. You're not going to change my mind, and I'm not going to change yours, so let's just drop it."

She thought about pressing the issue, but the look on his face told her the matter was closed. She issued a deep sigh. "Then I guess we should talk about our meeting with Reverend Walters."

"I think that might be a good idea."

"Our appointment with him is for Wednesday at two. I thought the afternoon would be best. Your morning will be free for classes and hospital rounds. It'll also allow me time to relieve Phyllis at the shop in the morning."

He nodded. "How did you get an appointment so quickly?"

"I told him we'd been referred by Eleanor Parker, and that money was no problem."

He gave her a sideways glance. "Just exactly how are we going to play this?"

Her mouth curved into a Mona Lisa smile. "We're going to give him enough rope to hang himself."

HE SAT IN THE TINY stall in the men's room, his head between his knees until his breathing returned to normal, until he was sure the expression and color of his face wouldn't betray his agitation. In the first moment when he'd realized the blonde was going to leave without drinking her coffee, he'd been so angry he had wanted to kill her right then and there. The blood had rushed to his head. It had taken all his willpower not to jump across the table, wrap his hands around her throat and squeeze—squeeze until her beady little eyes closed.

He drew a deep breath. He still couldn't believe she'd walked out. He had studied her movements for the past several days, until he had them down pat. She went to the library every night, always studied in the same secluded area in the back, and she always had at least two cups of coffee while she studied. Something had spooked her, he thought. Had he been a little too intense? Or perhaps she had seen what he'd done? But as quickly as the thought crossed his mind, he discarded it. No, it couldn't be that. He was too practiced in that area by now. Maybe she'd left because she thought he was trying to come on to her. That was it! She had made some comment about a husband, but he hadn't seen a wedding ring. Lying bitch.

He couldn't sit here forever. He had to get out of this bathroom, this library, and... And what? The blonde had really loused things up. She'd forced him to remain in the library longer than he'd planned to find another pigeon. He'd been so nervous, but he'd pulled it off.

Now he was going to have to scratch the other one. But he couldn't go home; he had to act tonight, or he'd lose a whole week. And that would throw everything off. He shook his head. He had to stay on schedule. He glanced at his watch. If he hurried, maybe he could still get to Smitty's in time.

He drew a deep breath, stood and pushed open the stall door. He walked over to the basin and studied his face in the water-spotted mirror above the sink. He'd unbuttoned the top buttons on his shirt, trying to get some air; he rebuttoned them now, readjusted the wig then smoothed back the hair with his palms. His forehead and upper lip were beaded with sweat. He looked at the paper-towel dispenser. It was empty. He stuck his hand in his pocket and reached for his handkerchief. However, his fingers touched a small slender object and he smiled.

He was glad now he'd decided to bring the extra vial with him tonight and keep it in the glove compartment of his car. He'd worried, though. What if the cops stopped him for something and asked to see his registration and asked him about the vial? He had no idea what he would do. But he'd decided to chance it and now he was glad he had.

He wiped his hands on his pants, then pushed the bathroom door open. Five minutes later he was in the car, belted, the items from the glove compartment on the seat next to him.

Twenty minutes later he glanced at the wall clock as he entered the popular sports bar. It was 9:23. He'd just made it. The bar was relatively quiet this time of the week. Not nearly as busy as he would have liked. Just a few regulars. It would be risky, but he thought he could pull it off. He spent a few minutes checking out the bar, formulating a new plan. Some people were sitting at tables, some standing at the bar. There was a young waitress taking a drink order. Was there another waiter or waitress somewhere in the room, or was he or she in back? He'd have to take the chance. The bartender was behind the bar, deep in conversation with a couple of patrons. He passed right by him, but the bartender didn't look up.

He forced himself to peruse the sports memorabilia that lined the walls as he worked his way toward the back of the room. There were lots of pictures of Chicago sports legends—from Michael Jordan to Ernie Banks to Dick Butkus to Tony Esposito. He paused, looking at a Chicago Cubs team picture. Now that he was settled, he might join a baseball team himself. He'd always liked the game. He continued his trek, skirting the pool table until he reached the back.

There was the door he wanted, the one next to the men's room. Do Not Enter—Employees Only. He glanced around. No one was looking his way. He turned the knob, pushed open the door, and slipped inside, prepared to make an excuse about thinking it was the men's room if anyone was there. But the room was empty. All he had to do was wait for the bartender to enter.

He didn't have to wait long. The bartender was a creature of habit. He always took a cigarette break at nine-thirty. He smelled the bartender's cologne as soon as he entered. The bartender didn't know he was hidden in the narrow triangle between the opening door and the wall, didn't sense his presence until it was too late. He gave the bartender a sharp whack on the back of the head with the side of his hand, but it only stunned him. He hit him twice more on the side of the face, before the man fell to his knees, then crumpled to the floor. It was only after he positioned him on the floor that he saw the bartender's bruised face. It wasn't the way he liked to do things, but it wasn't his fault. He'd been nervous. It was the blonde's fault. If she'd just drunk her coffee the way she was supposed to, he wouldn't have been forced to improvise.

He quickly removed the bartender's watch and ring, then went through his pockets, searching for his wallet. After he was done, he left the room as carefully as he entered it, armed with an excuse; but again, no one was looking. Then he meandered among the tables until he made his way back to the front of the bar and out the door.

The cool, crisp night air felt wonderful. He felt wonderful. Back in his apartment he removed the wig and tinted contact lenses, then took a long, hot shower, inhaling the steamy vapors. Hot water soon gave way to warm. He dried off, then slipped on freshly laundered pajamas and a robe. He walked down the hall to the study, where he poured himself a drink. He downed it in one greedy gulp, then poured himself another. Glass in hand, he crossed over to the large oak desk in the center of the room, found the photograph he wanted, then added it to his collection.

He stepped back and as he studied his handiwork, his mouth curved into a smile. "Two down, two to go."

Chapter Five

They found the little shop on Canal Street without too much trouble. It was tucked neatly on the corner, flanked by a boutique and a restaurant. The sign painted on the window simply read Reverend Charles Walters: Naturopathic Medicine.

Jeff held the door and Raven stepped inside. She'd expected to see the usual array of metaphysical paraphernalia: incense, oils, candles and crystals in various shapes and sizes. She wasn't disappointed. But the shop itself was something of a surprise. It was designed to resemble the waiting room of a doctor's office, complete with the usual rack of magazines and waiting-room chairs. A young, pretty black woman dressed in a long, flowing white robe looked up from the reception desk as they entered.

"May I help you?" she asked.

"I'm Rebecca Smith and this is Wade Jeffers," Raven said easily. "We have a two o'clock appointment with Reverend Walters."

"I'll let him know you're here." She pressed a button on her desk, and a soft chiming sound rang out. Then she turned to them, smiled and said, "He'll be right with you."

A moment later, a door opened and a slightly overweight, light-skinned black man swept into the room. He was dressed in a long, flowing deep purple robe that was gathered about his large waist by a gold braided rope belt. He reminded Raven of a peacock.

"Ms. Smith, Mr. Jeffers," he gushed. "It's a pleasure to meet you. My contemplation room is through here." Reverend Walters opened the door and held out his arm like a spokesperson pointing to a dream vacation.

Jeff threw Raven a telling look as they followed him through the doorway and down a narrow hall that opened into a small carpeted and heavily draped chamber. The room was dimly lit and sparsely furnished—just a couch, a round table, three chairs, several file cabinets, and a wall unit lined with canisters containing what she presumed were herbs. His work area was probably in another room, she thought.

"Please sit down." Reverend Walters lowered himself into one of the chairs and waited until they were seated, then looked at Jeff. "I understand you have a problem with impotence," he said delicately.

"Ah...that's correct," Jeff replied, his hazel eyes boring into Raven.

It took all her efforts to keep a straight face.

"I have a special herbal tonic that will help. It's a tad expensive." He named an amount that was more than Raven made in a week. "I can give it to you, and we can end the session right now, but I would only be treating the outward manifestation of a deeper psychic problem." He paused, leaned across the table and looked at them as if he were about to disclose some deep dark secret. "What I'd like to do is call upon my spiritual guide to show me the root of this problem. It will be slightly more expensive, but it's the difference between a quick fix and a permanent solution. I, personally, believe you can't put a price on good health. And I think you feel that way, too."

He reached across the table and took each of their hands in his. "Will you let me cure you? Will you let me do that for you?"

He was good, she thought. Just the right degree of sincerity.

Raven and Jeff both nodded.

"Good," he said, beaming. He then instructed them to keep their feet flat on the floor and place their hands, palms down, on the table. Then he closed his eyes and began to breathe deeply. After a moment, he began to speak, "The spirit says the two of you have been together through many incarnations. You are more than friends. You're soul mates. But in this lifetime there have been problems that prevented your coming together as one."

An eerie chill worked its way up Raven's spine. She shivered, causing her purse to slip from her fingers to the carpeted floor. In the quiet of the room, it had the effect of a gun going off.

Reverend Walters's eyes flew open and he looked at her, perturbed by the interruption. "Please, there must be absolute silence. Noises and unnecessary movement disrupts my communication."

"So, when do we get to ask questions?" Jeff asked innocently.

"After I'm done you may ask anything you like."

"But isn't the spirit gone by then?" Jeff persisted.

She could hear the laughter in his voice and threw him a warning look.

Reverend Walters's eyes narrowed. "The sessions are very tiring for me, and it takes several hours to renew my energies after a reading. For that reason, I see a limited number of clients daily and only by referral." He looked at them and frowned. "Didn't Mrs. Parker explain this to you?"

"Ah, yes, she did," Raven said hurriedly. The last thing she wanted was to have him get suspicious and clam up before they were able to question him.

For a moment he didn't say anything. She had a feeling he was about to call a halt to the session, but greed must have gotten the better of him, because he once again closed his eyes and began taking deep, cleansing breaths. There was a long period of silence, during which Raven felt her hands grow moist again. Jeff would laugh at her if he knew how anxious she felt at the moment. The man was a fraud. He could no more predict the future than she could. And yet some of the things he had said a moment ago were eerily close to the truth. She gave herself a mental shake. It had just been a lucky guess.

At first she thought the room was slowly getting darker, then she realized that it wasn't the room, but the area directly behind Reverend Walters that seemed to be glowing very faintly, giving the area behind his head a halo effect, like the ones in religious pictures. Probably some lighting trick, she surmised. No telling what gadgets were concealed in the wall behind him or in the table itself.

Finally, Reverend Walters began to speak. The words came out faintly as if from a great distance and with what sounded like a great deal of effort. Raven leaned forward, straining to hear clearly.

"The spirit says you are soul mates," Reverend Walters began. "But differences in this lifetime have kept you apart. For a while it seemed as if these differences were insurmountable...that led to separation. For the last few years you have traveled different paths." He frowned. "I don't understand...ah, yes, it becomes clearer. Your separation was necessary for your individual growth. You had different things you needed to learn before coming together in this lifetime, but now that period is over and your paths have crossed again. While you, Ms. Smith, have reconciled your differences, Mr. Jeffers has only done so on an emotional level. He has not done so intellectually." His eyes flew open and his pudgy face broke into a beaming smile.

"That's what is causing your impotence. It's an outward manifestation of this internal conflict, but I can help you."

So much for psychic abilities, she thought.

"You can cure impotence?" Jeff asked incredulously.

Reverend Walters gave him a smug, superior little smile. "Impotence, infertility, cancer, AIDS." He waved his hand dismissively. "I don't mean to brag, but you'll search far and wide, and you won't find another like me. I'm one in a million."

Thank God for that, Raven thought.

"I spent many years in the Far East, studying with some of the wisest men there," Reverend Walters continued. "They taught me many things—how to tap into the cosmic consciousness to diagnose physical illnesses, as well as the secret of herbal healing. Through those contacts, I have access to herbs that are not known by practitioners in this country but which have been used for centuries in other parts of the world. They are some of the finest and rarest on the planet." He named several that Raven knew were ineffective, and two that were illegal to import because of their toxicity.

Her heart began to pound with excitement. She schooled her features so as not to betray her excitement. "If these herbs are so rare just how are you able to get them?" she asked.

Reverend Walters's mouth curved into a smug little smile. "A good doctor never discloses his secrets, not for any amount of money."

"What about to stay out of jail?" Jeff asked bluntly.

"Oh, Lord!" Reverend Walters gasped. "You're police officers." His right hand flew to his mouth, and he looked from Jeff to Raven, his eyes wide with horror.

Jeff shook his head. "We're not from the police, but unless you want to spend the next couple of hours talking to them and the FDA, you'd better cooperate with us."

"Now I get it," he cried. "This is some kind of shakedown. How much do you want? Five hundred? A thousand?" Gone was the relaxed, easygoing, good-natured manner. His small beady eyes took on a cold, shrewd look.

Jeff shook his head again. "All we want is some information."

"What kind of information?" he asked cautiously.

"About two of your clients, Lauren Connor and Eleanor Parker. It's my understanding you've been seeing both women."

Walters shrugged offhandedly. "So what? There's no law against that."

"No," Jeff agreed, "there isn't, but there's a law against murder. It seems whatever herbal concoction you gave them may be killing them and others."

Walters's face drained of color. "Killing people! I—I don't know what you're talking about. I haven't done anything wrong."

"Those imported herbs you were just bragging about appear to have been contaminated."

Reverend Walters's head shook back and forth like a rag doll. "Look man, you're barking up the wrong tree. I—I was just talking. Embellishing my story." Beads of sweat dotted his brow as the words tripped out of his mouth so fast he was babbling. "My...my herbs aren't imported. It's just a line I feed the customers...to justify the cost."

"What about your herb garden?" Jeff asked.

"I d-don't have a garden," Walters stammered. "I tell people I do, but it's not true. Hell, I don't know anything about growing herbs. I get them from the local grocery store." He named a popular supermarket chain. His eyes swiveled from Jeff to Raven. "They couldn't hurt anyone."

"Maybe," Jeff said. "Let's start at the beginning. I want to know why Eleanor Parker and Lauren Connor came to see you, what herbs you gave them and for how long. I also want to know the last time you saw them and who else you gave that same herbal concoction."

For a moment, Walters didn't say anything.

Jeff gave him a hard look. "I can have the FDA here within the hour."

Raven knew they couldn't but hoped Walters bought the threat.

"All right," Walters said. He stood, walked over to one of the file cabinets, and rifled through a series of cards before pulling out two. He quickly skimmed one of the cards, then looked at Jeff. "Mrs. Parker wanted a love potion to keep her husband from straying. I made one for her, and then gave her an herbal tea to drink for seven days."

He named an herb that was known for its strong bitter taste, but wasn't harmful.

"What about Lauren Connor?" Jeff asked.

Reverend Walters took a moment to study the other card then said, "She was having money problems and wanted something to improve her luck with the lottery. I gave her a good luck charm and...ah...the same herbal tea that I gave Mrs. Parker."

"How many other people did you give that same tea?" Jeff asked.

Reverend Walters's eyes skidded off to the side. "Ah...I'm not sure."

"Was it ten? Twenty?"

"Look, I said I don't remember."

Raven's eyes widened as realization dawned. She looked at Jeff and saw the same horror reflected in his eyes. "My God, you gave everyone that came to you that same tea, didn't you?"

Hours later, Raven was still reeling from Reverend Walters's revelation. She and Jeff were sitting on the sofa in Jeff's office, sipping coffee and digesting what they had learned from their interview. "What do you think?" she asked. "You think Walters is the source of this bacterial contaminant?"

Jeff wearily ran his hand over his face. "If he is, he's not about to admit it."

Raven nodded. After Reverend Walters's initial disclosure, the ramifications of his admission must have hit him, because he'd suddenly clammed up. He'd not only refused to answer any more questions, but refused to give them the names of the other customers he'd given the herbal brew or provide them with a sample of his herbs. Even though he'd given them the name of the grocery store where he'd supposedly purchased the herbs, it was a large chain and there was no way to prove or disprove his claim.

"We could try threatening to report him to the Health Department?"

Jeff shook his head. "At this stage threats aren't going to work, we'd have to go through with it. And you know the hospital is still opposed to bringing in the CDC or the Health Department." He rubbed his temples. "Frankly, I don't know what to believe anymore. I was so sure the source of this thing had to be one of the suppliers."

"But Shay's preliminary testing has all but ruled out that possibility," Raven countered, recalling the report they'd just reviewed. "And he's not optimistic that further testing is going to change that conclusion."

"I know." Jeff sighed heavily.

"Walters has to be the source." When Jeff didn't respond, she tried again. "He's an alternative practitioner. I'd have thought you'd jump at the chance to pin this illness on one of us."

The moment the words were out of her mouth, she wished she could take them back.

Jeff recoiled as if she'd hit him. "What I did four years ago, I did because I thought it was for the best. I never wished you ill or derived any pleasure from what happened," he said quietly. His eyes seemed to plead for understanding.

"I know," she said.

He drew a deep breath as if he were trying to get his courage up. "My biggest regret is that I never talked to you about it. I've had four years to think about what happened, and I know you didn't do anything wrong. I don't know what caused Mr. Redmond's medical emergency or why Teresa lied.''

That was the last thing she'd expected him to say. "Did someone come forward?"

He shook his head. "Working in some of the remote locations I've been in the last two years gave me plenty of time to think. And I know you, and I know you'd never do something like that.''

This was what she'd longed to hear Jeff say, but now that he'd said it, she realized it really didn't change anything. His opinion of alternative health care hadn't changed. She knew he wanted her to say something, but she didn't know what to say.

She cleared her throat. "Why don't we put our heads together and review what we know about Reverend Walters? Maybe we can come up with something to tip the scale.''

He looked as if he wanted to say something more, but apparently thought better of it. He nodded. "That sounds like a good idea.''

"Let's start with Walters's initial claim that his herbs are imported,'' she said, settling back into the sofa cushions.

"We know that's probably a lie.'' Jeff said, stretching his arm across the back of the sofa. "If he wouldn't pay Flynn for his herbs, I can't see him paying double the price for imports. Besides, he didn't have to go to that kind of trouble or expense. None of his clients would be able to tell the difference between imported herbs and plain iced tea.''

Raven nodded in agreement. "If we rule out imports, then that takes us to his claim about growing his own. You know that actually fits,'' she said slowly, turning the idea over in her mind. "It's consistent with the type of scam he's running, and it's also consistent with what Harry heard about him.'' She leaned forward. "From that drivel he was giving us about the type of herbs he supposedly

patients, and the numbers of cases would probably be greater.''

"On the surface there was no apparent connection between Lauren Connor and Eleanor Parker, either,'' Raven countered. "But the connection was there. It was Grace Wells. She was the link. She knew both women and while she denies it, probably referred both of them to me and Reverend Walters.''

"Okay, you've convinced me. I'll go through the medical charts again.'' He flashed her another dazzling smile. "It would go faster if I had a helper.''

"I think I can hang around for a little while,'' she said, returning his smile. "Just let me call Phyllis to let her know that she needs to close for me.''

While she was making her call, Jeff got the files and placed them on the sofa table. For the next hour they painstakingly went through each chart, amassing diverse data on age, sex, lifestyle, occupation and living environment, then cross-referencing the information with each of the other patients. Raven recorded their findings in a notebook.

Next they turned to the admission log for each patient. Jeff had just finished reading Lauren Connor's log, when it suddenly hit her.

"Wait a minute,'' she said, flipping through her notes until she found the page she wanted. "Go back to the date of Lauren's admission. When was it?''

It took him a moment to find the section. "She was admitted on Thursday, June 23, at 3:16 a.m.''

"And Eleanor Parker?''

"Just a minute.'' She watched as he put one file aside, picked up another and flipped through several papers. "Parker was admitted on Wednesday, June 15, at 10:47 p.m.''

"What about Julie Hartman?''

"She was admitted on Wednesday, June 8, at 11:05 p.m.''

"I think there's a pattern here,'' she said excitedly. "All

of the patients were admitted on either a late Wednesday night or early Thursday morning.''

Jeff nodded. ''You may be on to something.''

Heart pounding, she waited while Jeff checked the other four charts. It was the same. Every patient had been admitted on either a Wednesday night or a Thursday morning.

''What do you think it means?'' she asked.

He gave her a thoughtful look. ''I don't know, but it must mean something. I've never heard of an illness that picks a specific day of the week to strike its victims and with such regularity. One patient a week for seven weeks.'' He shook his head. ''It doesn't feel right. Let's keep digging, maybe we'll come up with something else.''

They worked for close to two hours, going over patient information, looking for connections with Reverend Walters, as well as possible connections between patients. A little after ten, Jeff rubbed his hands over his face, leaned back into the sofa cushions, eyes closed.

''I gotta stop,'' he said. ''I'm losing my concentration. I'm sorry, but after I left you last night, I went back to the hospital and was there half the night.'' He rubbed the back of his neck. ''I haven't slept more than six hours in the past forty-eight hours.''

He did look tired, she thought. Tired, but extremely sexy and... There was a time when she would have leaned over and massaged his neck and shoulders.

Looking over at Jeff, she couldn't help but acknowledge that she still found him attractive. But there was no way she had any interest in rekindling a relationship with him. No matter how attracted she was to him, she knew nothing had changed. Jeff still regarded alternative medicine, her vocation, with disdain.

But something in the way she was looking at him must have telegraphed itself to Jeff. To her overactive imagination, it seemed his nostrils flared and his hazel eyes smoldered with passion.

The air, so calm and steady just moments before, now seemed charged with sexual tension. Suddenly, all she wanted to do was get out of his office and return to the safe cocoon of her apartment. "I'd better go," she said, hoping her voice didn't betray her nervousness.

"Okay," he said vaguely. "I'll drive you home."

Damn! She'd forgotten that he'd picked her up at the shop earlier. She would have preferred to take a cab, but didn't want to appear churlish. "Thanks," she mumbled. She stood and walked self-consciously over to his desk and began collecting her papers. She sensed rather than heard Jeff come up behind her.

"I really appreciate your letting me participate in the investigation," she whispered. He was standing so close she could feel his breath in her hair. "I'd be going crazy sitting around the shop, not knowing what was happening."

"I'm really sorry you got dragged into this, but we do make a good team." Jeff's breath seared her neck. A shudder ran through her body—not one of fear, but of arousal. Even without looking at him, she could sense his need, simmering to the surface. Before she could react, she felt his hands on her shoulders. The heat from his fingers seemed to sizzle right through her dress straight to her skin. Everything inside her told her to run, to get the hell out of there. But she didn't. She couldn't. She stood there waiting. Waiting until he slowly turned her around. For a moment they stood staring at each other.

And then slowly his head began to move toward her. She knew this was a bad idea, that she ought to push him away, but she could only watch, mesmerized as his mouth drew nearer.

"I've been dying to taste you again," he whispered before covering her mouth with his. Hot and hungry, that was the only way to describe his mouth as it moved over hers, mingling desire with something nameless.

A wild surge of pleasure racked her body. She felt blood

rushing through her body like a raging fire. Giving in to temptation and the attraction she had been fighting since seeing him again, she wound her arms around his neck and arched against him, quivering, as hot waves of desire consumed her.

At the same time, Jeff's hands were moving down her sides. Then she felt his hands lightly brush against the undercurve of her breasts, then cup them gently. She moaned as his thumbs stroked her nipples. His hands felt so good on her body. A wave of heat washed over her as she gave herself up to the pleasure of his mouth, his touch.

No words were spoken; there was only the low, aching moans of need. They were both breathing so hard, so fast, that her ears were filled with the sound. She scarcely heard the telephone ringing. Only when it had rung again and again did her feverish brain finally register what it was.

It took all her willpower to swim against the flood of desire. She struggled to pull away. "Th-the telephone—"

"Let it ring." His mouth slid down to her throat, scorching her flesh with his lips. His face burrowed through the thick strands of her hair to press hungrily against her neck. His fingers gripped her shoulders as if he were afraid she'd pull away. Her whole body was aching for him.

But the sound continued, grating and unrelenting, nagging with a sense of urgency.

"Jeff," she whispered breathlessly. "You'd better answer it. It could be important."

Groaning, he wrenched away and she saw the astonishment in his eyes. For a moment they stared at each other, neither of them able to believe what had just happened between them. The phone rang again.

Her thoughts in turmoil, she watched as Jeff leaned over the desk and picked up the receiver. She stared at him, aware of her hot tingling mouth, and her hot tingling body, aware of herself as a woman in a way she hadn't felt in years.

"Yeah," he said into the receiver.

He didn't say much, just listened then finally nodded. "I'll be right there."

He hung up and looked at Raven. "That was the hospital. Eleanor Parker went into cardiac arrest, but she's stable now."

Something in his tone made her look at him sharply. "But something else has happened." Her heart was pounding a mile a minute. "What is it?"

His expression was grim. "We just admitted another patient showing signs of the illness..."

"And today's Wednesday," she finished for him.

Chapter Six

What the hell kind of disease was he dealing with? Jeff asked himself angrily. His thoughts were in turmoil as he preceded Raven out of the elevator on the fifth floor of the hospital and down the pristine corridor toward the special intensive care unit he'd set up to handle this growing medical crisis. He'd always thought of himself as being a good doctor, but this disease had him second-guessing himself, doubting his own abilities. Not to mention, acting like a damn fool. How else could he explain his earlier behavior?

He looked at the woman walking alongside him. He couldn't believe he had kissed her like that. He'd totally lost it. He hadn't known what to say so he'd taken refuge in silence, acting as if the kiss had never occurred, talking only about the disease. For her part, Raven seemed to be working hard to do the same. But then he'd gone and asked her to accompany him to the hospital.

It certainly hadn't been necessary. He could have sent her home in a cab. But it felt so damn good being with her that he hadn't wanted to call a halt to the evening. Besides, she'd always been a good sounding board, and he was relieved to have someone he could talk to about this medical crisis.

But the moment he stepped through the set of double doors and entered the special intensive care unit, all thoughts of Raven were pushed out of his mind. This unit was identical to the sixth floor ICU, with its familiar back-drop of complicated electronic machinery. Everywhere there was a profusion of tubes, bottles and hissing machines. There was the smell of disinfectant, the sound of respirators and cardiac monitors. There was also the same high level of nursing activity.

"Are all the patients who've exhibited signs of the mysterious illness in this wing?" Raven asked.

He nodded. "Some of our most experienced personnel work here. Julie Hartman and Eleanor Parker are in the cubicles on the left, and Lauren Connor is on the right."

As they neared the nurses' station, he saw Glenn Myers walking toward them. "Dr. Myers, this is Raven Delaney," he said by way of introduction.

The young resident gave Raven a haggard smile before turning back to Jeff. "I'm sorry I had to interrupt your evening, but I thought you'd want to know about Mrs. Parker, as well as this latest admission."

Jeff nodded. "How's Mrs. Parker?" he asked, already moving down the corridor in the direction of her cubicle.

"Not good, but she's stable now."

"What happened?"

Dr. Myers frowned. "I'm not sure. She was having chest pains. Her husband said—"

Jeff looked at Dr. Myers, surprised. "Mr. Parker was here?"

"Still is. I knew you'd want to talk to him, so I asked him to stick around. Apparently his wife became distraught when he tried to leave, and that's what brought on this latest problem. We have her on a heart monitor."

Jeff's thoughts were grim as they moved in the direction of her cubicle. With her diabetes, he should have anticipated something like this, he thought.

The trio came to a stop outside Eleanor Parker's cubicle. Adjacent to the room was a small, open, closetlike area, containing shelving for linen and other supplies, a sink and a large laundry hamper. He looked at Raven and pointed to a small rack. "You'd better slip on a mask and gown," he said. "For obvious reasons, we're observing isolation precautions in dealing with these patients."

He watched as she slipped on the gown and helped herself to a hat, mask and latex gloves. He and Dr. Myers did likewise.

Unaware she was doing it, Raven breathed shallowly as she stepped into the tiny room and looked down at Eleanor Parker. She was shocked by the sight that greeted her. Mrs. Parker was incredibly dehydrated, her skin ashen, her eyes sunken into her head. She looked as if she were at death's door. She reminded Raven of victims she'd seen in prisoner of war photographs who were suffering from gross malnutrition. In addition to her malnourished state, there was a bruise over her right cheekbone.

She watched as Jeff checked her pulse, then listened to her heart and lungs. He made a few notations on the chart, then instructed Dr. Myers to increase the dose of medication.

They were about to leave, when Raven pointed to the abrasion under Eleanor Parker's right eye. "Any idea what that is?"

Jeff nodded. "She was mugged two days before she got sick. She hit her cheek on the pavement."

"Poor woman," Raven said, wincing at the misfortune. Her heart went out to the stricken woman.

"Okay," Dr. Myers said, following them out of the room. "What about the new patient?" he asked as the trio discarded their isolation apparel. "Do you want to see her?"

Jeff nodded. "Yeah, I think so."

As they walked down the corridor, Jeff couldn't shake the feeling that they were on the brink of a major epidemic. He couldn't hold off any longer. He was calling in the CDC. His only hope was he hadn't waited too long before sounding the alarm. True, he was only aware of seven, now possibly eight confirmed cases, but there could be others out there.

The new patient had been placed in the cubicle next to Lauren Connor. Jeff read the chart. She was a twenty-four-year-old law student by the name of Susan Kelly. Her temperature was 103. After again donning a protective gown, mask, hat, and gloves, he followed Raven and Dr. Myers into the tiny room.

"I'm Dr. Knight," he said, smiling down at the patient. "I understand you're not feeling well."

"I feel like I've been run over by a truck," the woman said, her voice a hoarse whisper. "I've never felt this bad in my life."

"Well, we'll try to make you more comfortable," he said reassuringly. He spent several minutes studying her chart, then turned to Dr. Myers, who was watching him expectantly. "What's been done thus far?" he asked.

"Well, doctor, we've given her aspirin, alcohol rubs and a refrigerated blanket to bring down her fever, which is now a hundred and three. She's also receiving an IV to replace fluids lost from sweating and diarrhea. She's severely acidotic, so she was given twelve ampoules of intravenous sodium bicarbonate, as well as potassium chloride, to correct an electrolyte imbalance."

"Good," he said before turning once again to the patient. "You told Dr. Myers you began feeling ill yesterday morning, is that right?"

"Yes." Jeff had to lean over to hear the woman.

"What was the first thing you noticed?"

"The fever, then the headache," Susan Kelly said. She tapped her fingers against the side of her forehead. "Right here is where I feel the pain. It's awful. Can you give me something for it?"

"The medication Dr. Myers gave you earlier should begin taking effect soon." He gave her arm a tiny squeeze then handed the chart to Dr. Myers. "I know you're not feeling well, but I need to examine you," he continued.

He pulled the stethoscope from around his shoulders. "I'll try to be as gentle as possible, but let me know if there's any discomfort. Okay?"

Susan nodded weakly, whispering through parched lips. "All right, doctor."

Raven steadied her as he listened to her heart, then checked her lungs. Straightening, he pulled the stethoscope from his ears and tucked it into the pocket of his lab coat then gently palpated her abdomen. Like the others, her liver and spleen were enlarged. She also had the same wicked-looking rash on her abdomen.

"Raven," he said over his shoulder. "Take a look at this."

She slipped in front of him. Jeff stayed right behind her and their bodies brushed as he leaned forward slightly, pointing to the area he wanted her to see. Her face was next to his, her breath warm on his cheek, and her scent was sweet and intoxicating. He was standing so close that he was practically holding her in an embrace. A wave of heat washed over him.

He tried to block out his awareness of her as she inspected the series of spots that dotted Susan Kelly's abdomen. But it was hard—damn hard. He couldn't breathe. He couldn't think. He could only feel. To his overactive brain, she seemed to be taking an inordinate amount of time to complete her inspection, but finally she stepped back. With her body no longer pressed against his from shoulder to thigh, he could breathe freely again.

The rest of the exam went quickly, then he asked Susan a series of questions geared to determine if she had any connection with any of the other patients or with Reverend Walters. All of his questions drew a negative response. He would have liked to question her further but it was soon clear that she was tiring.

He issued a few instructions to Dr. Myers, then asked him to give Mr. Parker an update on his wife's condition and to tell him he'd be out to see him in a few minutes.

He then took Raven's arm and left the room. Just outside the door there was a large frame holding a plastic bag. Both Raven and Jeff peeled off their isolation apparel, carefully scrubbed their hands, then retired to the doctors' lounge behind the nurses' station.

Raven took a seat on the lumpy couch, but he was too keyed up to sit. He felt restless, on edge. Raven seemed to understand what he was feeling and waited for him to speak.

"None of them are responding to the medication and the patient count is growing," he said finally. He raked his hand over his hair in frustration then stared at the ceiling. "I'm calling in the CDC."

Raven nodded. "I don't think you have any other choice."

Jeff looked into her lovely eyes. It was good having her to support his decision but then, except when he'd pushed her away, she'd always been there for him. He lifted the receiver. The first person he called was Henry Brockman, the hospital's administrator, to inform him of his decision and his rationale. Brockman reluctantly agreed. Next he called the CDC, then the Department of Public Health. When he was done, some of the tension he'd been feeling was gone.

"The CDC is sending out a team immediately," he said, plopping down on the couch next to Raven. "They'll be here tomorrow morning. I just hope they have some idea of what we're dealing with."

She gave him a reassuring smile. "I'm sure they'll be able to get to the bottom of this."

He rubbed the back of his neck and issued a weary sigh. "I'm not going to be able to take you home. Looks like I'm going to be stuck here for a while. After I talk to Mr. Parker, I'm going to have to get ready for tomorrow's meeting."

"Don't worry about it," she said. "I can take a cab."

She paused then added hesitantly, "If you like I can stick around and help you get the charts organized."

He looked at her profile admiringly. "I'd like that," he said. His eyes locked with hers and held. "Would you like to sit in on tomorrow's meeting?"

He forced back the warning signals going off in his brain. This wasn't a wise thing to do, but he was operating on feelings, not good sense. For one of the few times in his life, Jeff let his heart overrule his head.

She looked at him, surprised. "I'd like that but don't you think your Mr. Brockman might have a problem with my being there?"

Jeff gave her his best grin. "Probably, but I want you there. Hey, we're a team, remember."

"Are we really?" she asked.

He knew what she was asking: If his opposition to herbal medicine still remained. He didn't know what to say. He was trying to be more open-minded and receptive to her views. He'd read the books and studies she'd given him on herbal healing, and had to admit that in "limited" circumstances he might consider using an herbal remedy. But this was not one of them.

Thankfully, he was saved from having to answer by the charge nurse who stuck her head in the doorway. "Dr. Knight, would you mind speaking with Mr. Connor? He and his kids have been here all day. I tried to get him to leave, but he refused. He's pretty upset. Maybe if you talk to him, he'll calm down. The poor man looks as if he's at the end of his rope."

He nodded. He needed to speak to Mr. Connor, anyway. He left Raven organizing patient files and went in search of the family. He found them huddled together in the corner of the waiting room. Greg Connor was flanked by two small children, a boy and a girl, all three looking very scared. In contrast, a tall, slender, mahogany-skinned man, whom he presumed was Calvin Parker, sat drumming his fingers against the arm of his chair. He looked to be in his late forties.

Jeff scrutinized Greg Connor's face. He'd aged a lot in the last week, and Jeff was sorry that he had to be the harbinger of more anguish and suffering. It was one of the things about being a doctor that he hated most.

Mr. Connor stood as Jeff approached. "Doctor, what's wrong with Lauren? It's been over a week and she isn't any better."

Jeff could hear the fear in his voice and didn't want to alarm him unduly, but he knew he had to be as candid as possible. "We still haven't been able to identity the source of the problem," he said, steering Mr. Connor to a secluded corner of the waiting room, away from his young children. "As I told you before, it appears to be some kind of bacterial infection. Exactly what, we haven't been able to determine. We're still running tests."

"But it's been a week!" Greg Connor closed his eyes fighting back tears.

God, he hated this. "I know, but we're doing all we can."

Mr. Connor's shoulders sagged and his lower lip quivered. He looked across the room at his children, then back at Jeff. "Is...is she going to die?"

Jeff hesitated. It was not his way to pronounce death sentences. He always tried to put the best possible face on the prognosis, leaving unsaid the hard truth. He clapped the other man on the back. "Not if I can help it." He cleared his throat. "Why don't you and the kids go home and get some rest?"

Greg Connor drew a deep sigh, then nodded. Jeff watched as he collected his children and left the room. He sighed himself, then walked over to where Mr. Parker sat.

The other man looked up as he approached. "Dr. Knight?" After Jeff nodded, he added, "Dr. Myers said you wanted to see me?"

"That's right," Jeff said, pulling up a chair next to him. "You're a hard man to reach."

Calvin Parker shifted uncomfortably in his chair. "I'm on the road a lot. I'm a pharmaceutical sales rep for Dalton Laboratories."

"I see," Jeff said, though he wasn't sure what relevance his being on the road had to do with his ability to visit his wife. "What I wanted to talk to you about was your wife's medical history and her activities in the days leading up to the onset of her illness."

Calvin Parker frowned. "I already told Dr. Myers and Dr. Alexander everything I know."

Jeff wanted to yell at him, *Your wife is dying. Don't you care?* But instead he held his tongue. "It'll just take a few minutes."

Mr. Parker glanced at his watch. "All right, but make it quick. I have an appointment with a client."

Jeff went through a series of questions, geared to elicit as much information as possible about Eleanor's overall health, as well as her movements in the days leading up to her illness. Mr. Parker answered all of them, but he wasn't able to shed any light on the disease. The only interesting bit of information was his disclosure that Reverend Walters was treating his wife for diabetes. That wasn't what Reverend Walters had told them. Why had he lied? Jeff looked over at Raven who had entered the room sometime during the interview. He could tell she was wondering the same thing.

"I think it might help your wife's condition if you could spend more time with her."

Calvin Parker gave him a blank look. "What good would that do? According to Dr. Myers, half the time she's delirious, or so heavily sedated, she's only semiconscious."

Jeff nodded. "That's true, but she's aware of your presence. I think it would go a long way in aiding in her recovery if you visited more. If your job prevents your spending time with her during the day, we can arrange some special evening visiting hours for you."

Mr. Parker cleared his throat. "Thanks, but that really isn't necessary." He looked at his watch again. "Look, Dr. Knight, I really have to go." He was already moving toward the door.

Jeff stared in amazement at Calvin Parker's retreating back. "He seems to be more interested in his job than his wife."

"That's for sure," Raven said, coming to stand directly in front of him. "But do you know what's really odd?"

Something in her voice made him look up sharply. "No, what?"

"He never once asked how she was doing."

HE'D ALMOST LOST his nerve. He'd been going over this for days, but it still bothered him. He always rehearsed in front of his bathroom mirror so that he looked and sounded just right. But at that moment when he had stood directly behind the bartender, he'd been momentarily flustered, almost immobile.

The bartender was a pudgy guy. Almost as flabby as he'd once been. On the previous days when he'd watched the bartender to get his movements down, he had managed to push that fact to the farthest recesses of his mind. But in that storage room he hadn't been able to. It had caused him to hesitate. In the end, of course, he'd gone through with it. Later, he felt the satisfaction of another transaction successfully completed, but the heady excitement he'd experienced the first time wasn't there. The bartender had disturbed him; he'd felt an instant, unwelcome affinity for the obese man....

Whop!

The stinging blow came quickly, out of nowhere, knocking him from his seat to the floor.

"How many times have I told you about stuffing your

face with junk food, huh? How do you expect to lose that blubber if you keep shoving it in?''

''But I'm still hungry,'' he whined.

''Maybe if you did something besides sit on your lazy butt watching TV for hours on end, you wouldn't have time to think about food.''

''Johnny, he's a growing boy. He'll slim down.''

''Shut up! Was I talking to you, huh? Did you hear me ask your advice? He knows this is for his own good, don't you, boy?''

''Yes.''

''Yes, what?''

''Yes, sir.''

''Damn right. What did the doctor say today, Marge? Aren't there diet pills or something he can give us? Did you tell him I'm six-one and that my brothers are also over six feet? Never had a weight problem in my life.''

''Johnny, he doesn't need diet pills. He doesn't have your body structure. The doctor says he's absolutely normal in development.''

''Normal? Look at him, will you! Eleven years old and he's as wide as he is tall. It's your fault, Marge, for babying him.''

''Johnny, please. Can we talk about this later?''

They always talked about him as if he wasn't there. His father, his mother, the doctors. In later years, his teachers and the kids at school had done the same thing. He'd been powerless back then.

''Well, let me tell you something, missus, that is not a normal weight for someone in my family. What's he going to be, huh? The fat man in the circus? Not my son. My son's going to be a man, not some sissy-prissy jerk who's afraid of his own shadow, who lets people push him around. Marge, we're going down in the basement to lift weights for an hour. And for dinner, he gets a salad and a glass of milk. Salads are good for you, low in calories, or don't they teach you that in school, boy?''

"Johnny, you know he can't have leafy green vegetables. He—"

"Don't you start with that allergy nonsense, do you hear me? Allergies is just the doctors' excuse for taking our money. How the hell can the boy lose weight if we don't cut out all those calories? The boy knows I'm right. Don't you?"

"Yes, sir." Even as he muttered the words his father wanted to hear, he prayed the stomach cramps that always followed eating salads wouldn't be too bad.

"Good boy. Your mother, she means well, but she doesn't know how to raise a son—she doesn't know that a man's gotta be big and strong and powerful. Power's everything. I saw that when I was in the service. I see it every day down at the department. Power's what counts, boy. That's what makes people respect you. Don't forget it."

Well, he had power now, didn't he? He'd proved it eight times now.

His thin lips curled into a cruel little smile. And very soon he'd prove it again.

Chapter Seven

It was too late for second thoughts now. Raven's heart was beating faster than a speeding train as she followed Jeff into the hospital conference room. There were a number of people already assembled when they arrived.

A short, nervous-looking man looked up as they entered. His anxious look was replaced by a small smile when he spotted Jeff. He waved, then began to move in their direction.

"That's Henry Brockman, the hospital's chief of staff," Jeff whispered hurriedly.

"Am I glad to see you," Brockman said. He took Jeff by the arm and moved away from the others. "Whatever you told the CDC lit a fire under them. They sent their top epidemiologist, Joseph Hillman, to head up the investigation, and Public Health sent Eric Thacker. You know he's—" He stopped and frowned at Raven, noting her presence for the first time. "I'm sorry. I don't think we've met."

Raven held her breath. This was the moment she'd been dreading. When Jeff had invited her to sit in on the meeting, he'd been tired and overwrought, probably feeling obligated to ask her because of the assistance she'd given him over the past few days. But in the light of day, she couldn't help wondering if he regretted having asked her.

Well, if he wanted an out, Brockman had just presented him with the perfect opportunity to rescind the invitation.

Jeff stared into her eyes and smiled. "Henry Brockman, this is Raven Delaney. She's been helping me with the investigation."

The furrow between the administrator's brown eyes deepened even further. "You're not on staff, are you?"

"No," she said guardedly. "I run an herbal shop in the Windwood Mall." From Brockman's reaction, you'd have thought she'd just said she was an ax murderer.

His eyes instantly flew to Jeff. "Are you crazy?" he demanded then threw an anxious look over his shoulder, afraid his words might have been overheard. "She has no business being here. My God, what were you thinking?"

"That I needed help in this investigation," Jeff said coldly. "While you and the rest of the board have been busy trying to pretend we didn't have a problem, Raven's been helping me get a handle on this thing. Her assistance has been invaluable."

Brockman flushed. "Well, we don't need her help now. We've got the CDC and the state health officials." He gave Raven a condescending smile. "I'm sure you understand, Ms. Delaney."

"Well, I don't," Jeff said. "Ms. Delaney is eminently qualified to sit in on this discussion. She's not only a registered nurse, but has degrees in nutrition and pharmacology. I think she might be able to provide a different perspective on things."

She looked at him and blinked. Did he really think that? She was almost afraid to believe him.

Brockman snorted. "Really, Jeff, we have people on staff who can do that."

"Henry, I don't think you understand. This is not a subject open to debate. Raven is staying."

The hospital administrator looked as if he were about to blow a gasket. "All right, Jeff, I see there's no reasoning with you, but I want you to know I'm holding you personally responsible if anything happens." At that, he marched back across the room.

As much as she wanted to sit in on the discussion, she didn't want to cause dissention between Jeff and his colleagues. She looked at Jeff, her eyes troubled. "If my presence is going to cause problems for you, I'll leave."

He waved off her objection. "Don't worry. Brockman's bark is worse than his bite." He gave her a reassuring smile. "I want you to stay. Besides, if this meeting gets rough, it'll be good having someone on my side." He leaned over and whispered in a low, husky voice, "You *would* defend me, wouldn't you?"

Heat coursed through her at his look.

"Ladies and gentlemen, I see everyone has arrived," Brockman said over the hum of conversation. "Why don't we take our seats and begin." He motioned to the round conference table.

Jeff held her chair then took the seat next to her. She tried to focus on the introductions, but with Jeff's thigh pressed against her, it was damn hard. She drew a sigh of relief when he shifted position so that his thigh no longer touched her. She glanced around the table. The level of medical talent in this room was quite impressive. To her immediate right was Shay Alexander, whom Raven had known back when she and Jeff were dating. Next to Shay was Dr. Eric Thacker, a short, portly, red-faced man from the Department of Public Health.

Next to Dr. Thacker was Dr. Joseph Hillman. It seemed to Raven that Hillman was the Hollywood image of what a physician should look like—with his tawny brown hair combed back from his deeply lined but tanned and handsome face, he bore a remarkable resemblance to George Clooney, the hunky doctor on the TV series, "ER."

Alongside Dr. Hillman was the hospital's chief legal counsel, a Dan somebody—she missed his last name. He was strictly Ivy League, with sandy blond hair and boyish features. Also at the table were Brenda Holland, who was in charge of public relations, and a jovial-looking older woman named Leah Patterson who was with the CDC.

"Before I turn things over to Dr. Knight," Brockman said, "on behalf of the hospital, I want to thank you personally for being here and assure you that you have the full cooperation of the hospital. We'll help in any way we can." He paused for a moment then cleared his throat. "But we're also concerned about the negative impact public disclosure of this situation could have on the hospital. I'm sure you understand, we'd like to handle this matter as quietly as possible." He gave Raven a pointed look. "Ms. Delaney, I hope we can count on you to be discreet."

"Of course," she said, uncomfortably aware that all eyes in the room were staring at her. "As I told Dr. Knight, I won't say anything."

He gave her a cool nod. "Then I'll turn things over to Dr. Knight."

Jeff stood and proceeded to summarize the events of the past few weeks. His demeanor was confident and self-assured. He didn't embellish the facts, but spoke in a calm, direct matter which made the mysterious disease sound all the more sinister. When he finished speaking, she looked around the table, studying the reactions of the group. They looked suitably alarmed, and she was confident that the urgency of the situation had been heard and understood.

"What about deaths?" Eric Thacker asked.

"Four, to date," Jeff said. "But I must point out that the patients were at three different hospitals, and their deaths occurred prior to anyone drawing a connection between the cases." Jeff paused for a moment, letting that bit of information sink in. "Initially, we thought we might be dealing with a bacterial contaminant, and the culprit was herbs. We interviewed and collected samples from all the local herb suppliers in this area but, after extensive testing of those herbs and interviews with growers and

customers, we've pretty well ruled out that possibility."
He looked at Shay. "Is there anything you wish to add?"

Shay shook his head. "That pretty much sums things
up. None of the patients contracted this disease from the
herbs we tested." He scratched his head. "My testing did
uncover something disturbing with two of the suppliers,
but it's more of a criminal matter than a medical problem."

That sounds ominous, Raven thought, sitting up
straighter.

"It appears two of the suppliers—Flynn Imports and
Zook and Sons—are dealing drugs. Marijuana, to be specific. We founds traces of the plant."

Raven gasped. Harry dealing drugs? No, she thought, it
had to be a terrible mistake. He wouldn't do something
like that. Just last year, he'd chaired a local group dedicated to keeping kids off of drugs. And hadn't she heard
him say that drug dealers were the scum of the earth? But
as she listened to Shay's narrative, the facts were undis-
putable. She shook her head, struggling to take it in. It
seemed incomprehensible.

Brockman turned to Dr. Thacker. "Do you want to handle that?"

"Sure, we'll notify the police, as well as check both
facilities for possible public health violations."

Raven could feel Jeff's eyes on her. He looked concerned. She gave him a small smile indicating that she was
all right.

Jeff cleared his throat. "Eric, I'd like for you to also
check out a Reverend Walters. He's an alternative health
care practitioner with a history of using substandard products. At least two of the patients saw him right before they
were hospitalized. Lord knows what he gave them."

"You think he could be the source of the disease?"
Hillman asked.

"No, but I think he should be shut down."

Eric Thacker nodded. "We'll get a court order and go over to his place today."

"What about treatment?" Dr. Hillman asked. "What's been done thus far?"

"We've begun an aggressive drug therapy, but this thing hasn't responded to any treatment we've tried to date. Frankly, Dr. Alexander and I are out of ideas."

Hillman gave him a thoughtful look. "Any thoughts on what we're dealing with?"

Jeff hesitated. "I think there's a chance we've got something new. At least, it's new to us."

Hillman frowned. "Why do you say that?"

"I was with the World Health Organization for two years. I've seen and studied some of the most virulent diseases on the planet—cholera, bubonic plague, Ebola, AIDS—and I've never seen anything like this. It doesn't behave like any disease I've ever seen. It kills within a matter of a few weeks by totally destroying the person's immune system. I think we may be dealing with a new virus."

What kind of disease could destroy the immune system like that? Raven wondered. Nothing that she knew of and from the look on Hillman's and the others' faces, they didn't know either. Until now, she'd felt confident that the CDC would be able to quickly identify the deadly microbe, but now she wasn't sure. A shiver ran up her spine as the magnitude of the horror of the disease began to creep into her subconscious. If this really was a new virus, that meant they had no means of combating the disease.

She looked at Dr. Hillman who seemed to be taking an inordinate amount of time to light his pipe. Jeff's words had shaken him. He was pensive, worried, but trying not to show it.

"What's being done about quarantine?" he asked finally.

Jeff explained that while the infectious agent didn't appear to be contagious, all the patients had been isolated to one wing of the hospital.

"Good," Dr. Hillman said, nodding. "Then I guess we should begin by looking at the patients, then interviewing family members and everyone else who came into contact with them."

"Is that really necessary?" Brockman whined. "We're talking about Lord knows how many people."

"I'm afraid it is necessary," Dr. Hillman said firmly. "I know that's going to take a lot of manpower. If the hospital can't provide it, I'm sure we can tap the resources of the Public Health Department." He looked at Dr. Thacker, who nodded.

"It's not a question of manpower," Brockman sniffed. "We can handle that. It just seems to me that before we go off scaring people to death, shouldn't we wait until we actually have a diagnosis?"

Jeff shook his head. "We've already waited too long. We've got to get a handle on this thing as quickly as possible."

Dr. Hillman nodded in agreement. "We'll do what we can to keep a lid on things," he said, "but I can't promise anything."

"Then if there's nothing else, I guess we should begin by having you look at the patients," Jeff said. "Shay, why don't you take them up to the fifth floor. Ms. Delaney and I will be along in a moment."

She knew he wanted to talk about Harry, but she wasn't up to it right now. She wasn't sure how she felt. He was a good friend but she couldn't condone drug trafficking. Raven watched as the group filed out of the room, leaving just the two of them.

Jeff leaned over and gave her shoulder a little squeeze. His hand felt warm and reassuring. She would have loved to rest her head on his shoulder.

"I'm sorry about your friend Harry," he said softly.

She drew a deep breath then nodded. "You always

thought he was hiding something—'' Her voice broke and she blinked back tears. ''I must be the worst judge of men in history.''

The hand that had been stroking her shoulder stilled and he turned her toward him. ''Don't say that. You're sweet and kind and open. You look for the good in people. Just because Harry let you down, don't close yourself off to all men.''

She had the feeling he was talking about himself. She laid her hand against the side of his face. He smiled at her for a moment then turned his face and placed a kiss in the palm of her hand. It was a sweet, tender kiss that spoke of sharing and caring and held a promise of things to come. But so much lay between them, not the least being his disdain for alternative medicine.

''Come on,'' he said, taking her hand and standing. ''We'd better get out of here before they send a search party after us.''

THE DISEASE DESTROYS the patient's immune system.

Jeff's words stayed with Raven until late into the night. She reread the notes she'd taken during her hospital view today, as well as the notes she'd taken over the last week. It was becoming a nightly ritual. At first she'd done it as a way of keeping facts straight within their investigation, but as the days progressed she found she was just as obsessed with finding a treatment for this mysterious disease as Jeff was. However, where he leaned toward finding one with a drug base, she was looking at more unconventional methods.

In theory, she thought, as she studied the notes she'd compiled on the disease, if they could keep the patient's immune system intact, the body should be able to fight off the infection. She grimaced at the knowledge that the drugs they had used to date had focused solely on destroying the infection, not restoring the body's immune system. But that was exactly where the focus should be. It had worked with AIDS patients, and was now an accepted method of treatment for that disease. Why wouldn't it work here? The more she thought about the idea, the more she thought it was possible.

Unable to sleep, she got out of bed, slipped on a robe and headed to her study. She searched her library looking for several rare herb books she'd collected over the years. Finding them, she sank into the chair behind her desk and began to read. She pored through volume after volume before she found what she wanted—a series of herbs known for their abilities to help restore and maintain the body's immune system.

After that she was too excited to sleep. She was up at the crack of dawn, dressed and headed for Nature's Cure. As soon as it was appropriate, she'd called Harry. She had hesitated at first, but some of the herbs were quite rare and hard to obtain. Several others had to be shipped within hours of picking, as well as stored in refrigerated containers to retain their freshness. Harry was the only person she would trust with this kind of task.

He answered his phone on the first ring. Suddenly she felt flustered, not sure what she should say to him. He seemed equally uncomfortable. Finally, in a halting manner, she managed to tell him what she needed. He told her he'd make a few phone calls and see if he could locate the herbs. Then there was a long awkward pause which Harry broke by bringing up the subject of marijuana.

She heard him sigh. "I knew I'd made a colossal mistake the moment I took delivery of the plants." He sounded tired and depressed. "I haven't had a moment of peace since those plants came into my warehouse. They've been gone for more than a week and I still can't sleep at night."

"How in heaven's name did you get involved in something like that?" Raven asked, still trying to come to grips with her friend's behavior.

"I—I got into a financial bind and I needed a lot of cash

and I needed it fast. A business associate offered me a way out of my financial situation. All I had to do was store the plants in my warehouse for a few weeks.''

It still didn't justify drug trafficking, she thought, but Harry was human and subject to all the human foibles. ''What's going to happen now?'' she asked.

''I don't know,'' he said, his voice laced with frustration. ''Public Health came out yesterday and inspected the warehouse. I was also questioned by the police. My lawyer doesn't think any criminal charges will be filed because no one actually saw any plants on the premises, and he thinks Public Health is going to let me keep my license. I'll probably have to pay a hefty fine, and undergo a number of unannounced inspections for the next year or so, but I think that's a small price to pay for what I did. I've learned my lesson.'' He paused then asked, ''Are—are we still friends?''

She thought for a moment. He'd done a terrible thing, but she believed him when he said he'd learned his lesson.

''Yes,'' she said, ''we're friends.'' And she meant it.

''Thanks,'' he said. There was a catch in his voice. ''I'll get on your request right away.''

A few hours later, Harry called to tell her he'd located the herbs and would get them to her in a few days. She sat back and looked at the herbal formula she'd developed. Now, all she had to do was convince Jeff to use it.

THE BODY COUNT was now five.

Eleanor Parker lay on the narrow hospital bed. Calvin Parker stood next to the bed, staring down at his wife's lifeless body. He didn't stir at the sound of Jeff's footsteps. Jeff paused in the doorway and stared at the man. Calvin Parker was dry-eyed. The tears would probably come later, Jeff thought, once the reality of his wife's death sank in. He steeled himself for the inevitable pain and anger as he approached the other man.

''Mr. Parker.''

Calvin Parker looked up as he entered the room.

"I'm sorry about your wife," Jeff said. "I want you to know we did everything we could, but once the infection spread to her heart and lungs, she was just too weak to fight it off."

Calvin Parker nodded vaguely. "I'm sure you did your best. It was just her time to go."

Jeff looked at the other man, surprised by his words. Most people who'd just lost a loved one were angry, hurt, in shock. This kind of reaction—philosophical acceptance—normally came much later in the grieving process. But then, Calvin Parker didn't look much like the grieving husband, he thought, as he studied the other man more closely. He sighed. Who was he to say how a person should grieve?

Jeff looked at Eleanor Parker. She was incredibly dehydrated. Her skin was dry and cracked, and she'd lost so much weight that she looked almost mummified. Her abdomen was also strangely distended. It usually took weeks for the bacteria in the abdomen to multiply to the point where it became distended.

Jeff's brain whirled. What the hell kind of disease could do this? Just what the hell were they dealing with?

There was a strained silence while Jeff searched for something to say. "Mr. Parker," he said finally, "I want you to know we're going to get to the bottom of this. Hopefully, the autopsy will—"

Calvin Parker did a double take. "Autopsy? Who said anything about an autopsy?"

Jeff hesitated. He really didn't want to get into this with him. Now was not the time to be discussing something like that. "Why don't we talk about it later?"

Mr. Parker shook his head. "We'll talk about it now."

Jeff ran a hand through his hair impatiently. "It's the only way we have of finding out what killed your wife."

Calvin Parker shook his head again. "No autopsy." His

voice was firm and brooked no argument. "I just want this over and done with."

Jeff's eyes narrowed. He wanted to tell him that he didn't need his permission for an autopsy, but he didn't have the stomach for it now. He preferred the family members to be agreeable. He tried again. "I understand your concern. The autopsy will be performed as quickly as possible and with due regard for you and your family."

Calvin Parker sighed. "Dr. Knight, you don't understand. My wife was a very religious woman and didn't believe in such things. She would have viewed an autopsy as a desecration of one of God's creatures. I must honor her wishes."

"But without an autopsy we may never know what killed her," Jeff reasoned. When the other man continued to protest, he said, "Don't you want to know?"

"What kind of question is that?" Parker said with a trace of annoyance. "Of course I want to know, but knowing won't change the fact that she's dead."

"No, nothing is going to change that fact," Jeff said quietly. "But knowing what killed her might help save the lives of the three other patients who are suffering from the same disease that killed your wife."

Something in his manner must have telegraphed itself to the other man, for suddenly Calvin Parker underwent a stunning transformation. His shoulders sagged, his eyes filled with tears, and he seemed to be overcome with emotion. "You have to forgive me. I'm just shocked by Eleanor's death. Of course I want to know what killed her."

Jeff's gut reaction was that Parker was putting on an act for his benefit.

"All right, Dr. Knight. You do what you think is best."

Jeff nodded. After a few more minutes of strained conversation, he left Mr. Parker and stopped at the nurses' station. He instructed the nurse to have one of the hospital's grief counselors come down and talk to Mr. Parker. Though, from all accounts, it didn't look as if he needed it. Then Jeff headed for the morgue. Maybe the coroner would be able to tell him what had killed Eleanor Parker.

"Jeff, you did everything you could."

"Then why do I feel so lousy?" Jeff looked down at his hands, then back at Raven, his expression bleak. "I just feel so helpless. I couldn't even console Mr. Parker by telling him what killed his wife." His voice was laced with pain and frustration.

"I'm sure he knows you did everything possible." Raven reached over and took his hand in hers and smiled reassuringly. He didn't return the smile, but neither was he as grim as he'd been moments before when she'd opened the door to him. She'd taken one look at him and known that she was going to have to hold off talking to him about using her herbal mixture for a while.

"What's even worse, I ran into Greg Connor as I was leaving the hospital. He asked if I thought Lauren would be out of the hospital soon. He wants to plan his little girl's birthday party." For a moment Jeff seemed overcome with emotion. "He looked at me with such hope. I couldn't tell him the truth—that by this time next week his wife will probably be dead. I felt like such a fraud."

Her heart went out to him. This was the warm, sensitive man she'd fallen in love with four years ago. It took all her willpower not to take him in her arms.

"We expect a lot from doctors," she said. "We expect you to have all the answers, to do the impossible. It's easy to forget that you're human just like the rest of us, and that it's not easy for you to deal with the loss of a patient."

"The day it no longer bothers me is the day I'll no longer want to practice medicine. You have to care in order to be a decent doctor. Some days are just harder than others, and the death of a patient is something you never get used to." He looked at Raven and gave her a faint smile. "But having you to talk to helps," he said softly.

Raven swallowed, not knowing what to say.

She watched as his eyes swept over her face, her neck then dropped to the V of her dress. The top two buttons were undone, exposing the hollow of her throat and a couple inches of creamy brown skin. His hazel eyes darkened and she knew he wanted her.

Raven's eyes widened when she saw the look in his eyes. It was an unguarded moment, and something strong and sexual was telegraphing itself to her. Something warm and sensuous and utterly dangerous to her self-preservation. She wanted to enjoy it—but she knew she shouldn't. Ambiguous feelings began to jockey for position within her. She forced herself to look away. "I have all the confidence in the world that you're going to get to the bottom of this thing."

"Thanks," he said. "I'm sorry to go on like this, but I just feel so frustrated, like I'm beating my head against the wall."

"That's okay," she said gently. "You need to talk." Besides, his talking about the mysterious disease would allow her to broach the subject of using her herbal medicine.

"You sure you don't mind?" he asked, turning to face her on the sofa. As she shook her head, he settled back against the cushions. "Maybe talking will give me a fresh perspective on things." He drew a deep breath. "I've gone over it a zillion times in my mind and the more I think about this disease, the less sense it makes. It's like nothing I've ever seen before. It doesn't respond to any known antibiotic, or drug or chemical. Nothing!"

Raven frowned. "What about Dr. Hillman and the other members of the CDC team, don't they have any ideas?"

Jeff gave her a wan smile. "Ideas, yes, but if you're asking if they know what this thing is, the answer is no. They've sent tissue, blood and urine samples to the CDC in Atlanta, but I'm not holding my breath that they'll come up with anything soon."

She looked at him surprised. "But they've got some of the best minds in the world working there. Surely they'll come up with something."

"It's going to be damn hard," he said. "This disease doesn't follow any logical pattern. On the surface it appears to be a bacterial infection, but the way it fights off antibiotics suggests it's a virus. But if it were a virus, you'd expect the disease to spread from person to person. But the problem with that theory is that none of the patients' family members and friends have come down with the disease. Which brings up another interesting contradiction. It seems to show an extreme bias for women."

Raven frowned. "What do you mean?"

"Infectious diseases don't discriminate between sexes. Statistically speaking, men and women should be affected equally. However, this disease doesn't seem to know that and has a bias for women. Additionally, infectious diseases spread exponentially. A new infectious disease rapidly explodes in a population as microbes are transmitted from person to person. Then it declines within months because it is stopped by the elimination of susceptible victims either by death or, more often, by natural immunization. But that's not what's happening here."

"Why do you think that is?" she asked.

"I wish I knew that and a whole lot of other things about this disease." Jeff sighed. "But whatever it is, I think we're getting further away from finding an answer rather than closer."

His frustration gave Raven exactly the opening she needed in order to bring up using her herbal medicine. But before she could say anything, Jeff began talking about the course of the disease.

"This thing has to run its course soon," Jeff was saying. "It's already run longer than most infectious agents without mutating. But it's just a matter of time before it begins to mutate and, when it does, hopefully that'll give us some clues as to what we're dealing with."

"And what if it doesn't?"

"Then we'd better figure out how these people contacted the disease." He drew a deep breath. "Shay and Hillman have all but ruled out the possibility that this is a bacterial infection. We're moving into the area of viruses now."

Raven sucked in her breath. "I hope that's not the case. It'll be a lot tougher to come up with an effective treatment."

He nodded. "Tell me about it. There was a Dr. Ross with the CDC and he probably could have helped us, but he died about six months ago."

As he talked, he took her hand and laced her fingers with his, then ran the back of his other hand slowly up and down the right side of her face. She inhaled sharply. "I appreciate your letting me go on like this," he said, looking into her eyes. "You've been a lot of help."

His voice was deep and sensual, sending a ripple of excitement through her. The air around them crackled with sexual tension.

"Would...would you like some tea?" she gulped.

"Tea is not what I want," Jeff said smoothly, trapping her eyes with his so that she was unable to look away.

Her heart began to beat erratically as she tried to think of something to say to ease the sexual tension—but her mind was totally blank. The way he was looking at her...those hazel eyes of his...his warm, seductive voice... Raven felt heat rippling through her, which paradoxically, made her shiver.

"I really hurt you, didn't I?" he asked quietly. "By not believing you four years ago."

"You did what you believed was right."

He shook his head. "But it wasn't right, because it hurt you," he said, cupping her face with his hands. His fingers were so gentle. Raven felt the heat within her turn up a notch. "If I could do things over again, I'd do them differently. I'd listen to you, try to learn more about the things you believe in, not be so judgmental."

His voice was low and husky and made her want to think all kinds of silly things—things she should know by now were impossible. She moistened her lips and looked up at him.

"Raven, you're so beautiful—"

Desire. It was suddenly so palpable, it might have been a living thing, swirling around them, surrounding them, connecting them.

Raven knew the desire she could see in Jeff's eyes was mirrored in her own. Like him, she was helpless to hide it, powerless to conceal it. She could see it on his face, hear it in the way he breathed, feel it in his touch, in the heat of his skin.

She wanted him to touch her. She wanted to touch him. She wanted—

He kissed her.

Gently his mouth moved over hers in a kiss so sweet, Raven nearly cried out. It used to amaze her—it still amazed her—that a man who was so much larger than life, a man who lived his life so passionately, so intensely, could be so breathtakingly tender.

Even as he deepened the kiss, as his tongue sought entry into her mouth, even then he was unquestionably gentle. Raven felt herself melt. She felt her bones turn liquid, felt her body molding to fit against his as he took her into his arms and kissed her again and again.

His touch and his taste was so familiar, it seemed as if they'd last made love just yesterday. Her memories were incredibly vivid. In her mind's eye, she saw them lying on his bed, a double bed, kissing and touching, exploring...

Raven felt Jeff lift her onto his lap. She gasped as he pulled her so she sat astride his lap, facing him. Their legs intertwined, the roughness of his against the soft smoothness of hers. She could feel the hard bulge of his sex pressing against her as he kissed her again. He wanted her—it was undeniable.

She knew she could tell him that she wanted him, too, without saying a single word. All she'd have to do was to keep responding to his kisses. Or maybe, more obviously, she could unbutton his shirt and run her hands up and down his chest. He'd loved her touch. She remembered that—and much more.

She remembered the way he had once caressed every inch of her body as he made love to her. He had made her feel as if she were the most beautiful, most desirable woman in the world. She remembered how he had somehow seemed to know when to unleash his passion, when to leave his sweet tenderness behind. She remembered how he'd let himself lose control, giving himself over to her completely, crying out her name as waves of intense pleasure exploded around them both.

She remembered how totally, how absolutely, how with all her heart, she had loved him.

Her memory of that love was so strong, she could almost feel it. It was as if she'd been thrown backward in time, back four years, back before Jeff had said all those hateful things, back before she had known what he'd really thought of her and her profession.

She could make love to him again, as if it were four years ago. She could pretend that she was twenty-three again and in love for the first time in her life.

But tomorrow morning, when they woke up, it wouldn't be four years ago. It would be now, and they would be here, and the gulf that separated them—her views and practice of herbal medicine—would still be there.

She wiggled free, escaping his arms. He sat up as if to follow her, but stopped suddenly. She turned to look at him and saw the expression on his face as he realized what they'd been doing—what they'd been about to do.

"Oh, damn," he said. "Raven, I don't know what happened. I didn't intend to—"

"I know," she said. "It's...all right. It wasn't your fault—I mean, it was my fault, too." She looked at her hands clenched tightly in her lap. "But I'm not interested in going down this road again."

"Don't say that," Jeff said quietly.

She looked at him. He was watching her intently. His lean face looked mysterious and hauntingly handsome in the shadows. He didn't smile as she met his gaze.

"Can't we try again?" he asked softly, seriously.

Lovers. He was talking about them being lovers. Raven swallowed, remembering his taste, his touch.... It was tempting.

"I—I don't know." She turned away from him. "I won't pretend I'm not attracted to you, but it doesn't change anything. I'm still an herbalist and you're still a doctor. And the problems are still there."

He took her by the shoulders and turned her toward him. "How can you say that? We've changed. We're not the same people we were four years ago."

She bit her lower lip. "Maybe not, but we haven't changed on the points that matter."

Jeff frowned. "What do you mean?"

It was now or never. "Even though you talk about being more open-minded, you're still unwilling to consider an herbal treatment for your patients. You sit here and tell me how you're at a loss for coming up with any kind of treatment, yet you never once asked if I had any ideas."

He looked at her pleadingly. "I'm trying to keep an open mind, be more receptive to more unconventional forms of medical care, but here we're taking about a deadly virus."

She looked at him for a moment then walked over to the table in the corner, picked up the report she'd prepared on the use of herbs as a form of treatment for the virus, and handed it to him. "I want you to read this," she said.

He looked at the folder, frowning. "Okay. What is it?"

"It's my report on an herbal treatment for this virus."

"Raven—"

She held up a hand, halting his words. "Jeff, as you told Henry Brockman, I'm more than an herbalist. I hold degrees in pharmacology and nutrition. I probably know more about drugs and their effect on the body than anyone involved in this investigation. Yet you refuse to give any credence to my thoughts on a possible treatment because it doesn't fit into your view of what constitutes proper medical care. Open your mind, Jeff, the world is changing—"

She was interrupted by a shrill, insistent beeping. Jeff swore softly, got up from the sofa and reached for his jacket. He pulled a small cellular phone from the inside pocket of his sport jacket. "I'm sorry, Raven, but I'd better take this."

"I understand," she said, unable to keep the disappointment out of her voice. Damn, she needed to discuss her treatment, but at least he had a written copy of it. She tried not to listen to his conversation, busying herself with the papers on her desk. A few minutes later she heard him come up behind her. She turned and looked up at him. His face was grim.

"I gotta go," he said. "That was Shay Alexander. I'm afraid we have another case."

Chapter Eight

David Foster looked cadaverous. He was incredibly dehydrated, with sunken eyes, and mucous membranes so parched there was no saliva. Despite a temperature of 105 degrees, he was too dehydrated to sweat. A bad sign, Jeff thought, since sweating was the most natural and best way to rid the body of heat. He had to do something to bring down his temperature and fast. A temperature that high could lead to brain damage or cardiac arrest.

He looked at Dr. Hillman who was standing next to the nurse at the foot of the bed. "Any suggestion on how we can get this fever down?"

Hillman gave him a pensive look, then named a combination of drugs. They spent several minutes discussing the various drugs before deciding on one.

"I'll get it," Hillman said. He turned and strode from the room.

Jeff picked up the chart and quickly skimmed it. Foster had been transferred from St. John's Hospital where he'd been admitted the night before. He could see they'd tried to take a medical history over there, but Foster was just too sick to provide much information.

Jeff looked at the nurse. "It says here, his wife brought him in. Were you able to get anything out of her?"

The nurse shook her head. "Mrs. Foster is almost a basket case herself. We'll try again later."

Jeff nodded then leaned over the bed and caught Foster's head between his hands, holding it in place as he began asking him questions. Foster was babbling his answers. Though he was close to hallucinating from the fever, the history he gave was nearly identical to Eleanor Parker and the other patients. One moment he'd been fine, the next he'd been hit with a high fever and blinding headache, followed by severe abdominal cramps, vomiting and diarrhea.

And then there was the other similarity—the Wednesday-Thursday admission coincidence. Foster had been admitted at St. John's the night before—Wednesday night.

Jeff frowned. How could a disease strike with such regularity? The answer was—it couldn't. He knew of no disease that struck once a week and always on the same two weekdays.

He sighed and looked down at the patient. He began the examination, though it was a little hard with Foster thrashing around so much. The nurse steadied him with a hand on his back while Jeff quickly checked his chest, lungs and heart. His liver and spleen were enlarged.

As he lifted the gown to examine the abdomen, he saw the rash. It was exactly like the ones he'd seen on Eleanor Parker and the other patients, even down to the same location. He studied the angry red bumps carefully. There were a dozen of them in the upper quadrant of the abdomen, closely grouped, flat and macular. He estimated each one to be eight or nine millimeters in diameter and crescent shaped. The color struck him. The bumps were bright red, incongruous with his pale dry skin, like a vividly colored flower in a bleak desert.

He pulled the gown down, covering the abdomen, and looked at Mr. Foster. "How long have you had this rash?"

David Foster gave him a glassy-eyed stare. "What rats? There aren't any rats in my room, Mother." His face was beginning to twitch.

The nurse shot a puzzled glance at Jeff.

"His temperature is 105," he said by way of explanation. "Some confusion is to be expected." But it certainly complicated matters, he added silently. He needed answers to questions and he needed them now.

Even though it was probably a waste of time, he leaned over the bed and began to question him. "Mr. Foster, have you been seeing a holistic practitioner? A guy by the name of Reverend Walters?"

The twitching and the babbling stopped, and David Foster seemed suddenly lucid. "I've never been to see that man or anyone like him in my life," he sniffed, clearly offended by the question. "Superstitious bunk, nothing but a lot of mumbo jumbo." He continued to babble about people who threw their money away on charlatans.

Jeff sighed. It was clear he wasn't going to get anything more out of him. He instructed the nurse to have the patient moved to the isolation wing on the fifth floor.

Jeff was preparing to leave when Foster grabbed his jacket sleeve, halting his movement. For a man so seriously ill, he was amazingly strong.

"He did this to me," he said, giving Jeff a glassy-eyed stare.

Jeff looked at Foster and frowned. "Who?"

"The man that mugged me," Foster said impatiently.

A chill went up Jeff's spine.

"He thought I was unconscious, but I wasn't. I was awake, and I saw what he did."

"What did you see?"

Eyes wide, Foster stared at Jeff. "He stuck me with a hypodermic needle."

"Why would anyone do something like this?" Jeff asked. He paced back and forth, agitated.

Raven looked up at him. "You're really taking Foster's claim seriously, aren't you?"

He paused in his pacing. "Normally, I'd dismiss it as simply the ranting of a sick, delusional man, but I checked with the police and they confirmed Foster's story. He was mugged Monday night, and we did find a tiny puncture wound on his right leg. Eleanor Parker was also mugged just days before the onset of her illness, and the coroner found what appears to be a puncture wound on her right leg.''

Raven shrugged. "It could be just a coincidence."

"Yeah," he said. "It could."

She could tell from his tone of voice that he didn't believe that and tried again. "Jeff, it has to be a coincidence." When he didn't say anything, she looked at him with growing horror. "Do you realize what you're suggesting? That someone is deliberately causing this thing."

"Look, I know how crazy that sounds. But this disease doesn't feel right. And I'm having trouble scientifically explaining everything that's been going on." He looked up at her. "Actually, the idea of somebody deliberately spreading this virus is about the only way this does make any sense."

He looked so sad that she wanted to take him in her arms, but she checked the impulse.

"Let's look at this rationally," she said. "Eleanor Parker and David Foster were mugged. But neither Julie Hartman, nor any of the other patients were victims of a mugging, and yet they have the same illness."

"I know," he said, his voice weary.

"And what about the other patients? Did you find any puncture wounds on them?"

He shook his head. "No, I didn't. But that just means we'd better be damn sure of our facts before we say anything about someone deliberately spreading this virus." He placed his hand on a folder on his desk. "We've got a lot of work ahead of us."

Then he pulled out a sheet of paper and handed it to her. "I'd like for you to help me call the families and ask if anyone was mugged within a week of the onset of the disease."

It took almost an hour to track down all the family members and get the information. "Find anything?" she asked.

He shook his head. "What about you?"

"Zilch." She leaned back in her chair. "According to family members, none of them were mugged. So doesn't that prove the fallacy of your theory?"

"No," he said slowly. "I was thinking about that while I waited for you to finish your calls. I think what it means is that he used the hypodermic for just Foster and Parker."

She gave him a skeptical look.

"Hey, I'm not saying it makes sense. I'm simply saying that's what I think happened."

"Let's assume for the sake of argument that Foster and Parker did contract this thing..." she grimaced "...from an injection. If that's the case, then how did the others get it?"

"He used a different method." Jeff leaned forward slightly. "It would be easy enough to slip something in a person's drink. People don't watch their drinks, even when they're out in public. Just look at the recent rash of sexual assaults occurring around the country with the drug rohypnol."

"Are you suggesting food tampering?"

Jeff nodded. "We always thought exposure to the disease came through ingestion of a food product or drink, we just didn't know it was being done deliberately. Somewhere out there, someone is deliberately exposing people to a deadly virus."

"But why use two different methods to transmit the disease?"

Jeff shrugged. "Maybe the others were more susceptible to food tampering." He shrugged again. "I don't know."

Raven shuddered. "You make it sound so cold-blooded, but a person who would do something like this would have to be crazy."

Jeff shook his head. "I doubt it. There's too much premeditation and expertise involved. And this bug is dangerous to handle. Our killer may not be perfectly sane by society's standards but he knows what he's doing."

She shook her head still trying to take it all in. "But how could someone get their hands on something this deadly?"

"It's actually easier than you think. A strongly motivated person wouldn't have that great a problem."

"You've got to be kidding!"

"Nope. Some of the most deadly viruses on the planet are only a phone call away."

"My God! I thought outside of the CDC and maybe a few academic centers, obtaining an infectious disease would be virtually impossible."

Jeff shook his head. "There are several labs that maintain infectious microbes. They're made available to doctors and scientists for research and diagnostic purposes. Of course, you have to have proper clearance to obtain them."

"Obviously there are loopholes in the security system," she said dryly.

"It would appear so."

"What do we do now?"

"First we notify Hillman and the CDC of this new development. Then we call the police."

"You think they'll believe us?"

Jeff's eyes locked on Raven's. "They have to."

"THAT'S SOME STORY, Dr. Knight," Detective Valentine said when Jeff had laid out the events of the past few weeks and their belief that the mysterious illness was being deliberately spread.

Jeff nodded. "I know. I wouldn't believe it myself but for the fact that it all fits. The CDC, Public Health and hospital staff have all been working under the assumption that this disease was the result of an accident in nature." He threw Raven a look. "But from the very beginning it hasn't followed any kind of logical pattern."

Detective Valentine frowned. "What do you mean?"

"Normally, once the index case is identified, it's pretty easy to track the course of the disease. But that's never been the case here, and now we know why. In this case, we have two people who had the disease injected directly into their bloodstream. The others, no doubt, were infected by food tampering. He probably slipped something into their drinks. Since no one noticed, it's probably odorless, colorless and tasteless."

Detective Valentine raised his eyebrows. "Doc, are we talking poison?"

Jeff threw Raven a tiny smile. She could see he was visibly relieved that the young detective was taking their claim seriously. But she wasn't entirely surprised. Detective Valentine struck her as a man who liked the spotlight, liked being on the Big Case. No doubt he was out to make a name for himself. A case like this just might do it for him.

"So you believe us?" Jeff asked.

Detective Valentine nodded. "Actually, it's not that far-fetched. A couple of years ago, there was some nut running around the New York subways poking people with a hypodermic needle. But as far as I know, the substance inside turned out to be harmless."

"Unfortunately, that's not the case here," Jeff said. "It's definitely not a poison, but whatever it is, it's most certainly deadly." He hesitated before adding, "It looks like it might be a virus."

Detective Valentine whistled. "God, if the media get wind of that bit of information, it's going to be a circus." He shook his head. "How many deaths so far?"

"Five," Jeff replied. "And I'd like to keep it that way."

"That makes two of us. You got anything for us to go on? I mean, in the time you and Ms. Delaney have been working on this case, have you come across anything that might help in the investigation?"

Jeff threw her a smile that almost took her breath away. "Raven found something that might help."

Raven leaned forward. "I think the drink tampering and the injections always occur on a Monday," she said. "We arrived at that conclusion from information collected from David Foster and the other patients. Foster said he was mugged on a Monday and began feeling ill on Tuesday. He brought himself to the emergency room on a Wednesday night. It was pretty much the same with Eleanor Parker. Every patient has been admitted on either a Wednesday evening or Thursday morning."

"Hmm," Detective Valentine said thoughtfully. "That is interesting." He looked at Raven. "Sounds like he has Mondays off. That may be useful information when we have a suspect." He redirected his attention to Jeff. "So what are we talking here, a terrorist or what?"

Jeff shook his head. "I doubt it's a terrorist. No threats have been made and no group has come forward to take credit for these murders. Besides, the people that have been targeted are just plain everyday folks."

"Yeah, but folks who had the misfortune of being singled out by our killer." He pursed his lips. "It's curious though that he changed his method for Parker and Foster. Serial killers normally don't do that."

Jeff shrugged. "My guess would be that Foster and Parker weren't particularly susceptible to food tampering."

Detective Valentine considered his words for a moment. "That sounds reasonable, but what I want to know is how he got his hands on a live virus. Isn't something like that difficult to get?"

Raven shook her head. "Jeff tells me it's relatively simple." She explained to the young detective the relative ease by which a deadly microbe could be obtained.

Detective Valentine shuddered. "It's that easy?"

Jeff nodded. "I'm afraid so."

"God, that's scary."

Raven nodded. "But the average person wouldn't know that. The killer obviously has a fairly good medical background."

The young detective nodded. "I'd say that's a sure bet."

"So?" Jeff asked. "What's your take on the murders?"

"I think this is going to be a hard one to investigate." Detective Valentine ticked off the reasons. "We have no crime scene, no physical evidence, no fingerprints, no murder weapon and no witnesses. The killer has also done a damn good job of covering his tracks." He shook his head. "This guy's smart. He's not going to be easy to catch. And, frankly, this killer virus angle is a little outside the scope of my expertise. I'm going to need help from you and Ms. Delaney in investigating the murders."

"You got it," Jeff said. "Just tell us what you need."

"Well, for starters I need the names and addresses of all the patients and their family members so we can take statements." He grimaced. "Though from what you've said, none of these people can even say when or where the drug was slipped into their drinks."

Jeff shook his head.

"I'll also review David Foster's police report, check out his storage room, interview him. Hopefully, the killer left something behind that will help us."

"You might also want to check out a Reverend Walters," Raven interjected, then laid out in a brief but concise manner the case against him.

"What's the likelihood of your catching this guy?" Jeff asked.

Detective Valentine shook his head. "To be honest, I'm not all that optimistic. We're dealing with a very accomplished murderer."

Raven nodded. "That's what Jeff and I think."

"Unfortunately, serial killers are the hardest kind to track. They're seasoned professionals and know how to evade detection. Compounding the situation is the fact that there's no crime scene that we can use as a starting point. And, worst of all, like most serial murderers, he probably doesn't even know the people he's killing."

Raven shook her head. "I think he does know them.

This man is going to an awful lot of trouble, too much trouble as far as I'm concerned, to be killing a bunch of strangers.''

Valentine gestured to the file cabinets behind him. ''As those case files will attest, it happens all the time. You'd be surprised at the amount of planning a lot of killers go through, especially serial killers. They're predators, and they're good at what they do because they plan. I'm afraid that what we have here is a very clever psychopath, but I doubt if he knows his victims.''

DETECTIVE VALENTINE'S words stayed with Raven. She had no doubt that the killer was a psychopath, but she wasn't sure she bought the part about him not knowing his victims, and she said as much to Jeff. ''It's hard for me to accept the theory that these are just a series of random murders.''

Jeff nodded. ''I know, but Valentine seems to know his business. If he thinks these are random attacks committed by a serial killer, who are we to question it?''

Raven settled back against the cushions. ''We have five fatalities and no viable conventional means of combating this virus. We have to question it. If we don't figure out who's spreading the virus, we're going to have more victims and more deaths.''

Jeff rubbed the back of his neck. ''Yeah, you're right. We don't have time to waste on some wild-goose chase.''

She nodded. ''If Detective Valentine isn't going to pursue that line of inquiry, we're just going to have to do it ourselves.''

Jeff frowned. ''But we've already spent days looking for connections between the patients. Other than Lauren Connor and Eleanor Parker, there is no connection.''

She shook her head. ''But there's got to be some connection between the killer and his victims,'' she said adamantly. ''We just have to figure out what that connection is.''

Jeff looked at Raven and smiled. She could be so stubborn and single-minded about what she believed. "Maybe we should turn this around," he said. "They may not know him, but he sure as hell knows them. Not necessarily as friends," he added hurriedly. "The contact may have been casual, but it made an impact on him."

She turned the idea over in her mind. "That could be it. Maybe he has a personal vendetta against all of them. Or maybe it's only one of them," she said excitedly. The more she thought about it, the more the idea appealed to her. "This reminds me of the aspirin murders that we had here about a decade ago. That case involved a husband who wanted to do away with his wife. He was afraid of killing her outright, so he laced a number of aspirins with a deadly poison, then placed the bottles in stores throughout the city to draw suspicion from himself when his wife died."

"It's an interesting theory," Jeff said. "However, in that case the killer just placed the bottles back on the shelf and waited for random selection to take its course. Here, he's an active participant in every murder. It's almost as if he has to be a part of the kill. So how do we find him?"

Raven cocked her head to the side. "He obviously kills for a reason. We just have to figure out what that reason is. Wouldn't knowing why he kills tell us who he might be?"

Jeff shrugged. "It might—but who can really say why anyone does anything?"

"Don't go getting philosophical on me," she said, but her words were tempered by a warm smile. He returned the smile.

"I think his reason for killing is less important than how he kills. How did he get his hands on this deadly virus? How does he slip the virus into his victim's drink without detection and without leaving any clues as to his identity behind?"

"My point exactly. He has to know his victims. It would

explain how he's able to tamper with their food or drinks without detection, wouldn't it?''

Jeff's brow arched. ''But doesn't that contradict the theory that he's going after a single individual?''

She shook her head. ''Not necessarily. He's after a particular person but he's trying to divert attention from that fact by going after others. But there's deliberation even in the selection of the other people.''

''Sounds to me as if the killer is unpredictable which means he's going to be hard to track.'' Jeff leaned back against the sofa and steepled his hands beneath his chin. ''He may not have even infected the ultimate target at this point.''

Raven gave him a thoughtful look. ''That's true,'' she said, ''but the mugging of Eleanor and David Foster is awfully curious. Infection by injection adds a different dimension to this case. I wonder why they weren't as accessible as the others?''

Jeff gave her a quizzical look. ''Maybe it wasn't that they were less accessible. Maybe he wanted to make sure they died.''

HE TOOK A SWALLOW of beer, then stood back and studied the photographs on the bulletin board in his study. Killing is not a bad thing, he thought, especially if the person deserved to die. Well, not all of them, he amended. Some had been sacrificed to achieve the goals of The Plan. For the common good, he liked to think.

He took another swig of beer. Killing them had not been a snap decision on his part. He had thought about it long and hard, but in the end it was the only answer.

He walked over to his desk and reviewed The Plan. Things were progressing nicely, he thought. He'd gotten away with murder five times now. For a moment a furrow marred the smooth skin of his forehead. The murders had been detected. He'd underestimated the medical establishment here. He hadn't thought they'd discern a connection between the deaths this quickly but apparently they had. No doubt because of Lauren Connor.

He should have never selected her. He had known of her connection to Eleanor, but she'd been such an easy target that he hadn't been able to resist the temptation to do her. But he'd felt a twinge of remorse when he'd discovered she had small children, but by then it was too late, she'd already been added to The Plan, and The Plan had to be followed.

But he couldn't afford any more slipups like that. He was close to achieving his goal. He looked at the photograph he'd taken earlier that day, and smiled. It was a picture of his next victim.

Chapter Nine

Julie Hartman was dead.

Jeff knew he should have been prepared for it, but he wasn't. He'd hoped that with the CDC on board, they would identify the virus and suggest a viable treatment, but that hadn't happened. They had tried everything they could think of to halt the progression of the disease, but nothing had worked. Julie Hartman was now the killer's latest victim. He felt like screaming at someone, something.

But he didn't do either of those things. Instead, he swung his head around, surveying the group that had assembled in the hospital conference room: Shay, Dr. Hillman, Dr. Patterson and Henry Brockman. He knew that he had a precarious hold on his emotions, and it made it difficult to concentrate on what Dr. Hillman was saying.

"I'm sorry to say we weren't able to save Ms. Hartman. Whatever the killer infected her and the others with seems to have stumped even the CDC's top scientists. We're going to have to consider other possible forms of treatment...."

Listening halfheartedly, Jeff studied Dr. Joseph Hillman, who was giving them the CDC's assessment of the situation. Obviously Hillman had experienced scenes like this many times before and his stock phrase, "I'm sorry to say," had an overused, insincere ring. Jeff had the uncomfortable feeling that the man was enjoying himself, not in the same manner he'd enjoy a movie or a good meal, but in a more subtle, self-satisfied way—he was the center of attention in a crisis. This attitude grated on Jeff's already frayed nerves, especially since he seemed to speak about the patients as if they were case studies rather than actual people.

"—This serial killer angle adds an entirely new dimension to our investigation and treatment of the disease," Dr. Hillman was saying. "It's unfortunate that Dr. Ross is no longer with us. As you know he was one of the world's top scientists in the field of virology and would have been invaluable in trying to unlock the mysteries of this disease."

Jeff couldn't agree more. He'd met the aging scientist several years ago. If anyone could have isolated and identified this virus, it would have been Dr. Ross. That's why he'd asked Dr. Patterson to see if she could get copies of the doctor's latest writings. He'd didn't dare hope that Dr. Ross had ever come across this particular virus, but perhaps something similar, and had written about it. It was a long shot, but he was out of ideas. He sighed and turned his attention back to Dr. Hillman.

"It's unfortunate that the media has gotten wind of our problem. The inflammatory stories appearing daily certainly don't help matters. I suggest we forget about trying to identify the virus for now and focus on treatment. I hate to say it, but a cure may only come after the killer is apprehended and we can question him. In the meantime, I think we should switch gears and focus solely on treatment and halting the progression of the disease."

Jeff nodded. That sounded reasonable to him.

Hillman cleared his throat and looked directly at him. "I've been in contact with the Food and Drug Administration, and I'm pleased to report that they've given us permission to use a new drug—AST. We've observed very favorable results with aggressive viruses like this one in drug trials.''

Jeff frowned. He was familiar with the drug but he didn't view it in quite the same rosy light as Dr. Hillman apparently did. ''I realize that you think AST is the way we ought to go,'' he said, ''but I have reservations about using it. It's an extremely toxic drug, and as far as I know it's only been used in about a dozen Ebola cases in Africa. All the other trials have been conducted in the laboratory.''

Taking his glasses off, Dr. Hillman tried to think of how best to word his response. ''That's true, but it is not a constructive way to view the situation.''

''This isn't a situation,'' Jeff answered hotly. ''We're not dealing with laboratory rats. These are people.''

Jeff abruptly stood and walked to the window, watching the cars and the pedestrians on the street below as he continued to speak. ''And what do you suggest we tell the families about the survival rate for those patients who didn't respond to treatment? Or, for that matter, the likelihood of survival of their own loved ones?''

Dr. Hillman flushed then shifted uncomfortably. ''I'm not sure what good this line of inquiry does us.''

Jeff whirled around. ''What good it does? I'll tell you what good it does. The worst thing about a disease like this is the uncertainty. Humans are capable of adapting to anything as long as they know what they're up against. In this instance, what they can expect.''

Jeff crossed his arms over his chest and gave Dr. Hillman a hard look. ''Come on, Dr. Hillman, why don't you tell the others what the survival rate has been with this drug.''

Three pairs of eyes slid from Jeff to Hillman.

Hillman moved back in his chair, his chin resting on his hands. ''It's not good,'' he said finally.

''Be more specific,'' Jeff snapped.

''All right!'' Dr. Hillman burst out angrily. Jeff could

tell he didn't like being put in this position. "Days, a few weeks at the most."

Jeff didn't say anything. Having successfully backed Dr. Hillman into a corner, he was suddenly adrift. Slowly he sank back into his chair.

"This drug doesn't promise a cure, but it may buy us some time," Dr. Hillman said.

"But it's the quality of life the patients will have while on the drug that I'm concerned about," Jeff countered. "Shouldn't we take that into consideration?"

"Dr. Knight," Dr. Hillman said sharply, "as a physician I would expect your response to this medical crisis to be significantly different."

"Different from what?" Jeff cried. "These are *my* patients we're talking about. I have a duty to them and their loved ones. A duty not to cause them any additional harm or unnecessary suffering." He paused and looked at the others in the room. "Lauren Connor's condition is deteriorating rapidly. With the chance of halting the disease being so slight, is it worth subjecting her to the drug's potential side effects?" He began to tick off on his fingers a litany of possible complications—violent cramps, severe headaches, shortness of breath, kidney failure, high blood pressure.

There was a strained silence.

"Ah…I understand your concern, Jeff," Shay said, speaking for the first time. "But what other alternative is there?"

Jeff raked a hand over his hair in frustration. "I don't know."

Dr. Hillman nodded. "My point exactly. There is no other alternative."

Shay looked at Dr. Hillman. "You really think the drug will work?"

"There's no guarantee," Dr. Hillman hedged. "But, like I said, AST has shown promising results in drug trials."

Jeff shook his head, still trying to come to grips with what Hillman was proposing. "But those trials were with Ebola patients. Their cases were in no way similar to these."

"That's true," Dr. Hillman admitted grudgingly. "But there's a certain similarity between the Ebola virus and the one we're dealing with here." At Jeff's skeptical look, Hillman added quickly, "I know it's slight, but it's enough to make it worth the risk. I believe in aggressively treating all cases, whatever the chances are for survival. Every patient deserves a chance at life, whatever the risk."

"Even if the patient and family would rather end his or her suffering?" Jeff challenged. "Even when the chances of survival—let alone a cure—are less than fifteen percent?" He shook his head. "I just don't know if it's worth subjecting them to the additional pain."

Dr. Hillman stood up abruptly, pushing back his chair. "We obviously view the situation differently. I believe AST to be a truly remarkable weapon in the battle against this kind of deadly microbe."

Jeff groaned in frustration. "But what you're suggesting amounts to little more than experimental."

"Jeff, that's enough!" Brockman snapped. "The truth is, we're out of choices. We've got some nut out there infecting people with Lord knows what, cops swarming all over the place and the media breathing down our necks. We've got to do something."

Something, yes, Jeff thought bleakly. But was this the thing to do? His shoulders sagged under the weight of his impotence. Even though he wasn't entirely comfortable with using AST, he had nothing else to offer. *That's not true,* an inner voice whispered. *There's Raven's herbal treatment,* but as quickly as the thought crossed his mind he was discarding it. It was irresponsible to even consider using it. The AST had at least undergone some scientific testings, whereas Raven's was simply an unproven theory.

With a sigh, Jeff reluctantly nodded his head.

"Good, we're all agreed." Henry Brockman turned back to Dr. Hillman. "We'll use the AST."

Dr. Hillman walked back to his desk and pulled a sheet of paper from his briefcase. "All right," he said at length. "In addition to AST, our protocol for dealing with this virus also involves these drugs." He named several extremely toxic agents.

The drugs named stunned Jeff, but he forced himself to keep quiet, even though he felt uneasy about his decision. But as Dr. Hillman outlined the treatment schedule, Jeff's mind continued to torture him by running again through the drug's potential side effects...severe headaches, kidney failure, high blood pressure, shortness of breath...and from there it only got worse. Ultimately the drug would devastate the patient's immune system, making the patient susceptible to a host of infectious diseases. That was the downside. But, on the plus side, the drug just might work. Shouldn't he give it a try?

He sighed. "When do you want to start treatment?" he asked.

Hillman gave him a satisfied smile. "I suggest we start as soon as possible. In fact, I'd like to start today, immediately after the baseline studies are done. Of course, we are going to need consent from the family members to treat because of the nature of the drug."

Hillman's voice droned on, but Jeff was no longer listening. His thoughts were focused on one fact and one fact alone—the drug had to work.

God help them if it didn't.

"You're using AST? That's an experimental drug!" Raven plopped in the chair behind her desk in her office, stunned by Jeff's disclosure. "My God, the side effects can be horrendous."

"I know it's an extremely toxic agent, but we don't have any other choice. None of the patients have responded to any other form of treatment. We're dealing with an unknown virus. All bets for treatment are off.''

"But you don't have to go to that extreme," she argued. "You could use..." She named several powerful drugs used to treat stubborn viruses.

He shook his head. "We already considered those drugs and even tried two of them with Eleanor Parker and Julie Hartman, but they didn't work.''

"But still there are other less radical treatments that could be used.''

"Don't you think I would use them if there were?" His voice sounded tired and was laced with frustration. "I've been working my butt off trying to come up with something to combat this virus.''

"Have you really?" she challenged. "It seems to me you've only looked at conventional forms of medical treatments.''

At her words, he shifted in his seat next to her desk and looked down at his hands for a moment.

"I could understand and support your decision if you'd considered every possibility, but you haven't. There's a whole host of other forms of medical care out there.''

His eyes narrowed. "Don't start with me, Raven.''

"I'm damn well going to start," she snapped. "When are you going to get your head out of the sand? Even the National Institutes of Health has determined that alternative medicine has a role in standard health care. Just last year they recommended the inclusion of alternative healing to the curriculum for all medical schools. And they cited several reports on the effectiveness of herbs as healing tools.''

"Yeah, but the cases reported in those studies haven't gone through any scientific testing proving their effectiveness," he said defensively. "Until that happens, they're just a series of interesting anecdotes.''

"What about my paper on this disease?" she challenged. "Do you believe that's also just an interesting anecdote?"

He flushed and looked off to the side.

"You didn't read it, did you?" She jumped to her feet and glared down at him.

"Ah...I was going to but—"

Her eyes blazed with anger. "Why don't you just admit it, you didn't read it because you never once considered what I thought to be important?"

He looked at her with eyes pleading for understanding. "That's not true. I plan to read it. I just haven't had time. You know the hours I've been putting in at the hospital."

She planted her hands on her hips and glared at him. "I know you've been working hard, but if you'd been remotely interested in my thoughts on the subject of treatment, you'd have made time, the way you have for Dr. Ross's work and the other studies." She paced the room, agitated. "The treatment plan I laid out to you isn't something I just made up. There's plenty of data supporting the use of herbs in restoring the body's immune system. It's been used successfully with AIDS patients. While we're dealing with a different virus, I think it has an application in this situation, but you didn't even extend me the courtesy of reading the material."

He started to speak, but she cut him off with a jerk of her head. "You simply dismissed it out of hand. You haven't changed one iota. Same old Jeff."

"Raven, that's not true."

"I have to say, you had me fooled, but you're just as narrow-minded as you were four years ago. But this time your stubbornness is going to lead to the deaths of your patients."

Jeff bristled at her words. "Who do you think you are? These are my patients, and I determine the course of treatment. If I don't want to use some half-baked idea—"

Half-baked! That was too much. "How dare you—"

"I hope I'm not coming at a bad time."

Both their heads simultaneously swiveled in the direction of the sound. Nick Valentine stood in the doorway, looking at them curiously.

Raven threw Jeff an angry look before plastering a smile on her face. "No, of course not," she said, sitting back down. "Come on in."

Nick Valentine looked at them curiously as he moved into the office and took the seat she indicated. Even though the tension in the room was so thick you could cut it with a knife, the young detective acted as if everything was perfectly normal.

"I thought I'd drop by and bring you up-to-date on the investigation," he said, stretching his long legs out in front of him.

She felt the tension radiating from Jeff.

"We questioned Reverend Walters," he continued. "A lot of his story doesn't check out, but the guy doesn't seem to have the brains to have pulled off these murders. But more importantly, he has an alibi. He was with a client on the nights Parker and Foster were mugged, which suggests he couldn't have been involved in any of the murders. Nor did he have a motive for killing any of them, or for that matter, fit the FBI profile for a serial killer. I turned his case over to Vice. They'll shut him down, but I'm eliminating him as a suspect in these murders."

Well, that shoots that idea, she thought.

"We also ran the killer's MO through the FBI data files on serial killers for the last five years." He shook his head. "That was also a wash. Whoever our boy is, he hasn't committed any murders like this in any other jurisdiction."

"Or, " Jeff interjected, "left any evidence to that effect behind."

Detective Valentine looked at Jeff and nodded.

"What about your interviews with the patients and their family members?" Raven asked. Out of the corner of her eye, she saw Jeff staring at her, but she refused to look in his direction.

"With the exception of David Foster, none of the patients could think of anyone with an ax to grind or a vendetta against them. And in Foster's case, the threat was made almost two decades ago by a man who later committed suicide. A John Kramer threatened him, but the guy has been dead for almost twenty years.'' Detective Valentine paused and looked at Raven with something close to admiration. "But that line of inquiry did yield two possible suspects. Looks like you might have been on the right track after all about these not being random killings.''

Raven was so excited by his news, she forgot that she was angry with Jeff. She threw him a beaming smile. "That's great news,'' she said. "Please go on.''

"We think the killer is after a specific person and is trying to divert attention from that fact by killing others.''

Raven and Jeff exchanged looks.

"Like I said, we have two suspects. One is the husband of one of the victims, Calvin Parker,'' Nick leaned forward slightly. "It seems he wanted out of the marriage but his wife had made it plain that it would cost him dearly financially. Friends say she made it clear that it would only be, and I quote, 'Over her dead body.'''

"Interesting choice of words,'' Jeff mused.

The young detective nodded. "Tell me about it. Parker is a pharmaceutical sales rep. He had motive and possibly the means for killing his wife, as well as the others.''

"What about the other suspect?'' Raven asked.

"It's a guy by the name of Mark Daniels. He was involved with Julie Hartman. He's a con man with a long history of fraud and assaults. He's never served any prison time, probably because he intimidates his female victims. So they're afraid to press charges.''

"Sounds like a great, guy,'' Jeff said dryly.

"Yeah,'' Detective Valentine agreed. "He's the kind of guy you'd love to have twenty minutes alone with. Anyway, his latest ruse is that of posing as an investment broker, complete with a posh office in the Sears Tower. He bilked Hartman out of more than twenty-five thousand dollars. Seems she was threatening to press charges. But what's most interesting about Daniels is that early in his criminal career, his modus operandi was to slip rohypnol in his victim's drink.''

Jeff looked at him, surprised. "The date-rape drug?"

Detective Valentine nodded. "It's gotten a lot of publicity recently in that area, but Daniels used it to knock his victims out so he could rob them.''

If he could get his hands on rohypnol, what other drugs did he have access to? Raven wondered. Out of the corner of her eye, she looked at Jeff and knew he was wondering the same thing. "Have you questioned him?" she asked.

Detective Valentine shook his head. "I haven't questioned either man. I was going to do that as soon as I leave here.'' He looked at Jeff as he stood. "Would you like for me to drop you at the hospital? It's along the way.''

Jeff shook his head. "That's okay, I'm going to hang around here for a while.''

As far as she was concerned there was nothing to talk about. But from the determined look on Jeff's face, he wasn't going anywhere.

"Why don't I go along with you," she said hurriedly. "It might be good having another pair of eyes and ears along. Phyllis can handle things here.''

"I'll come, too," Jeff said, standing. "You never know when you'll need someone with a medical background along.''

She whirled around. "But don't you need to get back to the hospital?" she asked.

Jeff shook his head. "I don't have any classes or appointments this afternoon, I checked on my patients before I came over here, and I left them in Shay's capable hands.'' Jeff patted the inside breast pocket of his sport jacket where she knew he carried a cellular phone. "If he needs me, he'll call.''

For a moment Detective Valentine looked as if he was

going to refuse, then he surprised her by saying, "Since it was your lead that gave us these two, I guess I owe you this one."

THEIR FIRST STOP was at Calvin Parker's. He lived in a modest house in Oak Park, a middle-class suburb about thirty miles outside of Chicago. As Detective Valentine rapped the brass knocker on an elaborately carved door, Jeff looked over at Raven. She was doing her best to ignore him. He couldn't exactly blame her. He'd handled things badly back at her shop. He shouldn't have been so defensive about using AST, but her words had echoed his own fears and he had taken his anger and frustration out on her. He should have also known she'd ask him about her report and he should have leveled with her right off the bat. He just hoped she'd give him a chance to explain. But he'd really flubbed things up, it wasn't going to be easy.

His troubled thoughts were interrupted as the door swung open. Calvin Parker answered the door wearing a white shirt unbuttoned to his waist, holding a can of beer, and humming to the soulful strains of Luther Vandross singing in the background. He certainly didn't look like a man whose wife had died just days ago.

The smile that hovered on Calvin Parker's lips disappeared immediately, and was replaced by a cool stare. "Can I help you?"

Detective Valentine flashed his badge. "I'm sorry to bother you, but we'd like to talk to you." He tipped his head in Raven and Jeff's direction. "I believe you already know Dr. Knight and this is Raven Delaney."

Parker gave them a cursory glance, then turned back to the young cop. "I told the police officers that were here yesterday all I know."

Detective Valentine nodded. "I just have a few more questions. It won't take long."

"Oh…" Calvin Parker was unable to frame an objection. He nodded and moved aside to let them in. A moment later they were ushered into a sunlit sitting room off the entryway. He motioned Jeff and Raven to the sofa and took the love seat opposite. Nick elected to stand.

"We're sorry about your wife, Mr. Parker," Nick began. "I know the last few days have been difficult for you, but we must ask you some more questions. As you know five other people have died in the same way as your late wife."

Parker nodded. "Yes, I know."

"I know the police officers covered this same ground before but do you know anyone who would want to kill your wife?"

He shook his head. "Like I told them, my wife was a good, upstanding, churchgoing woman. She didn't have an enemy in the world."

Jeff leaned forward slightly. "It could have been a while back. Maybe before you were even married."

He gave Jeff a cool look. "Then I wouldn't know."

"What about yourself?" Nick asked, taking a seat directly in front of the older man.

Parker reacted with a surprised expression. "Me?"

"It's my understanding that you and Mrs. Parker weren't getting along, that you were having marital problems. In fact, you moved out and asked your wife for a divorce, but she refused to give it to you."

Parker rolled his eyes. "No doubt that old busybody Grace Wells has been giving you an earful, and as usual, she got it all wrong. Like all marriages, we had our ups and downs." He shrugged. "But we weren't discussing divorce."

"So you hadn't moved out?"

Parker shifted uncomfortably. "I left for a while. I needed my space. Eleanor understood."

"And you came back," Jeff said, "no doubt because you weren't willing to give up all of this." His hand made an arc in a gesture meant to encompass the house and all its furnishings.

A smile played about Parker's lips. "You think I killed Eleanor because I didn't want to give up my lifestyle?" He shook his head.

"It's been done before," Nick said dryly.

"I'm sure it has," Parker said smoothly, "but this time you're barking up the wrong tree. I didn't kill my wife or anyone else, for that matter." He shrugged. "I had no reason to kill Eleanor. Everything is in my name—the house, the car, everything. And she wouldn't have fought me in a divorce action to retain anything. She loved me."

That wasn't love, Jeff thought. It was a one-sided relationship where one party did all the giving and the other the taking. *Isn't that what you're doing with Raven?* an inner voice whispered. He turned the idea over in his mind. He never thought so, but maybe he had. She had always been there for him, encouraging him, supporting his interests, and what had he done for her? Rejected her profession, her ideas on alternative medicine without any kind of hearing. He'd spent hours reading medical journals, Dr. Ross's studies, and he'd never once picked up Raven's report. He was deeply ashamed.

Jeff looked over at Raven and found that she was watching him. She quickly looked off to the side focusing on what Parker was saying.

"It seems to me," Parker continued, "you ought to be questioning that Reverend Walters."

"We did," Nick said. "He has an airtight alibi."

Parker snorted. "So when all else fails, blame the husband."

Jeff shrugged. "Well, you have to admit you bear checking out. You work for a pharmaceutical company, where you no doubt have access to a lot of experimental drugs and infectious agents."

Parker shook his head vigorously. "Dalton Laboratories

doesn't manufacture any drugs that could produce the kind of symptoms my wife had."

Jeff's eyes narrowed. "And just how would you know something like that unless you had some knowledge of drugs yourself?"

"Give me a break," Parker said defensively. "I'm a good salesman. I read the company literature."

"We'll check it out," Nick said, picking up the questioning. "Can you account for your whereabouts for each Monday beginning with Monday, May 8, to date?"

The only outward sign that Parker was not comfortable with the question was a slight tremor in his voice. "Ah...I'm sure I had business meetings with clients on those dates."

Nick shook his head. "No, you didn't. Your boss at Dalton checked your itinerary and travel vouchers and you didn't work those days."

A flicker of apprehension flashed across Parker's face then it was gone. "Oh, you said Mondays. I guess I was at home with Eleanor."

Nick gave him a hard look. "You want to try again?"

Parker stood. "This interview is over. If you have any further questions, I suggest you contact my lawyer."

RAVEN WASN'T SURE what to make of Calvin Parker's claim. She kept running the conversation through her mind as they entered Mark Daniels's plush office on the sixty-third floor of the Sears Tower. Parker might not have been much of a husband, but she didn't see him as a killer. From her brief encounter with Eleanor Parker, she couldn't help but believe Calvin Parker's assessment of his wife was correct. She'd struck Raven as being the kind of woman who'd do anything for her man, even if that meant giving him every dime she had. And she doubted if a divorce would have changed that.

"Why so glum?" Jeff asked as they waited for the

young blond receptionist to announce their arrival. "I thought the interview with Parker went well."

She gave him a wan smile. "I'm not sure what to make of—"

They looked up as the door to the inner office opened, and a man walked out. Nick and Jeff stood.

Raven's first impression of Mark Daniels was of raw sex appeal. He exuded it—ripe, physical. He looked to be in his mid-thirties and was extremely good-looking. He was blond, blue-eyed, deeply tanned, and though he wasn't tall, he had a blatant virility that no doubt drew women to him like bees to honey.

He flashed a warm smile. "Why don't we step into my office."

Jeff, Raven and Detective Valentine followed him into a sparsely but tastefully decorated office.

He gestured toward the sofa and two small leather chairs before taking a seat behind his desk. "You wanted to talk to me about Julie Hartman."

"That's correct," Nick said. "I'm investigating her murder."

"Yes, I read about it in yesterday's paper." Daniels shrugged offhandedly. "I don't see how I can help you, though. I invested some money for her, but I barely knew her."

"You do know that someone slipped a deadly infectious agent into her food or drink," Nick said almost conversationally. "That's what killed her. Any idea who might have done something like that?"

"I just told you I barely knew her."

Nick gave him a hard look. "Mr. Daniels, let's not beat around the bush. We both know the two of you had more than a professional relationship. Isn't it true, you were an item up until about a month ago?"

"No, it isn't," he said easily.

"That's not what her neighbors say. It seems you were a frequent visitor at her apartment."

Daniels casually shrugged one shoulder. "I might have gone over there a time or two, but I can assure you it was strictly business."

Nick rolled his eyes. "Cut the crap. You wined and dined her until you got her to max out her credit cards and part with her life savings—twenty-five thousand dollars— then you dumped her."

"Hey, you got no business talking to me like that. I run a legitimate financial consulting business."

"Sure you do. And do you date all your clients?"

"It wasn't like that," Daniels insisted.

Nick's gaze never left Daniels's face. "Then why don't you tell us how it was?"

"We dated a few times, but like I said it was primarily a business relationship, at least on my part. But I guess she misread the situation. When things didn't work out professionally, as well as personally, she started making noises about wanting her money back or she'd make trouble for me. Things came to a head when I started seeing someone else. She went off the deep end. She called my apartment at all hours of the night. She followed me often. Threatened my friend." He shook his head and gave them a sad little smile. "It was very unpleasant."

Nick leaned back and regarded Mark Daniels steadily. "I see. You were just her fatal attraction." He shook his head. "That's quite a story. The only problem is, it doesn't square with the facts."

Daniels's throat worked as if he were having difficulty swallowing. "I don't know what you're talking about."

"Then let me spell it out for you," Nick said curtly. "Julie Hartman told friends that you conned her out of the money."

"Hey, they were legitimate investments."

Raven watched Daniels pull a pencil through his fingers again and again.

Nick shook his head. "There were no investments."

Mark Daniels's hand trembled slightly. Otherwise, his

outward demeanor didn't betray his thoughts. He'd make a hell of a poker player, Raven thought.

"Julie thought if she went to the police alone she might not be taken seriously, so she starting looking for other women that you had conned," Nick continued. "She found two. She was trying to get them to press charges against you when she was murdered. If she'd been successful, you'd have done some serious jail time."

The pencil broke with a quiet snap.

Nick gave him a hard look. "A handsome guy like you would definitely not like prison."

Raven watched Daniels's throat ripple as he swallowed. "You can't prove a thing."

"Oh, I think I can," Nick said easily.

Raven frowned. It seemed to her that Nick was enjoying this cat-and-mouse game.

"Julie wrote to her sister about you." Nick kept his eyes on Daniels now, waiting, measuring. "Her sister said Julie told her that she planned to press criminal charges, but she was afraid. You threatened her, assaulted her."

Daniels shook his head. "I never did any such thing."

"But your threats didn't work," Nick continued as if he'd not spoken. "She was still going to press charges. So you had to shut her up." He paused and gave Daniels a sideways glance. "It would have been easy enough for someone with your expertise to have slipped something in her drink. You're quite familiar with spiking drinks, aren't you?"

Daniels's eyes narrowed to tiny slits. "Don't try to pin this—"

Nick cut him off. "These murders have your fingerprints all over them. And you certainly had reason to want to kill Julie Hartman."

"That's a lie!"

Nick shook his head. "Look, Daniels, there's no point—"

He shot Nick an enraged look. "I didn't kill anyone!"

he shouted. He drew a deep breath, then said in a calmer voice, "Okay, I admit threatening Julie, but I swear I never laid a hand on her. And I certainly didn't kill her." He licked his lips and gave Nick a calculating look. "But I may have seen the guy that did."

Raven rolled her eyes. Now he claimed to have seen the killer. That was awfully convenient, she thought.

"I'm not saying anything else until I get some assurance from you. I want to know what kind of deal you can give me."

Nick gave him a hard look. "Listen, Daniels, six people have been murdered. All things considered, a fraud and forgery charge would be the least of your problems."

"Do we have a deal?" Daniels asked again.

Raven looked at Nick. She couldn't believe it, but he looked as if he was actually considering Daniels's proposal."

Nick sighed. "I can't make any promises, but if the information is useful, I'll talk to the state's attorney about reducing the charges."

For a moment Daniels didn't say anything, then he nodded as if he'd reached a decision. "I admit bilking the twenty-five thousand from Julie, but I didn't kill her," he said firmly. "I went to see her a couple of days before she went into the hospital. She wasn't home, so I sat outside her apartment in my car waiting for her. After a while I noticed this guy hanging around her apartment. It wasn't the first time I'd seen him."

"What was he doing?" Nick asked.

He seemed tense, as if he believed Daniels's story. Raven was surprised he was taking the claim seriously.

Daniels frowned. "Nothing at first, then as Julie approached he started taking pictures. I thought it was of both of us but now I realize it was probably just pictures of Julie. At the time I thought it was some kind of setup, so I walked over to confront the guy, but he took off running."

"Can you describe him?" Nick asked.

He shrugged. "He was some distance away but he looked to be about your height and weight. He moved pretty fast so I would guess he was in his late thirties or early forties."

"Was he black or white?"

"I couldn't tell. He was too far away. Oh, he was wearing a big floppy hat and sunglasses."

"Anything else?"

Daniels shook his head. "That's about it."

On impulse, Raven asked, "Do you remember what day of the week it was that you saw the man?"

Daniels shrugged. "I think it was a Monday."

"Why didn't you come forward and give this information to the police?" Raven asked.

Daniels issued a bitter laugh. "I've got a criminal record and I was seeing one of the murder victims. Who's going to believe me?"

"Don't you think the police are smart enough to separate fact from fiction?" Nick asked.

Mark Daniels shook his head. "It's not a question of being smart, but rather being pressed to make an arrest. As you pointed out, six people have been murdered. The press and the politicians are already clamoring for an arrest. That's why I didn't come forward. Put yourself in my place. Why should I place my neck in a noose for a woman who, if she'd lived, was trying to put me behind bars?"

Raven's eyes narrowed. He really was a piece of work.

"Besides," Daniels continued, "I really didn't think it was important until I read about the murders in yesterday's paper."

Nick gave him a sour look. "We'll check it out, but in the meantime, don't leave town."

Daniels rolled his eyes, but didn't say anything.

"One last question, can you account for your whereabouts every Monday night starting from May 8, to date?"

Mark Daniels threw Nick a cool look. "I was with Katherine Olsen. Not that it's any of your business, but we live together.''

Raven and Jeff exchanged looks. She knew he was thinking the same thing she was. Katherine Olsen was a prominent Chicago socialite. Although she was old enough to be Daniels's mother, she was rolling in money. He'd hit the jackpot this time.

''If you'd like to speak to her,'' he said with a grin, ''I'm sure she'll confirm my story.''

Raven didn't doubt it for one moment. It would take at least forty minutes for them to reach her Highland Park estate, which was certainly enough time for the two of them to have rehearsed their story.

''Thank you,'' Nick said, standing. Jeff and Raven followed suit. ''I think we'll do that.''

Daniels nodded. ''I'll call her and let her know you're on your way over. Now if you don't mind...''

''WELL, WHAT DO YOU THINK?'' Nick asked. They were seated in Raven's living room. She and Jeff had begged off going along with him to interview Katherine Olsen, and Nick had given them a ride back to her apartment.

''They're both strong suspects, but only one of them can be the killer,'' Raven said. ''The question is, which one?''

Jeff shook his head. ''Parker may have wanted his wife dead, and Daniels his girlfriend, but neither man strikes me as being cold-blooded enough to have killed anyone.''

Nick chuckled. ''You just haven't been around enough baby-faced killers.''

Raven leaned forward. ''I agree with Jeff about Calvin Parker, but Mark Daniels is another story. If anyone could do it, my guess is it would be him.''

Nick shook his head. ''Katherine Olsen is a pretty strong alibi witness. She takes him out of the equation to some degree. She was a big fish, and he could have used her money to buy Julie Hartman. And then there's the man Daniels saw outside Hartman's apartment.''

"*Claims* to have seen," Raven countered. "I wouldn't believe anything he says. The man's slime."

Nick shrugged. "Informants usually are, but generally the people that can help the police the most are not choirboys. I don't know if Daniels saw anyone or not, but I have to check it out. Frankly, at this stage, Parker seems to be the strongest suspect. He seems to have had motive, means and the opportunity. We'll check out both men, but my gut tells me that Parker's our man. Now I just have to prove it."

"I hope it's soon," Jeff said. "My patients can't hold on much longer."

That sobered Raven. She'd gotten so caught up in the investigation, she'd momentarily forgotten about the patients and her earlier argument with Jeff. But now it all came rushing back.

"I'll do what I can." Nick stood. "I'd better head over to Olsen."

As soon as she closed the door behind him, the atmosphere between Raven and Jeff changed. Now that they were alone, neither seemed to know what to say. Their earlier argument still hung in the air.

"I guess you're going to have to head back to the hospital," Raven said finally.

"Not just yet," he said quietly. "Shay is covering for me. He'll call if he needs me."

"I see," she said, searching for something to say. "I think it was nice of Nick to let us sit in on the interviews, don't you?"

Jeff smiled. "Frankly I was a little surprised that he let us strong-arm him like that."

"I'm not sure if we gave him much choice."

"Maybe not, but that's not what I want to talk about." He cleared his throat. I think we should talk about what happened earlier."

"Jeff, I don't see any point in continuing with that discussion. You—"

"Raven, I don't want this between us," he said. He walked across the room until he stood directly in front of her. "I want to clear the air."

"I think you made your position perfectly clear," she said, brushing past him.

"Listen to me," he said, holding her tightly to keep her from squirming away. "Just listen, damn it! I behaved like a jerk, and I'm sorry. I can only say that I wasn't thinking straight. I was frustrated and upset and I took it out on you."

When she still didn't say anything, he continued. "I don't think your ideas are half-baked. I think you have a very analytical mind. You've proven that numerous times in this investigation." He paused, then drew a deep breath. "I also want to apologize for not reading your report. You were right. I didn't treat your work the way I have the others and I'm truly sorry. I promise you, it won't happen again."

Raven's breath caught in her throat. He sounded so sincere. She wanted to believe him.

He looked into her eyes and smiled. "I'll read it today, and I promise I'll give it a fair evaluation."

She didn't want to read too much into his words, but she couldn't help but believe it was a positive sign. Maybe there was a chance for them after all.

"That's all I ask," she said. "That you look at the material, and assess it the way you would any other medical study. That's all I ever wanted."

"I know." Jeff touched her bare arm. "Will you forgive me?"

She nodded, smiling.

He issued a sigh of relief and returned the smile. "I care a great deal about you and I don't want to lose you...again," he said, his voice heavy with emotion. As he spoke he slid his fingers along her smooth skin from her shoulder to her head. His touch sent arrows of sensations shooting through her body. Raven shivered as he gently entangled his fingers in her hair.

"I know we have things to work out, but for now this is all that matters," Jeff murmured, pulling her head back so that she was looking directly up at him. The heat in his eyes was unmistakable, but Raven couldn't move. She had no desire to run away this time. He moistened his lips, and she closed her eyes as he lowered his mouth to hers in a tender kiss.

She heard his sudden intake of breath as she opened her mouth to him and willingly deepened the kiss. His taste was hot and sweet. As if her body had a mind of its own, her arms slid around his neck, drawing him closer. His tongue filled her mouth, and she angled her head, wanting more. Maybe she was reading too much into what he'd said. Maybe she was only kidding herself, maybe they didn't have the makings for a permanent relationship, but damn it, when he kissed her, touched her, she wanted to believe that there was a future for them, that a relationship founded on mutual respect of their different medical views was possible. She needed to believe that. She wanted to believe that. She wanted him.

"I want you, Ray," Jeff said breathlessly as he trailed hot kisses down her throat.

He swept her up in his arms and carried her through the apartment to her bedroom. He laid her on the bed then came down on top of her. She welcomed the weight of his muscular body on top of hers. She pulled him closer, drawing him between her legs and pressing upward to meet the hard evidence of his arousal.

He groaned—it was a low, guttural sound, born half of ecstasy, half of desire. Raven gasped as his hand covered her breast, as he caught her hardened nipple between his thumb and forefinger. She clung to him, hot with desire and dizzy from a barrage of emotions so intense she could barely breathe.

He pushed her sweater up and unfastened the front clasp of her bra. He stroked one rosy peak with his finger, sending a throbbing need through her. His mouth replaced his finger while he slowly caressed the other nipple. She moaned softly in need, aching for him.

"Your breasts are so beautiful," he murmured. "So firm and golden brown. I love touching them, kissing them."

She was lost. She closed her eyes and arched her back, the pleasure of his touch so intense.

He raised his head and whispered, "I could get drunk on the sight of you...the taste of you." His voice was thick with longing and need.

"You make me feel so good," she whispered, stroking his dark head as he resumed his devastating assault on her breasts. "So good." Then she breathed in short, sharp gasps as Jeff slid his hand inside her panties, caressing the inflamed source of her femininity.

Her breathing was sharp and shallow, and her nails were clenched so deeply into his shoulders she knew he would find marks there in the morning.

She unbuttoned his shirt and pulled it off as she slipped her own sweater over her head.

He caught her hand and asked, "Raven, are you sure—"

She reached up for him, answering him with the blazing heat of a kiss, with the shockingly intimate sensation of skin against skin, soft breasts against hard muscles. No, she wasn't sure. But she didn't want to think. She wanted only to feel.

Her long, slender fingers touched his hair, his shoulders, stroked his back, his arms. Jeff caught his breath as she reached between their bodies and unsnapped the top button of his jeans. The zipper stuck, and her touch was excruciatingly light as she attempted to pull it down. He took her hand and pressed it against him, against the hard bulge of his sex. He sucked in his breath.

"Yes...feel what you do to me," he whispered before groaning heavily. "Yes, like that." His breathing was heavy and labored, as if he'd just run a marathon. "Oh, Ray, we've got to stop." He drew a deep ragged breath then carefully but firmly lifted her hand and placed it on his chest.

She gazed up at him, her brown eyes luminous, the rose-colored tips off her full breasts taut with desire. Her chest rose and fell with each ragged breath she took as she touched him.

"I need you," she whispered.

The look he gave her was hot, like molten steel. And then he kissed her, returning her words with the urgency of his mouth against hers. She wanted this moment to last forever, this hot anticipation of knowing, of actually knowing, that he was going to make love to her. She wanted to be able to carry this memory with her always. She wanted to be able to look across a crowded room to meet Jeff's eyes, and to see a hint of this same liquid fire, to see this promise of paradise. She wanted *him.*

She pulled again at his zipper, and this time it opened. And instead of time standing still, things shifted into fast-forward. Raven pushed him over onto his back, and together they pulled his jeans and briefs down his legs. He pulled her astride him, burying his face in the exquisite softness of her breasts. His hands explored the smooth curve of her derriere as she noted with amazement that somehow, over the course of the past few seconds, the last of her clothes had disappeared.

Through her passion-filled haze, she felt Jeff take her by the hips and lift her up and off him.

"No," she breathed, kissing his mouth, his cheek, his neck. "I don't want to—"

"Don't worry, sweetheart," he said hoarsely, straining to reach his jeans and the wallet that was still in his back pocket. "We're not going to stop. I have to get some protection." A moment later he took her into his arms again.

"Now, we're ready," he whispered, as he pressed her back into the bedding. He gazed into her eyes as he entered her slowly. She gasped with the intensity of the pleasure that overtook her.

He took his time. Each stroke lasting an eternity, filling her deeply and ending with a kiss that claimed her completely. It was exquisite torture, stripping her to the last of her defenses, leaving her vulnerable, all her feelings exposed.

Raven closed her eyes, afraid that if she continued to hold Jeff's heated gaze, he'd see her for the fool that she was. He would know that…she still loved him.

She arched up toward him, pulling him down so that the full weight of his body was on top of her. She locked her legs around him, and he groaned, moving faster now, in sync with her every need.

"Ray," he breathed, and she opened her eyes.

He was still watching her, his eyes bright, almost feverish beneath his half-closed lids. His hair was damp, his skin was slick, and a bead of perspiration trailed down past his ear. Raven reached up to catch it with one finger, and he pressed his cheek into her palm.

"You're making me crazy," he said huskily. "We gotta slow down, or—"

But she didn't want to slow down. She pulled his mouth to hers and kissed him fiercely, increasing the slow rhythm of their bodies to a wild, primitive pace, each thrust harder and deeper than the last. She felt his arms tighten around her. She felt his body tense, then heard him cry out her name as he exploded inside her.

And then her body answered his, wave upon wave of exquisite pleasure surrounding her, lifting her, rocketing her to a height she'd only dreamed possible.

Then it was over. Tears stung her eyes as she drifted back to earth. He rolled off her and drew her into his arms, and she nestled against him. Her body entwined with his. The steady beat of his heart beneath her cheek provided security, and an overwhelming sense of peace and contentment.

He kissed the top of her head and slowly stroked her from her shoulder blade to her buttocks and then up again.

A tiny smile played at the corners of her mouth as she savored the memory of their lovemaking. He'd loved her so sweetly, so completely, she couldn't help but think they had the makings for a relationship after all.

IT WAS IMPORTANT to know the name of the person you intended to kill, he thought, as he looked back into the alley at his handiwork. The man lying unconscious and bleeding was named George Whitman.

He would regain consciousness soon. He might report the mugging to the police but two days from now he would become deathly ill, and that's when he would learn what Eleanor Parker and David Foster had already learned—that you reap as you have sown.

He chuckled to himself as he sauntered down the sidewalk. ''Three down, one to go.''

Chapter Ten

Something was wrong.

The moment his phone had rung, jarring him from a deep sleep, that thought had run through Jeff's mind. He'd picked up the receiver with trepidation, afraid that the caller was Raven calling to tell him that she'd regretted sleeping with him and didn't want to see him again. He castigated himself for not staying, but he hadn't wanted to crowd her, recognizing that she needed time to adjust to the fact that he was back in her life. Besides, he had to get back to the hospital. But he'd thought of nothing else since leaving her apartment. He'd gone directly to the hospital where he'd stayed until close to dawn, reading Raven's report, then reviewing Dr. Ross's reports and checking on his patients, but she had always been there in the back of his mind.

He issued a huge sigh of relief when the caller identified himself as Henry Brockman, but that relief was short-lived.

"I need to see you right away," the hospital administrator said without preamble.

He rubbed the sleep out of his eyes and looked at the clock on the nightstand. Nine-fifteen. He'd gotten four hours of sleep. "What's up?"

He heard the hesitation in the other man's voice. "I'd rather not go into it over the phone. I'll see you in my office in about thirty minutes."

A chill of foreboding ran up Jeff's spine. He tried to tell himself that he was just being an alarmist, that he'd just left the hospital five hours ago, that nothing could have happened in that time. But he couldn't shake this feeling of disaster. And it grew in intensity in direct proportion to his proximity to the hospital.

So by the time he stepped into Henry Brockman's office, he knew something was wrong. Dr. Patterson was leaning against the table, eyes glued on the floor. Dr. Hillman was sitting in a chair opposite from her, his legs crossed, his hands clasped together over his knees. He appeared to be examining the fabric of his slacks. No one spoke. Jeff felt the muscles in his stomach tighten as his eyes darted from one doctor to the other. There was a tension in the air. Something was coming. Something he wasn't going to like.

"All right," Jeff said challengingly. "What's happened?"

Dr. Patterson and Dr. Hillman started to speak simultaneously, then stopped.

"It's Lauren Connor," Dr. Hillman said with a sigh, looking up into Jeff's face for the first time. "She's not doing as well as we had hoped."

Jeff was stunned. "What do you mean? Has something happened?"

"She went into cardiac arrest," Dr. Hillman explained. "About an hour ago, but she's stable now. As best we can determine, she began experiencing breathing difficulties." Dr. Hillman gestured awkwardly to try to illustrate what he was saying. "But, for some reason, her heart stopped beating. We don't know why that happened yet. In any case, everything seems to be under control now. What's worrying me is that neither she nor the others seem to be responding to the AST."

"How can you say that?" Jeff asked. "You just started it."

"That's true," Dr. Hillman agreed. "However, viral infections of this type usually respond within the first twenty-four hours. This morning when we took her blood count, I was shocked to see that the drug has had almost no effect on the infection. Usually we give a second dose of the drug on the fourth day. But in light of the aggressiveness of this particular viral strain, I was afraid to wait that long. Instead I gave her another dose this morning.''

Jeff exploded. "You what! You gave her another dose of AST! By what authority did you change the medication?"

Brockman looked uncomfortable. "Ah...I authorized it.''

Jeff turned his anger on the hospital administrator. "Why wasn't I notified of the test results and consulted before a second dose of the drug was given?"

Brockman flushed. "I told the charge nurse not to notify you. You've been working around the clock here, helping with the police investigation. You're stretched to the limit. You needed the sleep." He paused and licked his lips. "When Dr. Hillman explained the situation to me, I approved the change. You would have done the same if you'd been here."

Dr. Hillman swallowed. "I didn't feel that we had any other alternative. We've got to knock down the level of infection in her system."

"But you just said a second dose of AST within a twenty-four-hour period is not the usual protocol," Jeff snapped.

"No, it's not," Dr. Hillman replied hesitantly, "but these aren't the usual cases. I wanted to try—"

"Try?" He couldn't believe the gall of the man. "Listen, Hillman," he said, pointing a finger in the other man's face. "My patients aren't guinea pigs for you to try things on.''

"Jeff!" Brockman said, his voice full of shock. "That's enough."

Jeff ignored him. "Hillman, you're so certain that Lauren and the others aren't going to make it, you're ready to abandon standard medical treatment and experiment. Well, I think your experimentation is lessening their chances. Just look at this cardiac problem with Lauren. She has no history of heart problems. The AST caused it, didn't it?''

Dr. Hillman cleared his throat. ''It might have. It's one of the possible side effects of the drug, but usually it doesn't occur this early in treatment. I don't know what to think about this complication, and that's why I asked for a cardiac consultation.''

''That's rich,'' Jeff said, his voice laced with sarcasm. ''You ask for a cardiac consultation when you damn well know the medication caused the problem. I agreed to the use of AST, but I assumed you would be using the standard dose. In view of the drug's toxicity, I can't agree to any kind of deviation.''

''Then I'd like to know what you suggest,'' Hillman said sharply.

''For starters, I think we should stop the drug completely.''

''No!'' Brockman said, clearly horrified at the mere suggestion. ''Jeff, the medication is their only chance.'' He turned to Dr. Hillman, ''Isn't that right?''

''Yes, it is,'' Dr. Hillman said. ''Increasing the AST, even if it is an unusual approach, is the only hope we have of knocking out this infection, and it has to happen quickly if Mrs. Connor and the others are going to make it.''

''But the drug isn't working!'' Jeff said angrily. ''She's not getting better. None of them are. If this latest crisis is any indication of what we can expect from using AST, then the drug is doing more harm than good, and I want it stopped right now.''

''What are you proposing, Jeff?'' Dr. Patterson sneered. ''To do nothing?''

Jeff's mind screamed for him to stop the medication. It wasn't working. The idea of causing his patients additional suffering went against everything he believed in, yet the idea of just allowing them to die without a fight was equally abhorrent. Yet, what other alternative did he have? Dr. Hillman was right about one thing. If there was a chance that AST would stop the disease then they should continue using it. But if it wouldn't help, then he was merely causing his patients and their families unnecessary pain.

He thought about Raven's treatment. He'd spent part of the evening reading her report and it seemed promising— more than promising. At least on paper, it appeared to work. His eyes widened as he realized the direction his mind was taking. But the more he thought about it, the more convinced he was that it was worth a try. Neither he nor his patients had anything to lose.

"Are you proposing we do nothing?" Dr. Patterson asked again.

Jeff shook his head. "No, that's not what I'm proposing. What I'd like to do is try a different approach." He couldn't believe what he was about to do. He drew a deep breath then for the next ten minutes, laid out in a systematic and detailed fashion the reasons for using Raven's treatment.

"I know it's only been used in a few limited circumstances, but the data suggest that it should be effective. More importantly, it lacks the toxicity of AST. So the patients won't suffer any of the horrendous side effects associated with that drug. The AST isn't working, and I have reason to believe this will. As you know, Ms. Delaney has degrees in pharmacology and nutrition and has worked extensively with herbs for a number of years."

As he spoke, Brockman stared at him with growing horror. When he finished Brockman's only comment was, "You're joking."

Jeff's eyes narrowed. "I've never been more serious about anything in my life."

"We can't use an unapproved method of treatment," Brockman wailed. "The board would never stand for it nor would the insurance company. We'd have no coverage in the event of a malpractice suit.'' He shook his head. ''I have to do what's best for the hospital, and I forbid your using that treatment here.''

Jeff argued with him for several minutes more, but Brockman stood firm. There wasn't a snowball's chance in hell he would agree to let Jeff use Raven's treatment. He was forced to settle for the elimination of the AST and the administration of a less toxic drug.

As he sat in his office later that day, he tried to think what he would tell Raven if the subject came up. His mouth curved into a wry smile. Who was he kidding? There was no way in hell she wouldn't ask about Lauren and the others. He just hoped she would understand.

RAVEN BEGAN HAVING second thoughts about rekindling a relationship with Jeff the moment he'd left her apartment. They had so many strikes against them, and working on this case with him only seemed to accentuate their differences, but he said he was going to try to be more open-minded, and he really seemed to be trying. Shouldn't she give him the benefit of the doubt?

She wanted to, especially after last night. She closed her eyes savoring the memory of their lovemaking. It had been devastating, and it had forced her to admit that she still had feelings for him—strong feelings. And those feelings scared her to death. She'd given her heart to him once before, and he'd broken it.

She swallowed, remembering the pain she'd felt. It had taken her a long time to put the past behind her. She couldn't go through that again. This time it would destroy her.

She was torn. She really wanted to be with him, but she was afraid. What if she was reading too much into his evaluating her report? Maybe Jeff would never accept her belief in herbal healing?

Those thoughts plagued her throughout the morning, so

she was no closer to reaching a decision when he came by the shop to give her a ride to the police station to see Nick later that day. Nick had called Jeff earlier asking him to come by the station after lunch. Jeff had called her and asked if she'd like to accompany him. She tried to tell herself not to make too much of that simple little gesture, but she couldn't help but think that it was another positive sign that he really did see them as a team.

A wave of heat had washed over her when he entered the shop, and remained with her during the ride to the police station. She felt like a schoolgirl in the throes of first love. But that feeling was pushed aside the moment they entered Nick's office. His face was grim and suddenly she had a feeling this was not just a casual briefing on the status of the investigation.

She looked over at Jeff, wondering if he felt it too, but he seemed distracted. She frowned. He'd been that way when he'd picked her up at the shop and during the ride over. No doubt his mind was on his patients, and her heart went out to him.

This had to be one of the worst times for him. It was hard for any doctor to stand helplessly by and watch his patients steadily decline and die, but especially for someone as kind and caring as Jeff. He was a dedicated doctor and gave one hundred percent of himself to his patients. That was one of the things she had always admired and respected about him.

But it was hard to sit back and say nothing, especially after last night. Once again the memories of their love-making flashed in her mind. They'd been so connected. She felt closer to him than any human being on the planet and wanted to share his burden. Before she could stop herself, she leaned over and covered his hand with hers.

He looked over at her and for a moment, it was as if they were the only two people in the world.

"The news isn't good," Nick said, pulling her back to

the matter at hand. "I'm afraid the investigation has stalled. We've hit a brick wall."

Raven tore her eyes from Jeff's and looked at Nick, alarmed. "What do you mean, you've hit a brick wall?"

Nick issued a weary sigh then looked at Jeff. "I'm sorry. I know you were counting on hearing something positive. That's why I wanted to tell you right away."

"What happened?" Raven asked, confused by this unexpected turn of events. "I thought you said Calvin Parker and Mark Daniels were strong suspects."

Nick shrugged. "That's how it appeared on the surface." He drew another deep sigh. "But over the last twenty-four hours there have been several new developments that pretty well take Daniels out of the picture. Maybe even Parker."

"How can that be?" Raven asked. "Daniels certainly had a motive for killing Julie Hartman. You said so yourself. He probably killed the others to divert suspicion from himself."

"Maybe," Nick answered cautiously. "But he also has an alibi. Katherine Olsen is willing to swear in court that he was with her every night for the last two months."

She frowned. "How does that change anything? We knew she was going to give him an alibi."

"That's true, but what we didn't know was that she would produce several prominent individuals who are also willing to swear that they were with Olsen and Daniels for the last eight Monday nights in question. While she might lie for him, I don't know why these other people would." He shook his head. "If that wasn't bad enough, other than Julie Hartman, we can't tie him to any of the other victims and definitely not to any virus. Hell, I don't even know what virus we're supposed to be looking for."

"What about Calvin Parker?" she asked.

Nick shook his head. "It's almost as bad. Parker's assertion that everything was in his name is true. The house, the car, even the checking and saving accounts. His wife's name wasn't on anything.''

"So our motive has gone out the window," she said slowly.

"You got it. He didn't have to kill her to get anything. He already had it all.''

Jeff frowned. "That's true only if you assume money was the motive. It seems to me, Parker might have had another reason for killing his wife that had nothing to do with money. She might have been his love slave, but that door swings both ways. She was quite a bit older than him, he was tired of her, and he wanted her out of his life, but the lady wouldn't go. What was it her friends said? 'Over my dead body.' Well, maybe that was the only way he could get her out of his life.''

Nick pulled on his lower lip as he considered Jeff's theory. "That's a possibility, but Parker gave us permission to search his house. We turned the place upside down, but we didn't find anything that would implicate him in her murder or that of the others. We also searched his car and his office and didn't find anything there, either.''

"What about his connection to Dalton Laboratories?" Jeff pressed. "Did you check with them about the various infectious agents they use in their research procedures?''

Nick nodded. "They weren't too forthcoming about anything initially. It was only after the state's attorney's office got involved and threatened to shut them down that they opened up." He grimaced. "For all the good that did. Apparently, you have to have special clearance to enter the research section of the plant or to receive any of its data.'' He shook his head. "And Parker didn't have it.''

"But how good is their security?" Jeff questioned. "Could he have breached it?''

Nick chewed his lower lip as he considered the question. "Possibly, but it would have been damn hard. They're equipped with the latest in high-tech security. To even enter the administrative portion of the facility requires the recognition of a palm print and to enter the actual lab requires a retinal eye scan identification.''

"So where does that leave us?" Raven asked.

Nick issued a weary sigh. "Not where I want us to be. The mayor's office is leaning on the captain, who's leaning on me. He wants me to move on, pursue other leads." He looked again at Jeff. "Considering the lack of progress we've made with these two, I can't justify the manpower. But I want you to know, I'm not dropping this line of inquiry completely. We'll keep digging into Parker's and Daniels's backgrounds.''

"If you don't mind my asking, do these other leads include the man Mark Daniels claims to have seen?" Raven asked.

Nick nodded his head. "He may not have been a figment of Daniels's imagination. At least one of Hartman's neighbors claims to have also seen a man fitting that same description in the days preceding her death. We're checking it out.

"Look, Jeff, I'm telling you this because I thought you ought to know it looks as if it's going to take some time to catch this guy. I promise you, I'm going to get to the bottom of these murders if it's the last thing I do.''

"I know you will," Jeff said, unable to hide his disappointment. "Our best just doesn't seem good enough.''

"How are your patients doing?" Nick asked.

Jeff rubbed the back of his neck. "Not good." He sighed. "I was really counting on you to help us.''

Nick glanced off to the side, unable to look Jeff in the eye.

"Well, thanks for giving us this update," Jeff said, standing. Raven followed suit.

Nick walked them to the door. They lingered in the open doorway for several minutes chatting.

She was about to ask if they'd been able to create a composite sketch of the man Daniels had seen when she caught a glimpse of Grace Wells. The older woman was standing some distance away at the sergeant's desk. From the way she was gesturing wildly, Raven sensed she was reading him the riot act.

Next to her, Raven heard Nick groan then mumble something about not wanting Grace to know he was in before he ducked into his office, closing the door.

Jeff chuckled. "Let's get out of here," he said. He took her arm and led her back to his car.

Once they were under way again, she leaned back. "You know, Nick Valentine is quite a man. He's smart, ambitious and a little overbearing, but he's also kind and extremely caring. I wonder what made him leave Atlanta."

Next to her she felt rather than saw Jeff shrug. He was unusually quiet. He'd been that way at the station, but she sensed it was more than disappointment with the progress of the police investigation.

She laid her hand on his thigh. "Jeff, is something wrong?" she asked gently.

He sighed, then nodded. "I stopped the AST," he said. Then he briefly recounted the events of the morning.

She sucked in her breath. It wasn't that she was surprised by the drug's side effects, but she had thought it would be days, not hours, before any appeared. "What are you going to do?"

He shrugged. "That's the sixty-four-thousand-dollar question. At this point there's nothing more we can do. We're out of options." He sighed again. "Other than make the patients as comfortable as possible and pray for a miracle, that's about it."

"It's that bad?"

"Yeah." He hesitated then added, "Bad enough that I even suggested using your treatment."

Her heart began to slam against the wall of her chest waiting for him to continue.

"I'm sorry," he said. He ran his hand over his hair. "I talked until I was blue in the face, but Brockman refused to even consider using it."

She searched his face. Had he really tried to convince them to use her treatment? she wondered. Or had he simply gone through the motions? It was more likely the latter. How often had he told her that alternative medicine went against everything he believed in? How persuasive could you be arguing for something you didn't believe in? Not very, she decided.

When was she going to get it through her thick skull that Jeff didn't believe in alternative medicine? He never had and probably never would. He'd probably only suggested using her treatment to his colleagues to appease her. No doubt, she thought cynically, he knew she would question him about it when she learned he'd stopped the AST and he'd wanted to defuse the situation.

She blinked back tears. She'd really thought he cared about her. Saw her as a whole person and was coming around on the issue of herbal medicine. Obviously, she'd pinned too much hope on his reading her report.

He glanced over at her. "If it were up to me I'd use it in a heartbeat, but it wasn't my decision alone."

Perhaps not, but he was the attending physician and his opinion carried more weight than anyone else's.

"You do understand, don't you?"

Unfortunately, she thought bleakly, she did. She stared straight ahead, not trusting herself to speak.

He looked at her quickly. "I don't think you understand at all." He tried to engage her in conversation, but the rest of the ride was accomplished in total silence. The moment the car came to a halt, she jumped out, heading for the shop.

Jeff was right behind her. He followed her past Phyllis's startled gaze through the shop into the back room.

"Raven," he said softly. He caught her hand and led her to the wing chair next to her desk then knelt on the floor in front of her. "I know you're disappointed that we aren't going to use your treatment, but as promising as it seems, the bottom line is it's not a recognized procedure.

Brockman is concerned about liability, but I think the potential benefits outweigh the risks. I assure you I'm not going to drop the matter.''

When she still didn't say anything, his eyes clouded. ''Don't shut me out.''

He looked so sad and sounded so sincere, she wanted to believe him. And for a moment, she almost relented. But she held back. She just wasn't sure of him.

She dropped her head, and he slid his hand up under her throat, lifting her chin. His fingertips were warm on her skin, and Raven stiffened, resisting not only the warmth, but the way it made her feel.

''You know I care a great deal about you,'' he said quietly. ''And I don't want to lose you.''

There was a long pause. ''I care about you, too, but my profession is also important to me.'' She turned her head to the side, blinking back tears. ''I'm not sure we have the makings for a relationship.''

''How can you say that?'' he cried. ''Didn't last night mean anything to you?''

''You know it did, but it's not enough.''

''Raven,'' he said softly. ''I don't want to lose you. I have the utmost respect for you—''

Suddenly, his beeper went off. ''Oh, hell,'' he said. ''That's probably the hospital. I've got to go, but I'll be back. And when I do we're going to talk this through. Okay?''

She drew a deep sigh then nodded. ''All right.''

He took her into his arms and gave her a brief, hard kiss, then stood and walked out the door.

She stared bleakly after him. God, what was she going to do?

AFTER JEFF LEFT Raven threw herself into her work, trying not to think about him. But it was no use. Her thoughts were in turmoil. Had he really tried to convince Dr. Hillman and the others to use her treatment? Her heart told her that she wasn't being fair to Jeff. That she was expecting too much of him, that the fact that he'd read her report and proposed its use ought to be enough. That he'd come a long way—from total rejection of the idea of using an alternative medicine to actually considering using her herbs. Even if his colleagues didn't agree, he had gone to bat for her. What more could she want?

You know, another voice whispered—she wanted his respect, plain and simple. He said he respected her, but did he really? During their conversation in the car then later at the shop, he had never once expressed his opinion of her treatment, which made her wonder what he really thought about it. As much as she cared about him, wanted to be with him, she couldn't live with a man who really didn't believe in her profession. In time she would grow resentful and her love would wilt and die like a rose on an unwatered vine.

But was she ready to call a halt to things? Or was she expecting too much and should give him more time? She dropped her head in her hands until raised voices in the front room penetrated her subconscious.

"You can't go in there!" she heard Phyllis yell.

"Get out of my way," a high-pitched voice screeched, and then Grace Wells marched into the room.

"Do you want me to call the police?" Phyllis asked, following Grace into the room.

For a moment Raven could only stare at the other woman, surprised. "It's okay, Phyllis," she said. Phyllis gave her a searching look, then nodded and returned to the outer room.

"Well, aren't you going to offer me a seat?" Grace asked in that whiny voice of hers.

Raven leaned back in her chair and regarded her steadily. "Frankly, I'm surprised to see you here. I thought I'd be the last person you'd want to see."

"Humph," Grace snorted, moving into the room as if she owned it. She settled herself in the chair next to Raven's desk with the stiffness of a carpenter's rule being folded up. The woman seemed absolutely rigid except in the joints.

"I know you didn't kill Eleanor," Grace sniffed.

When Raven didn't say anything, the other woman peered at her, frowning. "Don't you want to clear your name, find out who killed Eleanor and those other people?"

One dark eyebrow rose in surprise. No apology. Just that statement.

"At first—" Grace sniffed again "—I thought you were behind Eleanor's illness. But illness is one thing, murder is another. You didn't have any reason to kill her but that low-down husband of hers sure did."

When Raven still didn't say anything, the other woman added, "He's so happy that she's dead, he can't even act sorry. He hasn't shed a tear."

Was she the only person who questioned Parker's guilt? she wondered, but aloud said, "Perhaps he's simply one of those people who has difficulty displaying his emotions."

"Humph," Grace snorted. "I doubt if that's the case."

"So why do you think Mr. Parker killed his wife?"

"Seems to me, it's pretty self-evident. He killed her because he was tired of her but wanted her money."

Raven gave her a skeptical look. "It's my understanding he already had it. Everything they owned was in his name."

The other woman's face puckered into a frown. "Yeah, but a divorce would have put a whole new light on things. Eleanor would have come to her senses and fought for her fair share. Mark my word, she was not going to let him go easily. If she thought she could hold on to him by fighting for her share of their assets, she'd have done it."

Raven shook her head. "Not according to Mr. Parker. He said his wife would have given him anything—even a divorce."

It was now Grace who looked skeptical. "Don't let Calvin fool you. He talks a good story but he wasn't as sure of Eleanor as he makes out." She leaned forward slightly. "I know for a fact she threw him for a loop when she refused to sign some legal papers without reading them first."

Grace was getting on her nerves. Too much of what she said seemed to be nothing more than the vindictive claims of a very angry woman. "Do you have any evidence supporting all this?" Raven asked finally.

"Well, no," Grace said somewhat defensively, then added quickly, "but it's there. I don't know for how long, though. If I could get a little cooperation from our police department we could probably have enough evidence to make an arrest in no time."

"Why are you telling me this?"

"I saw you and Dr. Knight at the precinct today, talking to Detective Valentine. The three of you seemed awfully chummy." She fingered her purse strap as she looked at Raven from beneath lowered lids. It was a calculating look. "I thought if I told you my suspicions, you could tell Detective Valentine."

"Why don't you just tell him yourself?"

"I've tried, but he won't listen." Her eyes slid to the floor and she shifted slightly in her chair. "I don't think he likes me," she mumbled.

In other words, she'd made such a nuisance of herself that Nick was avoiding her. If the behavior she had observed earlier was any indication of what Nick had to deal with, she couldn't blame him.

"I've given all kinds of information to Detective Valentine," Grace continued, "but he just disregards it. Sometimes I wonder if he even wants to get to the bottom of these murders."

It was time to call a halt to the interview, Raven decided. "I'm sure he's working very hard to—"

"He's dragging his feet, that's what he is doing. Too

busy giving TV interviews and while he's doing that Calvin Parker is destroying evidence.''

"Do you know that for a fact?"

"Why else would he have Eleanor's body cremated, if he wasn't destroying evidence? He's going to get away with murder.''

"He may not have been a good husband but there's no evidence that he had anything to do with his wife's death. It's my understanding Mr. Parker isn't a strong suspect. Why, he even voluntarily agreed to let the police search the house.''

She looked at Raven as if she'd grown two heads. "Calvin's no fool. If he let the police search the house it was because he'd already removed any incriminating evidence. Probably stashed it at the apartment.''

That got her attention. "Apartment? What apartment?''

Grace gave her a sour look. "His apartment in Lincoln Park. Eleanor told me about it. She said that was where he entertained his lady friends—'' She paused and her mouth curved into a superior little smile. "He didn't tell you about it, did he?''

Chapter Eleven

For the zillionth time, Raven wished she'd never mentioned Grace Wells's name. But when Jeff had dropped by the shop at closing time, she still hadn't been ready to talk about what had happened earlier and skirted the issue by telling him about Grace's visit. When Jeff had suggested they check out her claim, she had no idea what he planned to do. If she had, she'd never have let him set foot outside her shop.

"You have to be out of your mind," she whispered as she slowly followed him down a plush corridor toward Parker's apartment. "What if someone's inside?"

Jeff caught her arm and dragged her along. "We'll ring the bell first. If anyone answers, we'll pretend we came by to get Parker's signature on a hospital form." He smiled and added, "Don't worry, this will be a piece of cake."

She shifted from one foot to the next as he pressed the doorbell and waited. There was no sound from inside the apartment.

"Good, no one's home," he said, looking around. "Keep watch."

"I don't like this!" she whispered hoarsely. Out of the corner of her eye, she watched as he pulled out a small file and went to work on the lock. After a moment of him fiddling with it, she heard a faint click, and the door swung open.

She looked at him in amazement. "How did you do that?"

He grinned at her. "A petty thief in Zaire taught me as compensation for medical treatment."

Raven watched as Jeff pushed the door open wider, stuck his hand inside, and flipped on the light switch. Then he pulled her inside the apartment and closed the door. The apartment was still and silent.

"Let's make this quick," Jeff said. "We'll both check out the living room, then we'll split up."

"What are we looking for?" she asked, following him into the living room and glancing around.

He shrugged. "Medical papers, drugs, vials, a syringe. Anything that looks like it came out of a medical lab. Something that might connect Parker to these murders."

"I still say we should have told Nick," she grumbled. "Let him handle it."

He shook his head. "Nick's hands are tied. There's no way he could get a search warrant for the apartment based solely on Grace's claim. We both know she's not the most reliable source. However, since Parker failed to tell Nick about his little love nest, makes you wonder if he isn't hiding something."

"Or maybe he thought it was none of Nick's business," she said, surveying the spacious room. It was a far cry from the modest house Parker had shared with Eleanor in Oak Park. The furnishings in the living room alone had cost a small fortune. In one corner of the room there was an expensive-looking entertainment center, complete with a big-screen TV and a fancy stereo system. A teak rolltop desk shared a wall with an oak bookcase and in another corner of the room was a small bar.

"This apartment presents a different picture of Calvin Parker," she said.

Jeff paused in his act of lifting a sofa cushion. "It certainly does," he said. "At the very least it seems to suggest he was making a new life for himself without a wife, which is interesting since he maintains that they weren't discussing divorce.''

Raven lifted a sculptured piece and peeked inside, then moved on to the sofa table near the entryway, checking the contents on top and inside. She found nothing of even remote interest. She sighed and moved on to the stereo system. She inspected the contents of the cabinet, but didn't find anything.

She turned and looked at Jeff. He was going through a stack of letters on the sofa table. The way he moved his head, reminded her of the way he looked last night, right before he kissed her. For a moment, she was suspended in time as her mind replayed the way he had held her, kissed her, loved her.

Suddenly, everything seemed crystal clear. What a fool she'd been. Of course, Jeff respected her and believed in her treatment. He never would have suggested its use for his patients if he hadn't. She'd just been too insecure to see that.

Jeff met her eyes and smiled, and it was only then that she realized that she'd been staring at him. She quickly looked away, but she had a feeling he'd known that she understood and accepted the decision not to use her herbal medicine. They needed to talk but this was not the place. She walked over to the oak bookcase and started going through the items on it.

They spent several more minutes checking out the living room, but didn't find anything.

"I'll take the hall closet, the den and the kitchen," Jeff said. "Why don't you check the bedroom and the bath."

Raven nodded and headed for the bedroom. She opened the door, flipped on the light switch, and froze in the doorway. *Wouldn't you just know it?* she thought. It was the consummate bachelor's bedroom, decorated with black satin sheets, a tiger-striped bedspread, and a mirrored ceiling above the bed. "How tacky," she muttered under her breath.

She walked over to the bed and went to work. There was nothing between the mattress and box spring, nothing under the bed itself. She moved on to the closet and found its wooden slat door open an inch or two. She pushed the door open farther and peeked inside, then whistled softly as she stared at the rows of designer suits, custom-made shirts, and a dozen or more cashmere sweaters. The man was certainly a clotheshorse. She sighed. It would take some time to go through the closet. She'd do it later. She closed the door and moved on to the bureau. She pulled open one drawer after another, but saw nothing of interest.

The bathroom was an equal washout. Nothing appeared to be secreted in the back of the toilet, or hidden among the color-coordinated towels or concealed in the extra roll of toilet paper. She went back into the bedroom and was checking the nightstand when Jeff appeared in the doorway.

"Any luck?"

Raven couldn't help the jolt of pleasure she experienced looking at his handsome face. "Nothing so far, but there's a closet full of clothes over there." She gestured toward the door with the wooden slats. "Why don't you check it out?"

He gave the room a critical look. "Be sure to check the wastebasket and curtains," he said as he headed for the closet.

For a moment she was incapable of moving. Her eyes roamed over him as he walked across the room. Broad-shouldered and slim-hipped, his body was that of an athlete, with the lithe grace that was born of ingrained confidence. He was wearing a blue denim work shirt and jeans that fit snugly in the back, molding to his long, muscular thighs and tight buttocks in what she found to be a thoroughly unnerving way. She felt her cheeks grow warm and forced herself to look away, shuffling instead through the papers and moving on to the next drawer. Out of the corner of her eye, she saw him pull back the closet doors. A moment later, she heard Jeff whistle, then say, "Well, well, well."

"What is it?" She turned and gave him a quizzical look.

"I don't think this is Mrs. Parker's." He held up a short pink, transparent nightgown.

Raven smiled. "I'd say that was a sure bet."

He continued to study the flimsy lingerie. "I wonder if the owner helped him buy these designer suits."

"Probably," Raven said offhandedly. "Looks like she likes expensive things herself. I've seen that same negligee at Victoria's Secret..." Her voice trailed off as his eyes met hers.

She knew he was remembering how she used to buy sexy lingerie at Victoria's Secret to wear for him. She groped for something to say.

"Did you notice that most of those suits don't look as if they've ever been worn?" she asked, trying to break the sexual tension that swirled around them.

Her question pulled them both back to the matter at hand. "Yeah, that's curious," he said. "We'd better get back to work."

She nodded, then went to inspect the curtains. Standing on tiptoe, she patted the top of the drapes and the sides.

"Ol' Calvin is certainly not what he seemed," Jeff drawled, holding up a scarf and a pair of handcuffs. "I wouldn't have thought his taste ran in that direction. Kinky."

"What do you mean, kinky?" Raven demanded, turning away from the curtains.

Jeff smiled. "Never you mind. Let's just say that Parker's interests are not particularly my cup of tea. After you finish up with the curtains, don't forget to check the wastebasket. I'm just about done with the closet."

"You think there might be something here?"

Jeff shrugged. "Who knows?" He glanced at the small silver clock on the nightstand next to the king-size bed.

"Hurry up, Raven. The sooner we get out of here, the better."

She would second that. They'd already been there twenty minutes.

She found the vials quite by accident. All her mental energy was spent castigating herself for not telling Jeff how she felt, and her search of the wastebasket was desultory, mindless, instinctive. But suddenly, the solid weight of a seemingly empty tissue box caught her attention. She knelt on the floor on the far side of the bed, turned the box upside down, and the tiny vials tumbled into her lap.

She stared at them for a long, speculative moment. There were four of them, unmarked, all filled with a clear liquid. She didn't even look up when Jeff closed the closet door.

"Nothing in there," he said. "Not even any videotapes. After finding the scarf and handcuffs, I had him pegged as the type."

"I think I found something," Raven said quietly.

"What?" She had his full attention now, and he materialized by her side immediately, squatting down next to her. She handed him one of the vials, and he held it up, studying the contents inside the small bottle. "I think we just hit pay dirt," he said, a rich note of satisfaction in his voice. His eyes searched her face, settling on her lips. For a moment, she thought he was going to kiss her. And, God help her, she wanted him to.

He must have read her mind because his lips curved into a sexy smile. "You pick the darnedest place to tell me I'm forgiven." He dropped his voice, saying in a low, husky drawl, "I *am* forgiven, aren't I?"

"Yes," she said, returning his smile.

"Good, then let's get out of here." He watched as Raven slipped the tiny vials inside her purse, then stood.

She was walking slightly in front of Jeff, and they'd made it almost through the living room when she heard a rustling sound. Swinging around, she saw a tall menacing figure, wearing a ski mask, dart from behind the sofa, charging toward them.

Jeff pushed her out of the way, but before he could take the offensive, the man slammed his fist into Jeff's abdomen, sending him sprawling to the floor. His head hit the corner of the sofa table, dazing him momentarily. The man grabbed a lamp off the sofa table, and raised it to drop it on Jeff's head.

Raven reacted automatically. She grabbed his wrist and pulled downward with all her might. The lamp crashed to the floor. The man whirled around, dislodging her hold. She staggered backward into the arm of the sofa. Before she could regain her balance, the man lunged forward, and wrapped an arm around her windpipe. She kicked at his legs and clawed at his arm, but the pressure only increased. Her mouth widened in gaping terror, all sound strangled except for a sickly gurgle. She struggled to stay conscious. But suddenly the man's grip was broken.

Jeff was behind him, an armlock around the other man's neck. He was twisting and turning, flailing his free arm trying to break free.

"See what you can find to use as a rope to tie him up," Jeff panted. "Hurry."

He didn't have to tell her twice. Her eyes darted about the room; seeing nothing they could use for a rope, she turned toward the kitchen. Out of the corner of her eye, she saw a metallic glint as the man pulled something from his pants pocket. Before she could warn Jeff, the man twisted, put the object against Jeff's side and pushed. Jeff recoiled. He doubled over slightly, his hand going to his side. The man broke free and bolted out of the apartment. Jeff turned to give chase, but Raven grabbed his arm.

"No!" The anguished cry tore from her lips. "I've got to get you to the hospital. My God, Jeff, he stuck you with a hypodermic needle!"

EVERYTHING AFTER THAT was a blur—the trip to the hospital, Dr. Hillman rushing Jeff into the examination room, giving the vials to Dr. Patterson, being shown to the waiting room and then the waiting.

Raven had sat there alone for what seemed like an eternity before Shay came out to talk to her. He told her that he had notified the police then he drew a deep breath and explained that Dr. Hillman was examining Jeff. He tried to sound upbeat and confident, assuring her that she had nothing to worry about now that they had the virus, that at this very moment the vials were being packed and would be sent to the CDC for analysis within the hour. He said he was confident the CDC would be able to identify the virus and develop a treatment.

But they both knew it wasn't that simple. It could be days, maybe even months, before the CDC had a handle on the virus, let alone any kind of treatment.

He tried to offer words of comfort but she noticed he couldn't look at her.

A few minutes later, Nick arrived. He walked over to where she sat and took both her hands in his. "I heard what happened," he said gently. "I'm really sorry."

"Thank you." She choked on the words as she spoke, blinking back tears. "He's going to be all right. He has to."

For a moment Nick didn't say anything, just stood there staring at her, shifting from one foot to another. It was the first time she'd ever seen the young detective at a loss for words. After a moment, he pulled up a chair next to the sofa.

"Do you feel up to making a statement?" he asked in that same gentle tone.

She closed her eyes and drew a deep, ragged breath. "I think so."

She felt Shay stiffen on the sofa beside her. "Detective Valentine, Ms. Delaney has been subjected to quite a shock," he said firmly. "Can't this wait until tomorrow?"

She placed her hand on Shay's arm. He looked at her, his expression one of concern. She gave him a reassuring smile. "It's okay." She drew another deep breath. "Frankly, I'd like to get this over with."

She watched as Nick pulled out a notepad and fountain pen. He seemed to be all thumbs. The pen slipped through his fingers and fell to the floor. She knelt down, picked it up and handed it to him. He mumbled a thanks and then stuck the pen back inside his pocket. When he realized what he'd done, he gave her a sheepish look, then took out a ballpoint pen. Apparently he was more upset about what had happened to Jeff than she'd realized.

"Ah…why don't we begin with your telling me what you and Jeff were doing in Calvin Parker's apartment," Nick said.

She drew a deep breath and then recounted her meeting with Grace Wells and Grace's assertion that Parker might have hidden evidence implicating him in his wife's murder at his apartment. She then explained how they'd found the vials. She didn't falter until she came to the part where they had been attacked.

Nick gave her a moment to compose herself then asked the question he'd probably wanted to ask from the very beginning. "Why didn't you call me?" Nick was all cop now.

"We didn't think you could do anything. You had no basis for obtaining a search warrant, but we also couldn't stand by and do nothing."

"It was a dumb and dangerous thing to do," Nick said.

"What was Jeff supposed to do?" Shay asked in astonishment. "Sit around while his patients died?"

Nick looked at him sternly. "I understand Jeff's frustration, but what he did was wrong. He had no business breaking into that apartment." He looked back at Raven. "You should have called me. As it is, the two of you may have put any case against Calvin Parker in a precarious position. If your attacker turns out to be Calvin Parker, I don't know if the state's attorney is going to be able to use any of the evidence you found because it was illegally obtained.''

"What?" Surely, she'd misunderstood.

"Let me get this straight," Shay snarled. "Parker attacks Jeff. Sticks him with a hypodermic needle thereby infecting him with a deadly virus, and you may not be able to make a case against him?"

Nick flushed. "I know it's not fair, but that's the law. We can't use evidence that was illegally obtained." There was an undercurrent of tension in his voice and she realized that he didn't think too much of the system.

"Some legal system," Shay said disgustedly.

Raven looked from Nick to Shay. "But this all presupposes that the man that attacked us was Parker."

Nick looked at her sharply. "Are you saying it wasn't?"

"Of course it was Parker," Shay answered. "Who else could it have been? He probably figured they'd found the vials and that's why he attacked them."

Nick threw him a sour look then turned back to Raven. "Was Calvin Parker the man that attacked you and Jeff?"

She turned the question over in her mind. It could have been Parker. It would certainly explain how the man had been able to slip into the apartment unnoticed. But their attacker had been quick and agile. And while Calvin Parker appeared to be in good physical condition, she doubted if he had the strength and agility demonstrated by the man who had attacked them. "I don't know," she said finally.

Nick gave her a reassuring smile. "It's okay. Let's start at the beginning. Did you see anyone when you arrived?"

She shook her head. "He must have slipped in while we were searching the bedroom. We were about to leave when he sprang out from behind the sofa and attacked us." Her hands shook as she relived the moment when Jeff was stuck by the needle.

"Did you get a look at the man?"

She shook her head again. "It all happened so fast.

We'd just turned out the living room lights and were leaving. That's when he—he…" She shuddered, remembering. God, would she ever be able to get that image out of her mind?

"Could you make out his features?"

"No," she said. "He was wearing a ski mask." Her head dropped as tears sprang to her eyes.

"It's all right," Nick said gently. "It would have made things a little easier if you could have ID'ed him, but I have a couple of police officers over at the apartment building right now interviewing neighbors. As soon as I leave here, I'm going to make a run over to the house to question Parker."

Suddenly all the hurt and the anger she'd been holding in came boiling to the surface. "I want you to catch the killer, Nick. I want to be there in court, pointing him out to the jury. I want him to get the death penalty. I want him to die!"

Nick gave her strange look. No doubt surprised by the venom in her voice. She'd shocked herself with her outburst.

"I understand your need for revenge," he said finally. Something in his eyes told her he did. No doubt it was hard for a cop like him to watch criminals evade punishment because of some legal technicality.

He leaned over and took her hand. "I promise you, one day, you'll get to see him face-to-face." With that he stood and walked out of the room.

A few minutes later, Shay returned to the examination room.

Raven sat alone, waiting.

"I'LL BE PERFECTLY blunt, I think your best chance for survival is to begin the AST immediately," Dr. Hillman said.

Jeff looked over at Raven and his heart melted. He was glad now that he'd insisted that she be allowed in the examination room as soon as Hillman had completed his testings. He'd been concerned about her sitting in the waiting room alone. She was trying to look brave, but she was failing badly. He could see the terror in her eyes, and he wanted to take her in his arms and tell her that it would be all right. But he couldn't. It was too soon to know if he would actually come down with the disease, but there was little doubt that he'd been exposed to the virus. Hillman's tests had confirmed that.

"I know we've had some problems with the drug," Dr. Hillman was saying, "but you're strong, healthy. Perhaps if we start the drug right away, before the onset of symptoms, we'll see a different result."

Jeff didn't say anything.

Hillman turned toward Shay. "Because of the drug's toxicity, I think we should admit him into the hospital tonight."

Shay nodded. "I can get a bed—"

"Please, stop talking about me as if I weren't here. My mind hasn't been affected. I'm perfectly capable of making my own decisions regarding medical treatment."

"Jeff, there's no decision to be made," his friend said. "We've got to begin treatment right away. It's your only hope."

He looked at Raven. Was it his only hope? The reality was, there was no hope. If he took AST perhaps his life could be prolonged—a few days, maybe even a few weeks. But in the end the outcome would be the same. The virus would kill him.

If he took AST as Hillman and Shay suggested, he would also have to be hospitalized, and he'd be sick the entire time. He didn't want that. What little time he had left, he wanted to spend with Raven. Taking her treatment would at least allow him to remain lucid and other drugs could be used to reduce the pain.

Pride and stubbornness had already caused him to waste four years. He wouldn't waste another moment.

"No," he said, turning to look at the woman who meant more to him than life itself. "Raven's herbal treatment is my only hope."

Dr. Hillman looked at him as if he'd gone mad. "Jeff, you're not thinking rationally."

Hazel eyes stared into chocolate brown ones. "On the contrary, I'm seeing things clearer than I've ever seen them in my life."

Raven's eyes widened and she shook her head. "Jeff, you don't have to prove anything to me. Listen to Dr. Hillman. Your life is at stake."

"See," Hillman said, his voice triumphant. "*She's* not even sure of her treatment." He then proceeded to tick off on his fingers the reasons against using it.

Jeff had to admit, everything Hillman said was true. But Hillman was dealing with logic, not emotions.

He walked over to Raven, took her hands and pulled her up. "Shay, if you and Dr. Hillman don't mind, I'd like to speak to Raven alone."

"Sure. We'll just be outside."

When the door closed behind the two men, he smiled down at her. "I meant what I said about taking your treatment. I think it'll work."

She dropped her head. He lifted her chin forcing her to look at him. "Raven, I never would have considered giving it to my patients if I hadn't believed that."

She blinked back tears. "Why don't we wait a few days? See what the CDC can tell us about the virus?"

He shook his head. "We can't wait. Hillman was right on that score, but he's dead wrong about AST. I think my chances are better taking your medication. Don't you?"

She looked down at her hands, unable to meet his eyes. He knew this was hard, but he wanted her to know that he believed in her and her treatment.

He lifted her chin. "Do you believe it will halt the virus?" he asked again.

Raven didn't know what to say. If he had asked that

same question last week, yesterday, or even earlier that day, she would have said yes. Not only that, she would have jumped at the chance of using it. But this was Jeff. The man she loved. Yes, she thought, she loved him. But she couldn't tell him that. Not now. She swallowed as she turned his question over in her mind. All her fears and uncertainties came crashing up to meet her. "I think it will work," she said finally, "but I'm not sure."

He gave her a reassuring smile. "You believed up until now that it would. Don't start doubting yourself."

"But what if I'm—"

He pressed a finger against her lips, halting her words. "We have to think positive."

"But if I'm wrong—"

He saw the anguish in her eyes, and wished he could take the pain away. He forced himself to sound upbeat and confident. "No more second-guessing." He wrapped his arm around her shoulders, tucking her securely against his side. "Let's get out of here," he whispered.

Arm in arm they walked out of the hospital to face an uncertain future.

Chapter Twelve

Their first stop was at Nature's Cure to get the various herbs and other items Raven would need to prepare the herbal medication, then she outlined the treatment schedule. Jeff would take one eight-ounce glass of the medication every four hours. Once she was sure they had everything they needed, they headed to Jeff's apartment.

When they reached his apartment, he came quickly around, opened the passenger door, and she wrapped her arms around him. Together they walked inside the building. She leaned against his shoulder, thinking how good it felt to be in his arms, how reassuring it was to have him with her now. She refused to think of a future without him.

As soon as they were inside, she made him take a seat on the sofa.

"I want you to just relax while I prepare the medicine."

"I feel as if that's all I've been doing for the last few hours," he told her, leaning back against the sofa cushions.

"Then you shouldn't have any trouble taking it easy for a little while longer," she said with a lightness she didn't feel.

"Okay, but first I want to check my phone messages."

"No problem." She nodded. "It'll take about twenty minutes to prepare the medication."

She watched him walk into the bedroom. He was still the same sexy, powerfully attractive man that had come into her shop two weeks ago. But so much had changed. She knew him better now, even better than she had four years ago, knew his fears and his pain and she had come to see how sensitive and loving he was. He was more than just a sexy man, or a *hunk* as Phyllis had called him. Oh, he was more than that. He was the man she loved. She wished she could tell him how she felt, but somehow now didn't seem to be the time.

When she thought of the nightmare days ahead, she felt a dull numbness, a disbelief that slowed the truth from registering in her brain. She had heard people talk about how they had coped with the terminal illness of a loved one, how they had blocked the pain by focusing only on the moment, but she had never understood it. Not until now, as she accepted it and was grateful for its presence. She was afraid that numbness was the only thing that could keep her sane in the days ahead. She had to be strong. She couldn't afford to be weak or frightened. Jeff was depending on her.

She straightened her shoulders and walked into the kitchen. She laid the items she needed on the counter and began meticulously preparing the herbal mixture. When she was done, she placed the ingredients into a teakettle to brew. While she waited, she walked to the window and stared out at the street below.

The world looked the same. It was the same for millions of people. Yet, for her and Jeff everything had changed— their world had not just been turned upside down—it had been shattered, and nothing was going to change that.

She shivered, stepping away from the window and feeling that same ominous feeling that had been lingering with her all day. She wondered if anyone or anything could stop this madman...the man who had... She swallowed, blinking back tears. What kind of human being could kill in such a cold-blooded way? But he wasn't human, he was an animal.

She turned around, trying to dispel her thoughts, and

saw Jeff standing in the doorway. He wore a navy robe, tied at the waist and open to reveal the smooth dark skin of his chest. The sight of him made her breath catch in her throat, and even in her sorrow, made a small flutter begin in the pit of her stomach. She walked to him and silently held out her arms, letting them slide around his slender waist as she cradled her head against his chest. For a moment she closed her eyes savoring the feel of his hard, muscled body against hers.

"Your medication is ready," she whispered. "Why don't you sit down while I get it."

A moment later she was back. She stood watching as he drank the herbal brew. Her eyes followed his every movement as he lifted the glass to his lips. He made a slight grimace then downed the contents and handed her the glass.

Then she drew a small bottle out of her pocket, shook out one white pill and handed it to him.

He frowned up at her. "What's this?"

"It's a sedative," she explained. "Dr. Hillman wants you to take it...so you can rest...and I agree with him," she added hurriedly. "It won't interfere with the medication. Okay?"

He nodded. The fact that he didn't put up a fuss was a testimonial to just how tired he was.

After he had taken the pill, they snuggled on the living room sofa. She held him, letting her hands move down his arms, murmuring soft words to him and holding him tight so that she could hear his breathing and his heartbeat.

"We need to talk about what happened," he began.

Her hand stilled. Talking would make it real. "We'll talk later...you need to rest now."

Jeff closed his eyes, feeling the effects of the sedative beginning to dull the edge of reality. He reached for Raven's hand and felt her warm fingers clutch his tightly.

"Don't leave me," he whispered.

"Never," she vowed softly.

He pulled her up from the couch and with his arms around her, moved with her toward the bedroom. He slid into bed beside her, drawing her to him and holding her close.

Soon the security of his arms, the quiet of the apartment, took its toll and she felt her eyes growing weary. And even though she woke several times during the night, Jeff was always there, quick to reach for her with arms that were solid and comforting.

Oh, how could she face the future without him?

JEFF WASN'T SURE how long he slept, but when he woke, it was morning. Bright light streamed through the curtains and settled across his face.

A faint sound made him look in the direction of the bathroom, and he saw Raven standing in the doorway wearing one of his shirts.

"I'm sorry," she said, her voice gentle and concerned. "I didn't mean to wake you." She walked over to the bed, switched on the lamp on the nightstand next to the bed.

"That's all right," he said, sitting up and feeling the pull of stiff muscles in his neck. His head ached a bit and he felt warm. "How...how long did I sleep?"

"About four hours," she said, taking a seat on the bed. "How do you feel?"

He saw the fear in her eyes, and knew what she was really asking. How *did* he feel? Like he was hung over, but it could be the result of lack of sleep and stress, not early symptoms of the virus. "Fine," he lied.

He didn't know if she believed him or not, but she didn't question him.

"Nick called," she said, changing the subject. "He'll be here in about an hour. Do you feel up to talking to him?"

"Sure." He nodded. Then regretted the head movement. "But first I think I'd like to take a shower."

She nodded. "I'll make breakfast."

"I don't want anything," he said, feeling his stomach churn slightly. "I'm not hungry."

"You've got to eat something. You have to keep your strength up." She smiled at him and her voice was quiet and persuasive.

He returned the smile, feeling the warm concern that radiated from her, feeling a deep, almost spiritual connection to her.

"All right," he relented. "But just tea and a piece of dry toast."

Later they sat at the small wooden table in the dining room, eating. The food helped more than he had expected and he had to admit he felt better. Raven kept up a constant stream of chatter, talking about everything but what they should be talking about—the virus, their relationship...and what to do next.

Jeff's eyes roamed over her lovely face and he saw the fear in her eyes. He reached for her hand across the table, holding it. He was about to tell her not to worry but before he could say anything, the doorbell rang.

"That's probably Nick," she said, standing. "Finish your coffee, I'll let him in."

A moment later Jeff stepped into the living room. Nick's blue eyes watched him and he saw sympathy there.

"How are you feeling?" the young cop asked.

"I'm fine," Jeff said, taking the seat next to Raven on the sofa.

"I just have a few questions for you about what happened last night."

He felt Raven stiffen beside him. He turned and saw the anguish in her eyes. He reached for her hand, holding it as Nick began to speak.

"Do you know if the man that attacked you was Calvin Parker?"

Jeff shrugged. "It could have been, but I'm not sure. The room was dark and he wore a ski mask."

"What about clothes? Do you remember what the guy was wearing?"

Jeff thought for a moment. "I'm not sure if he was wearing a jacket or shirt, whatever it was, it was made out of a slick kind of material," he answered. "So were his pants. I remember the fabric because it made holding on to him harder."

"That's good," Nick said excitedly. "One of Parker's neighbors reported seeing a man fitting Parker's description run from the apartment building about the time of your attack. She remembers because she was out walking her dog. She thought it was Parker because she's seen him jog about that time of night. The man she saw was also wearing a navy jogging suit."

He glanced over at Raven. "What about you? Now that you've had time to sleep on it, do you remember anything else?"

She shook her head. "No. I'm sorry."

"That's okay," he said, closing his notepad. "I think I have enough to call Parker in for questioning." At Jeff and Raven's look of surprise, he added, "Forensics checked the apartment door and there was no sign of forced entry, except, of course, yours. So the guy that attacked you..." Nick's voice trailed off when he saw the pain reflected in both their eyes.

"It's all right," Raven whispered, taking a deep breath. "Go on...I'm all right."

He cleared his throat. "I was just going to say the intruder didn't break into the apartment. Forensics was also able to lift a clear set of prints from the front door, the door facing, and the sofa lamp. They belong to Calvin Parker."

Raven frowned. "It's his apartment. I'd have thought it strange if his prints weren't there."

"Yeah, but I also learned that Calvin Parker took out a half-million-dollar life insurance policy on his wife three months ago. In my book, that's a powerful motive for murder.

"When you couple that with the vials you and Jeff found in his apartment...well, it looks like we may have found our killer."

Jeff nodded. It sounded like Nick had a pretty strong case against Parker. "Have you questioned him yet?" he asked.

Nick shook his head. "We haven't been able to locate him."

"You think he's fled the jurisdiction?"

"I don't think so," Nick said, standing. "I've got men covering the airport, train station and bus terminals, and no one has spotted him. He's around here somewhere. It's just a matter of time before we locate him."

"When you do," Jeff said, "call me. I'd like to be in on the questioning." At the puzzled look Nick threw him, he added, "I'd like to ask him about the vials we found at his apartment. We could develop a treatment, possibly even a cure, a lot quicker if Parker would cooperate and tell us where and how he got the virus. Without his help, it may take some time."

"Sure thing." Nick clapped him on the back.

"Are you going to stop investigating Daniels now that you have evidence implicating Parker in the murders?" Raven asked.

Nick frowned. "I don't see how I can justify continuing to investigate him. I think a good defense attorney could use that against us."

"You're right." She nodded. "It's just that if there's any possibility that you could be wrong about Parker..." Her chin quivered and she blinked back tears.

Jeff's response was quick. He pulled her back into his arms, cradling her head against his chest and stroking her back.

Nick cleared his throat. "I'll let myself out."

After Nick left, they sat on the couch, talking.

"Do you really think Parker is the killer?" she asked.

Jeff sighed, leaning his head back against the sofa. "I don't know. Nick seems to thinks so, and he makes a persuasive case for his guilt."

"I know." She twisted in his arms, looking up at him. "It's just that he's so anxious to make an arrest. I don't want him going off half-cocked."

Jeff shook his head. "He's ambitious, but he's a good cop. He seems to have a strong case against Parker." He glanced at his watch. "Listen, we'd better get going."

She looked up at him, surprised. "Where are we going?"

"I'm going to the hospital. You're going to work."

"Jeff, I don't think that's a good idea," she said, following him into the bedroom.

He frowned. "Why not?"

She made a flip-flop with her hand.

He took her by the shoulders and stared into her troubled eyes. "Whatever's going to happen will happen whether I'm here or at the hospital. I think it would be a lot healthier for both of us if we kept busy, and not sit around here letting our imaginations run wild."

For a moment he thought she was going to argue with him then she issued a sigh and nodded. "You'll call me if you need anything?"

"Of course, but nothing's going to happen."

"When she still didn't say anything he gave her a playful shake. "It's going to be all right," he murmured. "We've got the virus. The CDC should be able to give us some answers before too long. I've started your treatment." He smiled at her. "I'm going to be fine."

He kept up a steady stream of conversation until he dropped her at Nature's Cure. The moment she was out of the car, he leaned his head against the headrest, and closed his eyes.

It was funny, he thought, even though he dealt with life-and-death issues every day, he'd never really given any thought to his own mortality. He guessed, like everyone else, he'd always thought he would have plenty of time.

He slammed his palm against the steering wheel. It wasn't fair. He and Raven had finally put the past behind them and now this had happened. For a moment he couldn't see beyond his own misery. Then he gave himself a mental shake. It was time to take some of his own advice. He was going to think positive. He put the car in gear and headed for the hospital.

When he arrived at the hospital, he pulled into the parking lot adjacent to the emergency entrance to avoid any members of the press who might be camped out front.

Once inside, he headed straight for the research lab. He knew it was too soon to expect the results from the CDC, but he needed to talk to Shay. Then he'd check on his patients. As he stepped into the room, Shay looked up from the slide he was studying. He did a double take when he saw Jeff.

"What the hell are you doing here?"

"And hello to you, too," Jeff said, heading for the coffeemaker. He poured himself a cup and took a swallow. "How are Lauren and the others doing?"

"Jeff, I really don't think you should be here," Shay said, ignoring his question. "You ought to be in bed resting, conserving your strength."

"Don't *you* start on me."

Shay gave him a sour look. "Well, if you didn't listen to Raven then I guess you're not going to listen to me."

"That's perceptive of you," Jeff said with a grin. "Now, back to my question. How are Lauren and the others doing?"

Shay hesitated, then shook his head. "I wish I could tell you better, but they're not. And there was another patient admitted last night. A guy by the name of George Whitman. He's in bad shape."

The news depressed him. Jeff closed his eyes. He thought about going to Brockman and asking him to reconsider his decision to not use Raven's treatment, but knew it was futile.

"You also got another stack of documents from the CDC. They're in your office."

"Thanks. I'm going to make a round," he said, striding out of the room. His first stop was at the cubicle of George Whitman. According to the medical chart, he was a fifty-six-year-old city worker. Like Eleanor and David Foster, he'd had the virus injected directly into his system. His condition was listed as critical. Apparently he'd suffered a heart attack as a result of the mugging. Jeff rubbed his temple. He felt utterly frustrated and completely helpless.

He sighed, then moved on to Lauren's cubicle. Her condition was deteriorating. It was the same with Susan Kelly and David Foster. He then spent some time with Greg Connor and David Foster's wife. He wished he could give them some good news but he had to prepare them for the worst. That only depressed him further.

He spent the rest of the day cloistered in his office, updating patient files. He didn't know what the future held for him but thought it best that he put his files in order in the event someone had to take over his workload. Once that was done, he began working his way through the remaining stacks of Dr. Ross's writing. The man had been a prolific writer, chronicling virtually every aspect of his medical research. He was midway through the studies when Shay stuck his head in the doorway. He looked grim.

"We got the test results on the vials from the CDC," Shay said, moving into the room. The look he threw Jeff could only be described as one of pity.

Jeff's heart began to slam against his chest. It should have taken days, maybe even weeks for them to analyze the contents of the vials. He closed his eyes. If they had an answer now, it couldn't be good.

RAVEN STARED at the phone on her desk, debating whether she should call Jeff at the hospital. She tapped one manicured nail on the receiver. He's all right, she told herself. Shay or Dr. Hillman would have called her if he wasn't.

She was being an alarmist. He was fine. Besides, it was too soon for him to be exhibiting any symptoms. Jeff was right. Sitting here thinking the worst was getting her nowhere. She needed something to do to take her mind off Jeff and the disease.

Now was probably a good time to take inventory of her stock. She usually dreaded it, but today she threw herself into the job. But before too long she found herself going through her herb books double-checking, then triple-checking the herbal formula. She couldn't afford to make a mistake. Jeff's life depended on it. On paper, it seemed to work, but what if she was wrong? No, she thought, she wouldn't think that way. But it was hard.

If only she hadn't told Jeff about her meeting with Grace Wells. If only they hadn't gone to Calvin Parker's apartment. If she could turn back the hands of time, do it all over again, she'd do things differently. For one thing, she would have worked harder on her relationship with Jeff, and not let stubbornness and pride stand in the way. She'd always accused him of not being willing to listen to her views on alternative medicine. But, she'd done nothing to help him bridge the gap.

Oh God, she'd been such a fool.

"Can I come in?" a voice said, breaking into her troubled thoughts.

She looked up to see Nick Valentine standing in the doorway.

"Sure," she said, waving him in.

Nick's eyes swept the room before he plopped down on the sofa. "I thought I'd find Jeff here," he said.

She shook her head. "He's at the hospital."

One sandy eyebrow rose. "Shouldn't he be taking it easy?"

She raised one shoulder. "Probably, but he needs something to do. Something to take his mind off…"

Nick cleared his throat. "How long before you know—"

If he's infected? she completed the question in her mind. "Probably within the next twenty-four hours."

There was a strained silence.

She gave him a tight little smile. "What did you want to talk to Jeff about?"

"I just wanted him to know we put out an APB on Calvin Parker, but we haven't located him yet. But when we do, I'm going to take a great deal of pleasure in bringing him in."

"Well, you can't arrest him soon enough for me, but remember, don't spook him. Jeff needs to talk to him, find out as much as we can about this virus. And he's the only man who can give us that information."

Nick frowned. "We'll do what we can—"

"Detective Valentine," Phyllis interrupted from the doorway. "There's a call for you."

"You can take it here," Raven said, pointing to the phone on her desk.

She listened as he talked to the person at the end of the line. He didn't say much, just nodded. Finally, he said, "Good work. Listen, don't approach him...just watch him until I get there. I'm on my way." He hung up and turned to Raven. "Parker was spotted about three minutes ago going into his office building," Nick said. He was already moving toward the doorway.

"Wait, aren't you going to call Jeff?"

He looked hurriedly at his watch, then shook his head. "There's no time."

"Then I'm going with you."

He turned. "Now look—"

"You going to waste time arguing with me or go after Parker?"

Nick issued a deep sigh, knowing this was one battle he was not going to win. "Okay, let's go."

CALVIN PARKER WAS bent over his desk, haphazardly dumping papers into an opened briefcase, and didn't see them when they entered the office.

"Going somewhere?" Nick asked, moving into the room.

Parker's head snapped up. He looked terrible, Raven thought. His eyes were bloodshot, his clothes wrinkled as if he'd slept in them. He looked old and tired and scared.

Parker's mouth curved into the semblance of a smile. "I thought I'd get away for a few days. Eleanor's death affected me more than I thought."

Nick shook his head. "I'm afraid you're going to have to cancel your trip. I'd like for you to come down to headquarters. I want to talk to you about some vials we found at your apartment."

Parker's eyes grew as round as saucers. "Vials? Ah...I don't know what you're talking about."

"Of course not," Nick said, his voice laced with sarcasm. "So I guess you shouldn't have any problems coming down to headquarters to answer some questions."

Parker's eyes darted about the room as if he were looking for a way to escape. "Sure, just give me a few minutes to finish up here. Why don't you and Ms. Delaney wait for me in the conference room."

"This is fine," Nick said, settling into the chair in front of Parker's desk. Raven maintained her position off to the side. "We don't mind waiting here for you."

Parker was squirming now, fear flashing in his eyes. "I don't know why you keep hassling me."

"Give me a break," Nick said firmly. "Your protestation of innocence is getting a little tiresome. From where I sit, things don't look so good for you."

"I haven't done anything wrong. I swear."

"Things will go easier for you if you come clean." Nick gentled his voice. "Why don't you just get it off your chest? Maybe it's not your fault, what you've done. There are doctors who can help you."

Parker wasn't listening. "You're not going to pin this on me," he whispered in a hopeless monotone. "I didn't do anything and I'm not going to say I did."

"The evidence seems to suggest otherwise."

"Then you're reading it wrong," Parker said, picking up a small paperweight.

"What about that hefty life insurance policy you took out on Eleanor's life? And let's not forget about your fancy apartment and that closet full of designer suits. Am I reading that wrong?"

Parker was sweating bullets now. "You don't understand. I thought about it, but I—" Suddenly, he clammed up.

Raven stood up straighter. Had he been about to confess? Apparently Nick thought so because he pounced on his words. "What did you think about?"

Parker shook his head. "Nothing."

"Come on, Calvin. Talk to me. Get it off your chest."

Raven sensed Nick was running out of patience, and was pushing hard, maybe too hard.

Parker shook his head again, with the stubborn tearful defiance of a child. "But I didn't—"

"Okay, Parker," he said, standing. "That's the way you want to play it? Fine by me. Let's go—"

"No," he said, backing away. "Stay away from me."

Suddenly, Parker threw the paperweight he was holding at Nick's face, and bolted for the door.

Nick ducked. The paperweight nicked his cheek. Raven gasped at the trickle of blood that was running down his face, but Nick barely noticed. He was on his feet, running after Parker. Raven took off after him.

Parker's office opened onto a long, narrow corridor. Parker was running fast but sloppily, caroming off the walls like a pinball. Chuffs of breaths and piggish grunts rose over his slapping footsteps.

Raven caught a glimpse of Nick's face as he rounded the corner and ran down another corridor. His face was flushed, his eyes gleaming, and his hair bouncing everywhere. She flashed on the thought that this was a rush for him.

Suddenly the hallway veered to the left. Nick skidded and banged his shoulder. He winced, then muttered an expletive, but kept on running. She rounded the corner after him and saw they were in the general office area now.

Parker was just ahead, running through the office area, zigzagging among the desks and the dazed secretaries who sat glued in their chairs. Raven was right behind them. Startled faces snapped past her. She bumped into a man in a business suit and saw paper fly through the air. She mumbled an apology then she was running past the man, ducking furniture. Somewhere a woman was screaming for someone to call the police.

Ahead, Nick was gaining on Parker. A few steps shy of the front door he grabbed for Parker; his hand caught the end of a flapping shirttail that tore free.

One of the double doors swung wide open. Parker ran down the front steps of the building then sprinted for the parking lot. Nick followed, shouting at him to stop. Raven was right on his heels.

Parker ran to a parked car, a blue Mercedes, tugged open the door, and jumped inside. Nick was running for the car when the engine started. Parker pulled away, and Nick staggered to a stop, clutching his stomach, and gulping air. Then he was on the move again, running for his unmarked Chevy. Raven pulled open the passenger door and jumped inside as Nick was putting the keys in the ignition.

A moment later the car screamed away from the curb, straightened out and arrowed at the fleeing Mercedes. Nick grabbed a portable siren and attached it to the hood of the car. Parker took a sharp left turn down a side street. Nick swore then Raven felt herself thrown against the seat as Nick suddenly gunned the engine and made a sharp left turn. He jammed his foot on the accelerator. The passenger seat bucked as the Chevy shot forward. They were just inches away. Nick arrowed the Chevy at Parker's car, rammed his rear bumper with a crunch of bucking metal, and bulldozed him into a utility pole.

The impact tossed Raven forward then flung her backward against the headrest. Nick was already out the driver's door, gun in hand. She was fumbling with the door handle on the passenger side when a shot rang out.

She ducked down on the front seat while Nick took cover behind the driver's door of the Chevy. Nick returned the fire. She inched up and saw Parker leaning out the driver's side window, firing at Nick. She ducked down. Nick squeezed off a round that dimpled the Mercedes's door. Parker fired back. A bullet pinged off the Chevy's front bumper. Nick raised his head and fired another round. Raven huddled in her seat, her hands over her ears. The firing seemed to go on forever. Then suddenly it stopped.

She raised up and looked out the front window. She couldn't see Parker, couldn't determine his condition. Out of the corner of her eye, she saw Nick slowly stand. He emerged from behind the car door and slowly approached the Mercedes in a half-crouch position, gun drawn, ready to fire. At the passenger side of the car, he paused. She knew looking into the car would be the most dangerous moment. Parker could be lying in wait for Nick, poised to squeeze off a shot at close range....

She held her breath as Nick raised his head fast over the door frame, then quickly turned his head away. He lowered the gun and stared at her. His face told her everything she needed to know. She shook her head, refusing to believe it could be true. She jumped out of the car and ran to the Mercedes and looked inside. Calvin Parker was slumped over the steering wheel, a trickle of blood ran out the side of his mouth, and his eyes stared straight ahead.

He was dead.

Not wounded. Not unconscious, but dead.

Raven closed her eyes. Calvin Parker was dead.

Her body shook. Nick had said he'd take him alive. They needed him alive. And now he was dead.

A swell of nausea rose inside her. She turned away from the car, wrapped her arms tightly around her middle, as first one tear then another fell.

A moment later she felt Nick's hand on her shoulder. She turned and looked up at him. His face was etched in pain. "I tried to take him alive," he said, "but he tried to get away, started shooting."

"I know." Raven wiped her face with the back of her hand. "I know." She drew a shallow breath, then a deeper one.

"Damn it, I didn't mean to kill him. He shouldn't have run. Why did he run?"

She couldn't answer that. "I just wish...I wish..." The words stuck in her throat. She couldn't say it because she didn't want to think what the future held.

Nick drew a deep breath then nodded. "Thank God, you and Jeff found those vials. Everything's going to be all right."

Yes, she thought. Thank God for the vials.

WATER!

It had been plain tap water in the vials!

Raven watched Jeff's lips move, but she didn't hear his words. It was as if her mind had absorbed one shock too many and had shut down.

Her breathing became strained and she felt light-headed. She reached out and gripped the side of the sofa, steadying herself. It had never occurred to her that the vials could be anything other than what they appeared to be. She'd just assumed that because they'd found the vials hidden in a tissue box in Calvin Parker's wastebasket they contained the deadly virus.

"Could they be mistaken?" She knew she was grasping at straws.

Jeff shook his head. "There's no mistake. Just to be

sure, they ran the test three times on each vial, and every time it came out the same. It's just plain tap water.''

"It doesn't make sense. Why did Parker hide the vials if they only contained water? And why did he run?''

She watched as Jeff raked his hand over his hair. "I don't know. I'm afraid without Parker there are a lot of questions we aren't going to get answers to. If only Nick hadn't killed him. Maybe we could have gotten him to talk, tell us where or how he got his hands on this virus.'' He paused, looked up at the ceiling, his throat working. "Why couldn't Nick have taken him alive?''

She'd wondered that, too. And it always came back to the same thing—ambition. Nick had been so anxious to make an arrest, to be the hero, he hadn't bothered to call for backup. Now his ambition may have sealed Jeff's and the others' fate.

She felt cold. She didn't know what to do with her hands. "What happens now?''

Even as she asked the question, she knew the horror that lay ahead. Jeff knew it, too. He could barely look at her. His gaze shifted from her neck to her forehead. "We wait.'' His voice was strained and hoarse, as if the words themselves were strangling him. "We'll know in the next eighteen hours.''

Eighteen hours! How do you cram a lifetime of living into such a short time? she wondered. She walked over to him and wrapped her arms around him, savoring the feel of his hard, muscled body against hers.

"Hold me,'' she whispered. She felt his arms tighten around her, pulling her close. She closed her eyes, wishing they could remain this way forever, locked in each other's arms.

"Maybe I should double-check the formula,'' she said, pulling out of his arms.

"Don't. You've done all you can. Now—'' His voice broke. "Now we wait.''

"But there must be something else we can do." Her voice had a hollow ring even to her own ears.

"There is." He kissed her lips tenderly. "We think positive."

"I know," she said. "I want to be strong. I want to think positive, but I'm afraid."

"Don't, Ray..." he breathed, his hands moving, slowly, sensuously, down her back, over her hips. "Don't be afraid." He tilted her chin so that their eyes locked and held. "Nothing's ever going to take me away from you...nothing."

Then he covered her mouth with his in a mind-shattering kiss. The spark between them was hot and quick, running like a jolt of electricity through Raven. He wanted to make love to her. She could see it in his eyes, feel it in his touch, his kiss. He kissed her again and again, with an urgency...with all the intensity that was his.

"Raven..." he whispered against her mouth. "I need you.... I need you." His hands were warm and insistent, his mouth sweet and persuasive.

She didn't answer, but looked up into his eyes before moving with him toward the bedroom.

There was an intensity, a desperation in both of them that had not been there the last time...not even the first time they'd made love. All the events of the past few days, their fear of what was to come seemed to have them desperately in need. Raven was acutely aware of Jeff's vulnerability and the bittersweet way he held and kissed her, as if he thought this might be the last time they'd be together.

His kisses, hot and searching, left her breathless and aching for more. And his hands...the slow, seductive way they moved and stroked, the way he methodically removed her clothes, made her tremble.

"You've taught me so much, Raven," he whispered. "Do you know that?" His voice became muffled as his mouth touched the sensitive area just below her ear, as he nibbled and moved downward to the delicate skin of her shoulder. "You've taught me to dream again...to feel again. My life has been so empty without you."

Raven could no longer resist his mouth, pulling his head down so that she could taste him, and breathe in the seductive male scent of him. She shivered, tilting her head back, eyes closed, as she clung to his hard, muscled shoulders. He said she'd taught him to dream again, well, he'd taught her to dream again, too. She hadn't realized it, but without him, she'd only been half-alive. Now she was complete. It was like the sun breaking through the clouds.

There was no patience in either of them for waiting, no preliminaries as they fell onto the bed and he quickly took her with a soft impatiently muttered groan.

Raven saw his wistful smile and felt her heart melting. His look, his touch, made her crazy and as she moved beneath him, she felt herself growing hotter and more restless. She could not keep her hands from touching his spine, where the muscles moved so seductively beneath her fingers. His chest, so beautifully sculpted and hard as it moved downward, skimmed tantalizingly against the peaks of her breasts, then up again.

Jeff felt her response, felt the heat and pulled his hands down beneath her hips, holding her hard and tight, the feel of her making his muscles tremble with the excitement of loving her. Her soft groans and quiet breathy little gasps made him crazy, and even though he wanted to take it slow, wanted to remember every touch, every vision of her, he could feel the heat spiraling upward as both of them moved quickly out of control and past the slow heat of passion.

"Oh, Jeff," she gasped, moving almost frantically, and grasping his shoulders. "Oh..."

"Yes, sweetheart," he urged, holding her tight and feeling her own heat overtaking his body. "Let it go, sweetheart...just...let it go..." His last words were lost in a husky groan of pleasure, lost in the heat and passion that overtook both of them and left them trembling and clinging almost desperately to one another.

Later, they lay for long, silent moments in each other's arms. Jeff let his fingers move slowly back and forth along her neck, moving upward to her hair then back down to her shoulder.

Raven felt the cool air upon her heated skin, and she felt herself growing drowsy. And yet…deep inside her was this desperate need to hold on to him, just for another moment.

She was afraid of what tomorrow would bring. It ate at her, tore at her deep into her very soul, and it caused her to tremble.

"It's going to be all right," he whispered. He wrapped his arms around her until the shivers stopped.

How she wanted to believe him, needed to believe him, but time had run out for them. There was only one thing left to do—pray that her herbal treatment worked.

Chapter Thirteen

The first symptom Jeff noticed was a sudden rash that appeared on his chest. As he examined it, the rash seemed to spread quickly from his chest to his abdomen. With his index fingers, he spread the skin at the site of the blotches to see if it would blanch with pressure. Not only did it not blanch, the pressure deepened the color.

Then, as quickly as the skin eruption appeared, it began to itch. Although at first Jeff tried to ignore the sensation, it increased in intensity to the point where he had to scratch. An application of the topical antibiotic hydrocortisone relieved the itch...but then came the fever.

It started to rise slowly, but once it got past a hundred degrees, it shot up. Soon Jeff's forehead was awash with perspiration.

When he looked at himself in the bathroom mirror and saw his face flushed and eyes sunken, he was horrified. A few minutes later he began to experience difficulty breathing. Even with deep breaths, he was gasping for air.

Then his head began to pound like a drum with each beat of his heart. The seriousness of his condition was obvious. Jeff knew the virus was spreading rapidly throughout his body, destroying his immune system and other vital organs. Somehow he'd skipped the initial stage and gone directly to the final stage of the disease in a matter of hours. He was going to die!

Jeff's eyes flew open and he jolted upright. For a moment he didn't know where he was. He felt disoriented and confused. His eyes dropped to his abdomen to look at his rash, but it had disappeared. Only then did Jeff realize that he'd been dreaming. He drew a deep breath, a nightmare would be a more apt description.

He looked at Raven who was sleeping peacefully next to him. Even though the air conditioner was going full blast, he felt hot. He looked down at his pillow and bedsheet; they were drenched in sweat. He threw back the sheet and swung his legs over the side of the bed. He felt a clanging noise inside his head, as if someone was beating him over the head with a sledgehammer.

When he stood his legs felt rubbery, and he swayed slightly. He was glad Raven was asleep and didn't see him like this. No doubt it would frighten her. It frightened him.

He walked gingerly into the bathroom and closed the door. The cool tiles felt good on his feet. He leaned on the sink and recoiled at the remembrance of the nightmare. It had been so frighteningly real. He even looked at his chest and abdomen again to make sure he didn't have a rash. Thankfully, he didn't. But he definitely had a headache, which he prayed was due to stress and sleep deprivation, and not the virus.

Looking into the mirror, he saw that his eyes were red, and he was in dire need of a shave and shower.

He stepped into the shower stall and let the hot steaming water pour over him and tried not to think about the next twelve hours, but it was impossible. He had so much to live for, he loved Raven and wanted to spend his life with her, have children with her, grow old with her.

Suddenly it was all too much for him. His shoulders slumped and he fell back against the shower stall, eyes closed; he let the pain and fear he'd held at bay for the last twenty-four hours wash over him. He didn't know how long he stood there before he was able to pull himself together.

By the time he'd showered and shaved, he felt a world of difference from when he'd awakened, but he did not feel up to par. He still had a headache and the muscles of his legs were sore. So was his lower back. He couldn't help but worry that he was exhibiting symptoms of the disease. If he was coming down with the virus, he didn't want Raven to know, not yet anyway.

Jeff slipped on a robe and returned to the bedroom. He sat down on the edge of the bed and brushed a strand of hair from Raven's face, trying to store up a lifetime of memories in a few hours. The past day and a half shimmered in his memory like a dream, and last night had been wonderful. Except for a quick dinner and a couple of hours at the hospital, they'd spent the evening in this room, in this bed. The memory of exquisite lovemaking wove in and out of the dream like a shining thread of gold, but even more precious was the way Raven had shared herself. They talked for hours.

She talked about her childhood, growing up with an older brother, and what had made her go into herbal medicine. She told him about opening Nature's Cure, about her work and how much she loved it. They'd talked of everything and nothing, from their favorite movies and books to their preferred restaurants.

Never once had she pressed him to talk about the future. As a result, he'd found himself opening up to her, telling her things he had never told anyone—his dreams, his hopes, his fears. And all the time she'd listened and held his hand, wrapping her arms around him and resting her cheek against his chest while he spoke.

He couldn't remember ever feeling this connected to anyone in his life, or ever wanting anybody more. They'd made love countless times in the past couple of days, but as he watched her sleep he found that he wanted her even more than he had before they'd made love the first time.

He didn't want to look at his watch, because this was the day. He swallowed. By tonight the symptoms would...

He brushed the thought aside and thought of Raven. She was his rock, his beacon, his love. For a moment he permitted himself to fantasize about a life with her—waking up every morning next to her, coming home to her every night, making love. He couldn't help but hope that maybe, just maybe, he would beat the odds.

"Hi, there," he heard her say, her voice low and incredibly sexy. Raising up on one elbow, she ran her hand down his chest where his robe parted.

"Don't tempt me," he teased, smiling down at her.

She frowned. "You're going to the hospital?"

"Yes," he whispered against her mouth. Then he kissed away her frown.

"Are you feeling okay?" she asked, running her hand over his face and down his shoulder.

He pulled back, not wanting her to know that he wasn't feeling well. "I'm fine," he said, then he leaned over to brush another kiss across her lips. Easing himself off the bed, he stood up and stretched, enjoying the way she looked at him. Grinning at her again, he said, "Come on, you've got to get up and feed me."

She shook her head. "I'm going to shower, while you make breakfast." With a jaunty little smile, she slipped out of the bed and disappeared into the bathroom, and he stood staring after her delectable body.

His body had hardened instantly. An image of making love to her in the shower flashed through his brain. He reminded himself that he needed to concentrate on what he had to do today, not lovemaking. He frowned when he thought of the workday ahead. In addition to checking on Lauren and the others, he still had a few patient records to write notes on, and a stack of Dr. Ross's files to go through. He wanted to know he had done everything he could for his patients and to identify the virus.

He quickly dressed and was making breakfast when Raven walked into the kitchen. He felt her come up behind him, inhaled the intoxicating smell of her perfume mixed with her own sweet womanly scent as she pressed against his back.

"Did you remember to take your medicine?" she asked. She tried to make her voice sound light, but he heard the undercurrent of fear.

"Yes, I did." He turned and slid his arms around her and smiled down at her. "I don't think I've told you but I want you to know how proud I am of you for your work on this virus."

"Oh, Jeff." He felt her shiver in his arms, then burrow deeper. "I would feel better if I could be with you today."

"I'd like that, but we both know I wouldn't get any work done with you there." His arms tightened around her, then he stepped away. He gave her fanny a playful swat. "If we don't get some food soon, I can't be responsible for my actions."

"Then we'd better get this food on the table. I'm afraid to see what might happen."

He watched her as she went about setting the table. He loved this woman. He wanted to promise her the stars, the moon, that everything would be all right, that they would have a tomorrow. But in his heart, he feared they only had today.

RAVEN STOPPED PACING and looked out the window. She chewed her lower lip then glanced at her watch again. When she'd talked to Jeff at noon, he had said he was leaving the hospital by five-thirty so they could spend the evening together. It wasn't like him not to call if he was going to be late. Something was wrong. Maybe she should just drive over to the hospital.

No, she told herself, she wouldn't think that way. She had to think positive.

She went into her small kitchen and turned the burner beneath the teakettle. Using the few minutes it took to heat the water, she closed the greenhouse window over the kitchen sink against the warm sunny air and watered the collection of herbs growing in ceramic pots.

The teapot whistled and the phone rang at the same time, jangling her nerves.

She snatched it up on the second ring. "Jeff?"

There was a pause. "No, it's Nick."

"Oh…how are you?" She couldn't keep the disappointment out of her voice.

"Raven, I hope I'm not calling at a bad time."

He sounded tired and a little down. Raven straightened. "No, I was just waiting for Jeff to get home from the hospital." She glanced at her watch. Six forty-five. Surely, Jeff was on his way.

"How is he?"

She swallowed a sudden lump in her throat. "I…I think he's showing signs of the virus."

There was a silence at the other end of the line.

"It's still early," Nick said finally. "Your treatment could still halt the disease. Maybe even cure it."

She closed her eyes. "I hope so. H-have you found anything new?"

For a moment Nick didn't say anything. Then he drew a deep breath. "Look, Raven, I don't want you to get your hopes up," he said gruffly, "but you may have been right about Mark Daniels."

Her heart began to beat double time. "But isn't the case closed? I thought Parker was the killer."

"I thought so, but Katherine Olsen paid me a visit today."

"Mark Daniels's girlfriend?"

"I guess you should say, his former girlfriend, and she's singing a different tune. Seems Daniels wasn't with her and her friends all those Monday nights after all."

"She could just be a woman scorned—out for revenge."

"She probably is, but she also brought in an interesting piece of information—a social security card belonging to Mark Daniels. However, the name on the card was

Daniel Martin and the social security number was different from Mark Daniels's. I've been working around the clock the last eight hours, and I hit pay dirt. It seems under the alias Daniel Martin, Daniels has worked in the medical field. Get this, his most recent stint was in a medical research lab as recently as a year ago.''

She tried to hang on to her excitement. ''Are you going to arrest him?''

''I wish I could, but the case is officially closed. I'm going to need hard evidence to take to the captain in order to get the case reopened. My gut tells me he's our man. I just can't prove it.''

She couldn't believe what she was hearing. ''Can't you at least call him in for questioning?''

''I could, but that would tip him off that we're on to him, and I don't want him fleeing the jurisdiction before we can build a case.''

''Nick, you've got to do something now to make him talk. Jeff doesn't have much time.''

''I know,'' he said, his voice laced with frustration, ''but I've got to be damn sure of the facts.''

''I know, but there's got to be something you can do?''

''I really don't think—'' He paused in midsentence.

''What? Did you think of something?''

''Yeah, I did.'' She could hear the excitement in his voice. ''I don't know if it will work,'' he said cautiously, ''but it's definitely worth a try. This is what I'd—'' He broke off and she heard the telltale squeak of a chair coming upright. ''Can you hold a minute?''

''Sure.''

She heard him muttering beneath his breath, as he talked to someone in the background. A moment later he came back on the line. ''Raven, I gotta go,'' he said hurriedly. ''Something's come up. But listen, I want you to meet me at Daniels's office in the Sears Tower at seven-thirty. I can't explain now, but be there.'' He hung up, breaking the connection before she could ask any questions.

She glanced at her watch. It was almost seven. If she was going to make it to the Sears Towers by seven-thirty, she'd have to leave now. She chewed her lower lip. She would have preferred to wait for Jeff, but there was no time. She scribbled a hasty note, recounting her conversation with Nick and asking him to meet them at the Sears Tower, then scurried out the door.

AT THE SAME TIME Raven was talking to Nick, Jeff was pacing the floor in his office waiting for the results of the second battery of tests he'd undergone that afternoon. He'd seen little point in all this testing, but Dr. Hillman had insisted, especially after he had told him about the symptoms he was experiencing.

He glanced at his watch. He'd tried calling Raven to tell her he was running late, but the line had been busy. It was just as well that he hadn't gotten through, he thought. No doubt she'd want to know what was keeping him, and he didn't know what to tell her.

He sighed and looked at the one remaining pile of Dr. Ross's reports he had to go through. He'd already spent several hours earlier that day going through his documents, and hadn't found anything that shed any light on the mysterious virus. Nor, for that matter, had any of the other numerous studies and reports by Dr. Ross that he'd perused over the last week and a half. He saw little point pursuing this line of inquiry further, but he had nothing better to do. He sighed again. It would at least be a more productive way to pass the time than brooding.

He crossed the room, plopped into the chair behind his desk, picked up another report and began reading. Once again he had to marvel at the detail and meticulous manner in which Dr. Ross had chronicled his work. He'd been a brilliant scientist and his death six months ago had been a loss to the medical community. Thankfully, his work would live on through his writings.

As Jeff read, he realized the documents he was now

looking at chronicled the doctor's work during the last three years of his life. Like a lot of scientists, Dr. Ross had been deeply interested in finding a cure for AIDS, and his writing reflected that interest. He'd done an amazing amount of research on the subject. It was fascinating reading.

Jeff skimmed several more reports. It seemed interest had progressed to the development of a theory regarding a cure for AIDS. Dr. Ross postulated that the disease could be cured by introducing another virus—a supervirus—into the infected person's system which would kill the AIDS. Jeff sat up straighter in his chair. The CDC, however, had refused to fund the project on the grounds that it was too dangerous. Their concern was that the supervirus was too unstable. That it wouldn't be able to distinguish between good cells and bad cells. It would attack various parts of the body indiscriminately, as well as destroy the immune system—

Jeff felt the hair on the back of his head bristle. Dr. Ross's supervirus sounded a lot like the virus they had been dealing with. He set the report aside and stood. He paced for a while, thinking. He crossed to the window and stared out at the street below without really seeing it. He had a terrible suspicion that Dr. Ross's virus and the one they were dealing with were one and the same.

He began to pace again. If that was the case, it would mean that Dr. Ross had gone ahead with his research, and after he died someone had gotten their hands on his papers and developed the virus. Assuming that had been the case, the person would have to have had access to a number of live viruses, not to mention, possess the expertise to develop Dr. Ross's supervirus. He chewed his lower lip. With the exception of a handful of scientists at the CDC such as Dr. Hillman, there were few people that possessed that kind of ability. And then there was the problem with timing. Dr. Ross had been dead for about six months. The virus had appeared two months ago. Could it have been developed that quickly?

Then an even more frightening thought occurred to him. What if the person hadn't stolen the doctor's papers, but the actual virus? Of course that presupposed that Dr. Ross had gone ahead and secretly developed it. It would have been totally irresponsible on his part to do such a thing, but he had been almost obsessed with finding a cure for AIDS. The more Jeff though about it, the more certain he became that that was exactly what had happened. It also meant Dr. Ross had probably left a paper trail. Given his propensity to meticulously chronicle his projects, he thought it was a sure bet.

He went back to his desk and began to quickly go through the remaining reports. After about twenty minutes of searching, he hit pay dirt. It wasn't much, just some preliminary notes on the research project, but it spurred him on. He was so engrossed in looking for more project information that he almost missed the dog-eared color photograph.

It was stuck to the back of one of the pages and appeared to have been taken a number of years ago. It showed a smiling Dr. Ross, and a very familiar looking man. Jeff sat for a moment, staring at the picture, stunned. Suddenly all the pieces clicked into place.

Jeff wasted no time. He snatched up the phone on his desk and was dialing the police when he heard the door open behind him. He glanced over his shoulder and saw Shay, followed by Dr. Hillman, barge into the room.

"I know who the killer is," he said hurriedly. "You're—"

"Jeff, put the phone down," Dr. Hillman ordered. "We have something to tell you."

He could hear the urgency in the other man's voice, and a sense of foreboding washed over him. He wanted to run away, to put his hands over his ears, anything to not hear Hillman's pronouncement.

But he did none of those things. Instead he lowered the phone back into the cradle and sat perfectly still, waiting for Dr. Hillman to tell him what he'd known since the moment he'd awakened that morning—that he had the virus.

Chapter Fourteen

Raven drove fast, making it into the Chicago Loop in record time, since the nighttime traffic was fairly light. The anxiety she had felt all day increased in direct portion to how close she got to the Sears Tower. By the time she parked her car across the street from the high-rise office building, her heart was pumping hard. She looked for Nick's unmarked Chevy, but didn't see it. She'd either gotten there before him, or he'd parked on one of the side streets. She chewed her lower lip trying to decide what to do. She glanced at her watch. It was seven-thirty.

Figuring that he was probably already inside, she locked the car and approached the tall, imposing building. As she reached the revolving door leading into the building lobby, a young couple exited, allowing Raven to slip inside.

It took a moment for the elevator to arrive. Leaning back against the wall, she forced herself to breathe deeply and let the silence of the building calm her nerves. By the time she finally stepped into the elevator, her heart had stopped its wild hammering. The doors slid closed. The elevator whined upward. She felt a strange sense of unreality as she watch the lights flash in succession: thirty, forty-five, fifty-five. Except for a faint hydraulic hum, the ride was silent.

On the sixty-third floor, the doors slid open.

Raven stepped out of the elevator and took a left, moving through a set of double doors leading into a suite of offices. The first thing she noticed was that, except for the emergency overhead lighting, the lights were off in this wing. She listened for the sound of voices or activity, but heard nothing.

"Nick?" she called.

There was no answer.

She proceeded down the deserted corridor, pausing when she came to a door labeled Conference Room. The door was closed, but there was a ribbon of light on the floor. Could Nick and Daniels be inside? she wondered. Nick had said he would meet her in Daniels's office, but maybe it was the conference room. She pushed open the door and peeked inside. The lights were on, but there was no sign of Nick or Mark Daniels.

Frowning, she closed the door, stepped back into the corridor, and continued down the narrow hall. The smell of coffee brewing drew her to the tiny kitchen area. Raven saw a fresh pot of coffee and a half-filled mug on the countertop. Well, someone was here. Nick was probably in Daniels's office.

She'd only gone a few steps when she thought she heard something.

Scrape.

She spun around quickly and peered down the corridor, straining to hear.

Scrape.

It took her a moment to realize that the sound was coming from the hallway on the other side of the corridor. It sounded like footsteps, quiet and quick, almost as if someone was walking on tiptoe. She stared wide-eyed into the dimly lit corridor before calling out, "Nick? Is that you?"

She was greeted with silence.

"Hello? Who's there?" she called again.

The footsteps hurried on, and then she heard a slight clanking sound like that of an elevator door closing, and then nothing. For a moment, all the horror stories of

women being assaulted in deserted offices flashed through
her mind. She gave herself a mental shake. She was being
a paranoid alarmist. "Don't be silly," she muttered to herself. "It's probably just somebody who works here, who's
anxious to get home." But, all the same, she quickly
walked the short distance to Mark Daniels's office. At the
door of the outer office, she drew a deep breath, then
knocked. There was no answer.

"Nick? Are you in there?"

Still no answer.

She turned the knob and stuck her head inside. The
lights were off, and there was no sign of the young detective or Mark Daniels. Nick must have gotten held up at
the police station. She sighed and leaned against the doorjamb, trying to decide if she should wait here for him or
go outside and wait for him in her car.

But as the minutes ticked by, her nervousness returned.
She'd wait for him outside.

She was about to leave when she thought she heard a
noise coming from Mark Daniels's office. She walked
across the room, pushed the door open a crack, paused and
peered inside.

"Mr. Daniels?" she called softly. "Nick?"

There was no answer.

She gave the door a little shove. Slowly it swung farther
open and she stepped inside. It took her eyes a moment to
adjust to the darkness and the sight that greeted her—the
toppled chair, the scattered papers. Clearly there had been
a struggle, she thought. Nick and Daniels must—

Suddenly her toe caught and she pitched forward into
the darkness. Her knees and outstretched hands slammed
into something on the carpeted floor. Something that cush-
ioned her fall. She groped blindly. One hand sank into
wetness and she recoiled. But even as she did, the realization hit her. There was blood on the floor, and she was
touching a body.

She fell back on her haunches as a wave of dizziness

swept over her. All her medical training and years of working around blood couldn't prevent this totally visceral response.

A groan shuddered the silence. The sound was like an alarm, screaming at her to move, to take action. She knelt next to the body.

"What happened?" she cried. "Where are you hurt?"

She found an arm, then ran her hands over the chest. A man's chest. Her fingers traced the outline of his face. "Nick?"

He turned his head slightly and his lips moved against her skin.

"Oh, God," she moaned. "Nick!"

"Listen." The word was little more than a whisper. "Not much time..." He coughed, and she leaned closer. "Police..." There was another groan, then a word she couldn't understand.

"Don't try to talk," she ordered gently. "Just lie still. I'll go for help."

He grasped her arm, clutching the sleeve of her sweater as she tried to rise. "No," he whispered. "I have to..." He coughed and sputtered as he tried to sit up, but his efforts proved futile, and he fell back, gasping in pain.

"You're going to be all right. But I've got to call for help," she explained to him as gently as one would reassure a frightened child.

His right hand slowly slid down her arm and groped for her trembling hand. Finding it, he squeezed with strength born of desperation. "No," he cried. She sensed he was staring straight ahead. "Too late," he whimpered, his voice fading. "You got..."

His body shuddered. Then he went still. His head rolled to the side, and the hand that had clutched her hand fell to the floor.

"Nick!" Raven cried, shaking his shoulder. He didn't respond. He couldn't respond. He was dead.

Her hand flew to her mouth as realization dawned. Nick

had confronted Mark Daniels, and Daniels had killed him! Her eyes darted frantically about the room. He could still be in the building. Maybe even in the vicinity. *Get out of there!* an inner voice screamed, but it was already too late. As if in slow motion, Raven saw the door explode inward, and a man charge toward her.

JEFF READ RAVEN'S note again. Moments later he was in his car headed for the Sears Tower. The expression on his face was grim. He pressed on the accelerator, ignoring red lights and speed limits, his eyes trained on the highway. He'd called the police and passed on the information from his car phone, but he was unwilling to entrust her safety solely to them. He had to get to the Sears Tower as quickly as possible. He just prayed he wasn't too late.

A SCREAM DIED in her throat. "My God, Nick, I thought you were dead," Raven said, slowly getting to her feet and walking toward him.

Nick Valentine stood in the doorway, not saying anything, taking in the scene before him.

"Am I glad to see—" she paused in midsentence, frowned and looked back at the body lying on the floor. If the man wasn't Nick then who was it? She leaned over and flipped on the desk lamp. It was Mark Daniels. She quickly turned her head away from the ghastly sight. It took a moment for her to compose herself, and then she voiced the question that tickled at her subconscious.

"If Mark Daniels is dead, then—" she began.

"—he couldn't be the killer," Nick finished for her.

Her eyes flew to his face. He hadn't moved from the doorway. He just stood there, shoulders hunched under the sport jacket he wore, one hand shoved deep into his coat pocket.

"Well, aren't you going to do something? The killer could still be here."

He glanced briefly at the body then back at Raven. "I'm sure he is." His normally warm voice sounded odd.

"Shouldn't you call for backup or at least building security and have them secure the building?" she asked, confused by his demeanor.

An elusive emotion danced in his eyes. "That won't be necessary."

"But the killer will get away!"

Nick chuckled. "Yeah, he will, won't he?"

Raven looked at him as a cold chill worked its way up her spine. Nick pushed himself away from the doorway and took a step toward her. She took a step back, suddenly afraid.

"You know, you're a little too clever for your own good," Nick said, taking another step forward. As he spoke, he slowly drew his hand from his coat pocket. "It's just too bad no one ever told you that curiosity killed the cat."

Raven was about to ask him what on earth he was talking about, when she noticed the snub-nosed revolver held loosely in his hand. Staring into the black hole of the two-inch barrel, she tried to swallow, but her throat muscles wouldn't obey. The words that rattled through her mind like a runaway freight train could not fight their way through the dryness of her mouth.

"I see you've nothing to say." He shrugged. "It's just as well. I don't have time for a lot of chitchat. I have an appointment to keep for my alibi."

"You killed Daniels? But why?"

He smirked. "Oh, come on, Raven, you disappoint me. I killed him because he saw me outside Julie Hartman's apartment."

She frowned. "But the man he saw was—"

"—the killer," he finished for her. "That's right, I'm your man." He flickered a disparaging glance toward Mark Daniels's body. "I'm not sure if that little worm actually knew it was me he saw, but I'm not taking any chances."

Stall. *Keep him talking,* an inner voice screamed. Jeff knew she was here. She hoped he was already on his way.

"But all those people? Why did you do it? They never did anything to you."

He shrugged. "It was like you and Jeff said. It was a smoke screen to divert attention from the four that I wanted to kill—Eleanor Parker, David Foster, George Whitman and Ned Rodgers." At the mention of the last name, he tilted his head and gave her a thoughtful look. "You didn't know about Ned Rodgers because I just infected him. And now my work is done." He smiled then. "You know I was really impressed with your and Jeff's analysis of this case. Too bad you won't live long enough for anyone to know how smart you are."

Raven hoped she didn't look as frightened as his words made her feel. "But what did they do to you?"

He shook his head. "Not me...my father. Did you know he was a Chicago cop? He was a great guy...well-liked, good reputation. He was in line for lieutenant and he would've made it too—if they hadn't taken it all away from him."

She sensed this was an emotional subject for him. If she could keep him talking maybe she could get closer to the doorway, and when he wasn't looking make a run for it. "How did they hurt your father?" she asked.

"He was accused of being the bag man for a local mobster." His voice took on a bitter note. "On the dates the hood claimed Dad was collecting protection money for him, he was working. On the first Monday, he issued a verbal warning to Eleanor Parker for speeding. On the second Monday he was having lunch at David Foster's diner. On the third Monday, he talked to George Whitman about a domestic disturbance at his place. And on the fourth Monday, Ned Rodgers, the Internal Affairs investigator on the case, handed in his report, recommending Dad's dismissal from the department."

Raven swallowed. "So this has all been about revenge," she said quietly.

"Yeah." The smile that spread across Nick's face turned him from the person she'd once thought of as a friend into a cold-blooded killer. "Parker, Foster, Whitman—they all knew the truth, they could have given Dad an alibi, but they didn't give a damn about him. If they'd just cooperated or if Rodgers had done a decent job of investigating the allegations, Dad would be alive today. Eleanor Parker didn't even bother to keep her interview with Rodgers, and David Foster claimed he didn't remember what day it was that Dad had lunch at the diner. Whitman flat-out refused to even talk to him." Nick's voice had risen steadily as he talked. "Not one of them lifted a finger to help clear an innocent man. These good citizens didn't want to get involved, and their apathy cost a man his life."

Raven wondered if there might be more behind their reluctance to get involved than he had realized. It could have been fear of or actual threats from the mobster that had kept them silent, but she didn't think it was wise to contradict a man holding a gun on her. As Nick continued to rail against his victims, she took another step back.

"They took away everything he'd worked for—his job, his pension, his pride, his dignity, his good name. They destroyed him. He had nothing to live for and he took his own life." Nick's eyes hardened. "I was eleven when Dad died and I swore that I'd make them pay. It took years of planning, but I pulled it off."

She frowned. "But we looked for connections between the patients, and we never found any of this."

He nodded. "They never knew about each other. Only Internal Affairs knew the identity of the people who were questioned. Ned Rodgers was recently diagnosed as having Alzheimer's. So I wasn't worried about him. The man barely remembers his own name. And the others—" He gave a bitter little laugh. "It meant nothing to them. The only one of them who even remembered the incident was Foster.''

"What about you?'' she asked. "How come none of this was uncovered in your background check to get on the force?''

His mouth curved into the semblance of a grin. "Right after Dad died, we moved to Atlanta. A year later, my mother remarried, and her husband adopted me. As you know, adoption records are sealed. My birth certificate lists Barry Valentine, not John Kramer, as my father.''

"I see,'' she said slowly. "But how did you get your hands on a virus that no one has ever heard of?''

She watched as he almost preened with pride. "It took years and a lot of planning,'' he explained proudly. "After I graduated from the police academy in Atlanta, I moonlighted as a security guard. A lot of cops do, so no one thought anything of it. I kept my nose clean and eventually got on with a firm supplying security guards for the CDC.''

She stared at him in horror.

"That's right,'' he said smugly. "I got the virus from the CDC.''

"Bu-but how could they not recognize their own virus?''

He grinned. "Because Dr. Ross, its creator, didn't share his discovery with his superiors. Well, actually,'' he amended, "he couldn't. You see, he wasn't supposed to be doing research in that particular area.''

"Then how did you know about it?''

He smirked. "Dr. Ross was a brilliant man, but a social misfit. He had no family and no real close friends. Work was the only thing he knew and loved. Right after I came to the CDC, I thought I might be able to use him so I cultivated his friendship. Over the years, I gained his trust and confidence. I knew about his research project. I encouraged him to go ahead with it, so naturally I was the only person he told about his creation of a supervirus.''

His eyes hardened. "And I killed him right on the spot and made it look like a mugging."

Raven trembled violently at the cold, matter-of-fact manner in which he spoke of killing his friend.

"Then I destroyed the relevant portions of the doctor's research and stole the virus." He spared her a hard look then. "I know you are hoping for a cure, but as far as I know there isn't one."

That was too much. She grasped the corner of the desk to keep from falling, overcome by the horror of his words. "You killed eight innocent people."

"Only five." He shrugged. "I had to divert attention from myself. My only slipup was in choosing Lauren Connor. She was too closely connected to Eleanor Parker." He shook his head. "That was sloppy."

She had to agree with him. But for Lauren, Jeff may never have come to see her, and she wouldn't have gotten involved in the medical or criminal investigation. In fact, there may never have been a criminal investigation. "You spent your whole life in search of revenge. You're mad!"

He gave her an icy cold stare. "Like Dad used to say— I don't get mad, I get even."

He waved the barrel of the gun with a jerk. "Move away from the desk, and put your hands behind your back."

Hesitating only a moment, Raven did as she was told, moving so that she now stood with her back to the open doorway. Her voice was barely a squeak. "What are you going to do?" she asked as she watched him take several steps backward until his back was to the only window in the room.

Nick smiled and answered almost pleasantly. "Tie up loose ends. It seems you committed suicide. You were so distraught over Jeff's impending death, you convinced yourself that Mark Daniels was the killer. You somehow got his gun away from him, then killed him before taking your own life."

"No one is going to believe that!"

"I think they will. Everyone knows how much you love Jeff. You've also made it plain that you thought Mark Daniels was the killer. Once I remind Dr. Alexander of your outburst at the hospital about wanting to see the killer dead...well, I think he'll make a fine grand jury witness."

She moistened her lips. "W-was any of the stuff you said about Daniels true?"

He shook his head. "Not a word, but I knew it would get you here." With his free hand he proceeded to undo the lock on the window. She had no doubt what he planned to do.

"I know you find this hard to believe," he said conversationally, "but I'm really sorry about this. Under other circumstances I think the three of us could have become good friends but you and Jeff left me no other choice." He shook his head. "Too bad the two of you decided to burglarize Parker's apartment at the exact time I was there. I thought I could spare you but after you saw the hypodermic—"

She shook her head. "I didn't see any—"

"It was at the hospital," he explained. With his free hand he pulled a fountain pen out of his coat pocket. "It looks like a writing pen, doesn't it? But I assure you, it's quite unique. It allowed me to get close enough to my target so that I could..." He pressed the top of the pen and a small stream of clear liquid squirted out of the point. "I can either squirt it into a drink or inject it directly into a vein. You see, it was all quite simple. But unfortunately, you saw the pen at Parker's, then later at the hospital. I was afraid one day you'd remember what you saw and put the pieces together. So, as much as I like you, I have to kill you."

Raven blanched and whispered hoarsely, "You'll never get away with it."

Nick's smile was wicked. "I already have."

She watched as he slipped the hypodermic pen back into his pocket and fumbled with the window. It was apparent he was having difficulty lifting the window with one hand. He's going to have to put the gun down, she thought. And when he did, she would make her move. She doubted he would shoot her in the back since he wanted her death to look like a suicide. She had to keep him talking, distract him as he fumbled with the window.

"What about the vials we found at Parker's apartment?" she asked. "Did you plant them?"

"Sure did. He was the perfect fall guy. But don't lose any sleep over him. While I was planting the vials, I found several bottles of insulin. I think he was planning to kill his wife with an insulin overdose. That's why he took out the insurance policy and that's why he ran. He thought I was talking about *his* murder plan." Nick laid the gun on the table next to the window and looked away for just a moment in order to raise the window. It was only for a moment, but it was enough for her to make her move.

She turned, bolted out of the room, and sprinted down the corridor. To her terrified eyes, the long, narrow corridor seemed to stretch out endlessly before her. She heard her own screams echo off the walls.

Surely someone was working late on this floor or the next and would hear her! Someone who would answer her cry for help. It was her only hope.

She pounded on the first door that she came to. She turned the doorknob. It was locked tight. She ran to the next one. She screamed and pounded, but there was no answer.

She heard Nick's footsteps coming down the corridor, coming closer. She took off running.

The corridor curved to the right. She looked back over her shoulder so she didn't see the computer table until she ran smack into it. Pain shot through her leg. Blinking back tears, she stumbled to her feet and took off again.

Her purse flew off her shoulder but she couldn't stop to retrieve it. Her leg was screaming with pain as she ran toward the office door directly ahead. Was it locked, as well? Were they all locked? Should she make a try for the elevators, or were her chances better in the stairwell? Could she make it down sixty-three flights of stairs? And if she did what would she find? A parking lot? An alley? Is that where they'd find her body in the morning?

She kept running. She could hear Nick behind her. Getting closer.

She sprinted for the door dead ahead. It was unlocked. Stumbling through, she found herself in a large room filled with computer equipment. Her eyes darted about the room, looking for a place to hide. Just as the door flew open again, she ducked behind a tall file cabinet.

She heard him prowling the room. Her heart was thumping so loudly, she was surprised he didn't hear it. She held her breath, and waited. An object clattered to the floor, echoing like a pistol shot in the darkened room.

She tried in vain to locate the source but the sound seemed to come from a dozen different directions at once. "Oh, Jeff," she whispered. "Where are you?"

The echoes faded, leaving total silence. The minutes ticked by, and she heard nothing. Had he left? she wondered. It had been quite a while since she'd heard any movement. Slowly she inched her head around and peered from behind the file cabinet. What she saw made her reel back in horror.

Nick was on the other side of the room and moving toward her.

She jumped up and took off like a jackrabbit, but Nick was faster. He caught her around the legs and she went down. She tried to crawl away, but he held on. He flipped her over then his hands were on her throat, squeezing hard and long as he shouted things at her, things she couldn't hear because her brain was screaming for air. But she could see. She could see the way rage had distorted his handsome face, seized it, claimed it, and she knew she was going to die here, now.

Then his hands flew away from her throat as though

someone had grabbed them. She gasped for air, gulped at it, sucked at it, coughing and rubbing her throat.

"I ought to kill you right now," he panted. "You pull another stunt like that and I will." He jerked her up, twisted her arm behind her, and pushed her toward the door.

The walk back to Mark Daniels's office seemed to take seconds and before she knew it, they were standing in the doorway. Her eyes flew to the opened window, and fear unlike anything she'd ever felt flashed through her. She'd believed Jeff would come. But time had run out. An image of Jeff's handsome face came to her. A wave of tears threatened, and she fought them back.

With a rough nudge, Nick pushed her back into the darkened office. "Now, we'll walk slowly across the room."

But her feet wouldn't cooperate, and he gave her another shove. She thrashed, twisted, pried with her free hand, struggled to get free. "You're not going to get away with this. Jeff knows I'm here with you."

"You're lying!" As if to emphasize his words, he gave the arm he held a vicious twist.

She cried out in pain. "No, I'm not," she gasped. "I left a note for him, telling him about your call and your asking me to meet you here."

Nick froze.

"You didn't think of that did you?" she asked, taking advantage of his momentary hesitation to pull out of his grasp and put some distance between her and the open window. "Jeff will know you're lying."

"Shut up! I need to think." He chewed his lower lip as he paced, agitated.

"You ought to let me go," Raven said. "Jeff will be here—"

"Well, he's not here now!" He lunged for her then but she sidestepped his hands. He grabbed her by the arm and shoved her hard. She nearly fell and grabbed on to the corner of a bookcase. She dug her hand into the wood, holding on for dear life.

"I've come too far to let you mess things up now," Nick sneered. "After I kill you, I'll just have to kill Jeff, too. I'll make it look like a double suicide. Then I'll be home free." He pried her hand from the bookcase, and grabbed her about the waist.

But she was not going down without a fight. With the strength adrenaline was pumping into her veins, she gouged at his eyes; her nails tore into his flesh.

He reared back, slapping her hard. For a moment, stars danced before her eyes. He began dragging her across the room. She thought of Jeff and tried to form words to leave behind in this world for him. "Jeff, I love you..."

"How touching," Nick taunted. They were just inches away from the window now. "I'll be sure to give him your love before I kill him."

"That won't be necessary."

The voice came from the darkness behind them. Nick whirled around. At the same time, a small black object sailed through the room, hitting him squarely in the face.

With a cry of anguish, Nick released Raven.

Out of the darkness, a larger shape rushed into the room. With the impact of a linebacker, Jeff struck Nick in the midriff, pushing him back against the desk. Nick was up instantly, swinging. Jeff used his quickness to sidestep a blow. Nick pulled the hypodermic pen from his pocket, clicked the cap so the needle point gleamed in the darkened room. Holding it like a knife, Nick came at him.

He took a swing at Jeff, barely missing his arm. Nick pivoted and brought the hypodermic down again. Jeff knocked the pen from Nick's hand, and kicked it away. Nick lunged at him, but his foot slipped on the pen on the floor and he fell backward—toward the opened window.

Nick's face was paralyzed in stunned disbelief as he scrabbled for something to hold on to and his hand locked on Raven's wrist.

She felt herself falling.

She heard screams, cries, curses, but couldn't tell where they came from. Nick was screaming, surely; she could see his open mouth as she was inexorably dragged toward the open window ledge by his weight. Maybe she was even screaming herself; she simply didn't know.

Then strong arms clamped around her waist and stopped her slippery progress over the window ledge. Her shoulder was burning with agony from the strain of Nick's weight. His hand was locked like a vise around her wrist on the area where she wore her watch.

"Jeff, please don't let me fall." Nick was babbling, his handsome face white, his eyes terrified.

"Give me your hand!" Jeff shouted. He dug in his heels, straining backward with every ounce of strength in his body, one arm wrapped tightly around Raven, and the other stretched forward reaching for Nick. "Take my hand," he ordered.

"I can't reach it," Nick screamed.

Jeff leaned out as far as he dared, and reached for the other man. Raven wasn't making a sound. Nick was still screaming and kicking wildly, pleading with him not to let him fall.

"Damn it, hold still!"

Nick either didn't hear or didn't understand, senseless to everything except his own terror and the emptiness beneath him.

"Shut up! Shut up and listen to me!" The raw fury in Jeff's voice must have gotten through, for Nick abruptly stopped screaming. The sudden silence was as nerve-racking, in its way, as the screaming had been.

"Hold still," Jeff ordered, his voice tight. "Give me your hand. I'm going to try to pull you up."

Nick's gaze was blank with terror, but somehow he focused on Jeff. "Okay," he said, the word barely audible.

In the distance he heard the faint sound of police sirens. Help was coming but Jeff couldn't wait. He leaned forward, reaching out a hand toward Nick's swaying arm. All he wanted was to grab Nick's hand and pull him up. But the other man had had a change of heart. As if in slow motion, he watched with growing horror as Nick stuck his hand inside his jacket and drew out a gun. His intent was clear.

"Oh, my God!" Jeff whispered. He had to dislodge Nick's hold on Raven. But how? His eyes fell on Raven's watchband. Jeff went to work on the buckle, frantically trying to undo the clasp on her watchband. Out of the corner of his eye, he saw the other man point the gun at him. Jeff doubled his efforts. Beads of sweat dotted his brow and he felt as if his heart were beating out of control. He heard a click like the barrel of a gun being pulled back. He glanced down and saw Nick's finger squeeze back slowly on the trigger.

"Say bye-bye." He smiled.

At that same moment, the clasp on Raven's watchband sprang open and the watch slipped from her wrist and along with it—Nick Valentine. Nick's screams rent the night air. And then there was silence.

"Oh, Jeff," Raven sobbed as he gathered her close and buried her face against his chest. "Nick was the killer. He killed them all."

"I know," he said, leading her away from the window and into the outer office. "It's over, sweetheart. It's over…" He blinked back tears when he thought how close he'd come to losing her. "It's over…he can't hurt you or anyone anymore." He held her for a long moment, telling her about the things he'd learned from Dr. Ross's files, how the virus had been developed and Nick's theft of the virus.

"The virus!" she gasped then pulled out of his arms. "We've got to get over to Nick's apartment right away," she said. "Maybe he was lying about destroying Dr. Ross's paper. If we—"

Jeff caught her about the waist, holding her in place. At

her stricken look, he shook his head. "We don't need them now."

"Oh, God, no," she moaned then slumped against him. "It's too late."

"It's not what you think," he said quickly when he realized she'd misunderstood his words. "Your treatment worked." He gave her a lopsided smile. "I'm going to be fine."

She stared into his eyes for a full minute before his words finally sank in. "Are you sure?" Her voice was full of wonder, as if she couldn't quite take it in.

"Yes." He laughed then hugged her close for a moment before setting her away again. "Thanks to you, I am fine. Dr. Hillman gave me a clean bill of health."

She couldn't believe it. Her herbal medication had worked.

"I gave a batch of your medication to Dr. Hillman. He and Shay are working on Lauren and the others right now. I think they'll all make a full recovery. Hillman agrees."

"That's wonderful," she said, blinking back tears of joy.

"No, you're wonderful," he said, smiling down at her, "and soon the entire world is going to know it. Your herbal treatment has turned the medical community and its view of alternative medicine on its head. Hillman thinks it has applications for a number of infectious diseases. The medical community is going to be at your door."

She looked at him, her eyes brimming with love. "You're the only person whose opinion I care about. You believed in me when no one else did…when I didn't believe in myself."

He framed her face in his hands and kissed her tenderly. "How could I not? I love you, and I'm going to spend the rest of my life showing you just how much."

Her face broke into a brilliant smile. "And I love you."

"You are my life," he told her with a fierceness that brought tears to her eyes. "My rock, my beacon. Your love and the pleasure of being with you is all I want. All I'll ever need.''

In the background he heard the sound of heavy pounding like footsteps running down the corridor. ''Looks like the police have arrived. Do you feel up to making a statement?''

''I can do anything as long as you're by my side.''

He pulled her close so that her body was flush against his. And then he kissed her. A long, slow, hot kiss that promised a lifetime of joy and happiness and love.

This Valentine's Day Harlequin brings you
all the essentials—romance, chocolate
and jewelry—in:

Matchmaking chocolate-shop owner Papa Valentine
dispenses sinful desserts, mouth-watering
chocolates...and advice to the lovelorn, in this
collection of three delightfully romantic stories
by Meryl Sawyer, Kate Hoffmann and Gina Wilkins.

As our special Valentine's Day gift to you, each copy
of *Valentine Delights* will have a beautiful, filigreed,
heart-shaped brooch attached to the cover.

Make this your most delicious Valentine's Day
ever with *Valentine Delights!*

Available in February wherever
Harlequin books are sold.

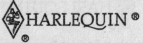

Heartbreak RANCH

Four generations of independent women...
Four heartwarming, romantic stories of the West...
Four incredible authors...

Fern Michaels
Jill Marie Landis
Dorsey Kelley
Chelley Kitzmiller

Saddle up with Heartbreak Ranch, an outstanding
Western collection that will take you on a whirlwind
trip through four generations and the exciting,
romantic adventures of four strong women who
have inherited the ranch from Bella Duprey,
famed Barbary Coast madam.

Available in March,
wherever Harlequin books are sold.

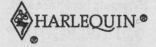

HARLEQUIN ®

LOVE *or* MONEY?
Why not Love *and* Money!
After all, millionaires
need love, too!

How to Marry a
MILLIONAIRE

**Suzanne Forster,
Muriel Jensen
and
Judith Arnold**

bring you three original stories
about finding that one-in-a million man!

Harlequin also brings you
a million-dollar sweepstakes—enter
for your chance to win a fortune!

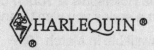 HARLEQUIN ®

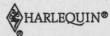

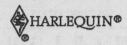 **HARLEQUIN®**

Not The Same Old Story!

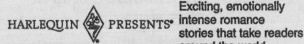 Exciting, emotionally intense romance stories that take readers around the world.

 Vibrant stories of captivating women and irresistible men experiencing the magic of falling in love!

 Bold and adventurous— Temptation is strong women, bad boys, great sex!

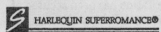 Provocative, passionate, contemporary stories that celebrate life and love.

 Romantic adventure where anything is possible and where dreams come true.

 Heart-stopping, suspenseful adventures that combine the best of romance and mystery.

LOVE & LAUGHTER Entertaining and fun, humorous and romantic—stories that capture the lighter side of love.

Look us up on-line at: http://www.romance.net   HGENERIC